Issue 17
October - November 2019

Lezli Robyn & Tina Smith, Editors
Shahid Mahmud, Publisher

Published by Arc Manor/Heart's Nest Press
P.O. Box 10339
Rockville, MD 20849-0339

Heart's Kiss is published in February, April, June, August, October and December.

www.HeartsKiss.com

Pleaee refer to our website for information on how to submit material for *Heart's Kiss* magazine.

Available by subscription (www.HeartsKiss.com) or through your favorite online store (Amazon.com, BN.com, etc.).

ISBN: 978-1-61242-477-4

FOREIGN LANGUAGE RIGHTS: Please refer all inquiries pertaining to foreign language rights to Shahid Mahmud, Arc Manor, P.O. Box 10339, Rockville, MD 20849-0339. Tel: 1-240-645-2214. Fax 1-310-388-8440. Email admin@ArcManor.com.

Contents

OPENING EDITORIAL

by Tina Smith

Fall is brimming with new possibilities. Summer's last bursts of heat fade and the autumn brings transition. It's the season for change and new beginnings. I've always loved the spring and fall for those reasons. The symbolic nature of the time of year always works well with schools starting back up from a long summer break, and other events and projects seem to ebb and flow from that beginning.

We have some great new-to-us writers and some returning favorites. Many of the authors have a terrific fan base and we're so lucky to have them appear on our pages. Our featured novellas this issue are Kayla Perrin's *One Night in Paris* and Kathryn Nolan's *Queen Cleopatra and the Baseball God*. We are so very excited to have Kayla, a *USA Today* and Essence bestselling writer in this latest issue. Kayla has written for Harlequin and we're delighted to feature her breathtaking novella. And great news for *Heart's Kiss* readers is that we plan to publish more stories from this series. In *Queen Cleopatra and the Baseball God*, Nolan showcases her ability to write fun and flirty characters that stick with you long after you read the last sentence. Kathryn Nolan is a rising star in indie romance. Her novels have quickly become romance fan favorites and we

will not be surprised to see her on the bestseller lists very soon.

We also have three *Heart's Kiss* regulars, with Olivette Devaux's *The Music of Loose Spring*, David H. Hendrickson's *The Boy in Boxers*, and Tonya D. Price's *In Tuscan Twilight*. In *The Music of Loose Spring*, , a small town local finds himself befriending two new arrivals, twins, and falls for one who swears to stay away from romance because of his health condition—but we all know love never quite works that way. Hendrickson's story prepares us for the holiday season where a Swedish pastry chef makes a delivery to a family and ends up spending time with her perfect match, who happens to be in his boxers at the time of their meet-cute. Our readers were so delighted by Price's Greek story, we brought her back for another destination love story, *In Tuscan Twilight*.

And, of course, with every issue we have some non-fiction articles for our readers to stay in touch with recent topics in the romance genre. *Recommended Books* will keep readers up-to-date on new releases as well as may-have-been-missed gems. Julie Pitzel has a new topic in her *You Read That?* column, this time covering the topic *Saved by Romance*.

Well, the winds are changing as I am outside writing this at my house on the west coast. Our summers tend to linger, but this week we've had a mild break. As I mentioned, autumn is the time of change and we have wonderful changes ahead for *Heart's Kiss*. I will be stepping down as co-editor of the magazine to have more time for writing. I'm also taking more hours as counselor, as there is a need in our area after the Camp Fires in Northern California. I'm so excited for Lezli to continue the work we've both started here and I'm confident she will do fantastic running the magazine solo. I'll be involved much less from this point forward, but *Heart's Kiss* will always hold a special place in my heart. Thank you for reading and enjoying—I will soon join you as a fan of the magazine. Hold a place for me at the reading circle on the comfy chairs. I'll bring the hot chocolate and blankets.

Kayla Perrin is a multi-published, award-winning USA Today *and* Essence ® *bestselling author with over 50 novels and novellas in print. She is a trailblazer in the African-American fiction arena. She has written for many major publishers including St. Martin's Press, HarperCollins Publishers, and Harlequin. In 2001, after only four years in the business, Kayla was awarded the* Romantic Times *Career Achievement Award for excellence in multicultural romance. In 2007, her novel,* Midnight Dreams, *was the Borders bestselling multicultural romance of the year. In 2011, she received the prestigious Harry Jerome Award in Canada for excellence in the arts.*

ONE NIGHT IN PARIS

by Kayla Perrin

CHAPTER ONE

I downed the last of my wine, then snatched up my Samsung Galaxy smart phone from my dining room table. My decision was made. "I'm gonna call her."

"Oh, no no no." Holly Krebs, one of my two best friends, reached for my hand, trying to pry the phone from my fingers.

"What are you doing?" I asked. I jerked my arm upward, but Holly held on, successfully wrestling my phone from my hand. "Stop it!"

"You're not going to call her," Holly said, fixing me with a determined stare.

"Ow." I rubbed my wrist, which stung—but not as much as my ego. Then I said, "Yes, I am." I reached for Holly's hand, but she pulled it back. "Come on, Holly. Gimme back my phone."

Holly tossed the phone to Vivica James, my other best friend, who was sitting across the table from us. Vivica caught it and stuffed the phone into her purse.

"Seriously, guys," I said, annoyed. "Cut it out."

"You can't do this," Holly said. Her tone was nononsense, which matched her look. Her light-brown face was thin, her cheekbones high, and her short black hair was slicked back with gel. People often looked at her and judged her as uptight.

"We won't let you," Vivica added. She was the prettiest of us three, at least I thought so. With her flawless dark skin, shoulder-length curly hair, and a big, bright smile, she came across as warm and bubbly to everyone who met her. But even she was giving me a stern look that said she meant business.

"She deserves to know," I insisted. "*Someone* has to tell her."

"And she *will* find out," Vivica stressed. "Trust me. How do you think I learned about Craig? He slipped up. And Steven will, too."

I whimpered. I wanted to call Steven's fiancée—*now*. The fiancée he was apparently going to marry tomorrow. Thanks to the fact that she had linked her cell phone to her Facebook account, I'd been able to find her number. And now, after polishing off half a bottle of wine, I had enough liquid courage to call and tell her just how big of an asshole Steven was.

If only my friends would let me do it.

"You two are supposed to be in *my* corner." I frowned at each of them in turn. "You should want me to expose the bastard."

"And ruin a woman's wedding day?" Holly asked. "No, you're better than that."

"Like hell I am." Right now, I wanted to blow up Steven's game. I mean, how dare he date me for five months, only to tell me that I was the other woman?

I'd come home from a business trip to Canada and had called him the moment my plane touched down. *Babe, I need to see you*, I had all but purred in my best bedroom voice. Steven's reply had been an abrupt, "I can't." Which had made me raise my eyebrow. That wasn't like Steven. There had been no, "I'll call you later." Or, "I'll come by when I'm free." Normally, he was ready to pounce on me when I came home from my business trips.

Naturally, I pressed him as to what was going on—which was when he'd told me in an almost impatient tone that it was over between us and that he was getting married on Saturday.

"M-married?" I'd sputtered, my head starting to spin as I tried to process what he'd just said.

"You knew it was never going to work between us," Steven had replied, not a trace of guilt or contrition in his tone. "You're hardly ever in town."

Those words had been like a stab in my heart. I'd even gasped, garnering the attention of those around me on the plane, but I'd just been so shocked. Steven had told me often that he liked my independence … and suddenly I knew why.

The very fact that I had a job that required a lot of travel meant I wasn't around to keep tabs on a man. Which was fine with me. I didn't want to have to monitor a guy's every movement to ensure that he wasn't cheating on me.

But that reality had also made it super easy for Steven to have a whole other life I didn't know about. One I found after clicking on friends of his friends via Facebook for hours, and finally discovering Dominique Kissinger. The woman who had been boasting for months that she was getting married to "the best man in the world" in May.

"He's been living a lie, with me and with her," I said, thinking again of his wretched betrayal. "It's not like I was away and he decided to cheat one me. I went back a year on Dominique's Facebook page and saw that that's when they got engaged! He started seeing me five months ago. I'd want someone to tell me if I were about to marry a pig."

"Maybe if she was a good friend of yours, you could tell her," Vivica said. "But if you call Dominique and ruin her wedding day, you're going to look like the bad guy. Like some bitch with a vendetta. He'll explain away your story real easily, trust me. Like I said, Steven will screw things up for himself soon enough. And when he does, your conscience will be clear."

As much as I hated to admit it, Vivica had a point. Steven would likely smooth things over with Dominique and she'd marry him anyway. But damn, I wanted Steven to feel as much pain as he had caused me. I wanted to show up at the wedding and be that person who stood up when the minister asked, *If there is anyone here who has a reason why these two should not be wed …*.

I wanted to claw his eyes out for what he had done to me. Take a golf club to his head. Burn all his belongings on my front lawn.

You get the idea.

But at the end of the day, I knew I would do none of those things. And I wouldn't allow myself to be the bitch who destroyed a woman's happiness on the most important day of her life.

However, I was still devastated. Devastated that I'd believed Steven loved me, when in fact he had been screwing me over. How had I been so wrong about him?

"Married?" I croaked. "I'm the other woman, and he tells me two days before the wedding?"

"Oh, hon." Holly wrapped an arm around my shoulder and pulled me close. "Don't cry. You're gonna be okay. I promise you that."

I didn't even realize that I'd been about to cry until Holly said that, and that's when the tears started to spill from my eyes. I brushed them away angrily, not wanting to cry over Steven. Not after what he'd done to me. But how could I not? He'd hurt me. Trampled on my dreams. Broken my trusting heart.

"Guess my mother's right about me," I said, sniffling and wiping at my tears.

"No, Bella," Vivica said. "She's not. You're going to find love. Look at you. You're gorgeous. How can you not?"

My mother liked to say that I was unlucky in love. My long-term relationship in my twenties had ended when Chad decided that he wanted a woman who was ready to start having babies. In my early thirties, I'd gotten married—only to separate six weeks later. (I met the guy on a trip to Vegas, don't ask). And ever since that breakup, my mother had started talking about how some people were just plain old unlucky in love, and that I was one of them.

I'd started to feel like I was going to be alone for the rest of my life. Until Steven.

Steven made me believe that I'd found a man who could accept me for me. One who could accept the long hours I had to dedicate to my job. Unlike other guys, he'd embraced my career as an internal corporate auditor, and didn't mind that I pulled in a higher salary than he did. The bastard had made me believe in love again.

"When Dominique learns his true colors," Vivica began gently, "you can sit back and say that your hands are clean. If you tell her now, she'll likely write you off as a jealous stalker, one who is upset that Steven is getting married. But when she starts to piece together the facts for herself, she'll realize for herself that he's a lying asshole."

Brushing away my tears, I nodded at Vivica. I knew that she was speaking the truth. And sadly, she was doing so from experience. She had learned her husband of thirteen years was cheating on her, and she'd handled the situation with strength. She'd dumped his lying ass, no looking back.

"I never did like Steven," Holly commented.

Looking at her, I narrowed my eyes. "Since when?"

"Since the first time I met him. He seemed ... I dunno ... like he was putting on an act."

"An act?" Now I was even more stunned.

"Not an act about liking you. I guess it just seemed he was trying too hard to seem perfect." Holly shrugged. "I don't know. I just know that I didn't completely trust him."

My gaze went to Vivica, I guess seeking her opinion as well. I couldn't have been more surprised when she said, "I didn't like him, either."

"Why the hell not?"

"I agree with Holly. He came off as a little too perfect. Doted on you as though you were the only woman in the world. Maybe I'm just suspicious of that kind of public display of affection."

And I had loved it. Craved it, after so long a dry spell. "That's silly," I said. "Craig was never the touchy-feely type, but that doesn't mean that you have to be suspicious of a guy who is."

"Call it a feeling, then," Vivica said. "I can't explain it."

What had they seen that I hadn't? "You could have shared your feelings with me."

"It wasn't our place to say," Holly said. "Our not liking someone isn't a reason you shouldn't date him."

"So friggin' reasonable, both of you. Next time, tell me when you think I'm getting involved with an idiot. Maybe if you both had told me you didn't have a good feeling about Steven, I would have kicked him to the curb and saved myself this heartbreak."

Vivica and Holly exchanged a doubtful look. And I couldn't blame them. I likely would have dated Steven anyway.

Pushing my chair back, I got to my feet and started for the nearby kitchen. "I need more wine."

"I think you've had enough," Vivica said.

I turned to stare at her. "My boyfriend just dumped me—and now it's the night before his wedding to a fiancée I didn't know about. I haven't had enough. Not hardly."

❖

I didn't sleep well that night. My mind was plagued with the grief of being dumped—and the reality that I'd been wooed by an ass who'd had a fiancée. I very seriously wanted to go to the church the next day to stop the wedding, because I was still pissed off. And I just might have—if I hadn't been suffering the worst hangover in the history of the world. My head hurt when I opened my eyes. Getting out of bed and getting dressed wasn't even a possible option. I was glad that I'd had my friends come to my place last night, that we hadn't had this catch up session at one of their homes, which would have required me to crash in a bed other than my own. It was the kind of day where I wanted to stay my bed with the covers pulled over my head ... and I did exactly that.

Despite my heartbreak, I vowed to move on—even though I was livid that Steven had had the gall to treat me with such little respect. I wouldn't text him, no matter how much I wanted to send him one good long message giving him a piece of my mind. I would let him be.

Lesson learned the excruciatingly hard way.

In the days that followed, I became Angry Bella. Gone was the sweet and trusting and hopeful Bella. The Bella who believed that true love existed beyond the pages of fairy tales. Two bottles of wine and a wicked hangover, I'd emerged from my awful break-up with a new outlook on love.

Men sucked.

I was going to harden my heart and not let anyone penetrate it. I'd buy some toys. Satisfy myself. Lots of women got through the lonely, horny moments that way.

My anger was evident everywhere. If a man looked my way, I practically snarled when I met his gaze. About three weeks later in the grocery store, one man dared to wink at me and got my venomous stare in return. It startled him so badly that he turned and bumped into a rack of peanut butter, knocking over several jars. I'd smiled, as though that had been a bit of payback on men in general.

Given my sour attitude—which I couldn't even quite hide at the office—men would assume that I had issues.

I didn't care. Because I did have issues. I had issues with all men.

And I wanted nothing to do with any of them, except my father and brother. And my adorable two-year old nephew, Josiah—who had not yet been corrupted by the rest of his species.

In the six weeks following my breakup, I didn't think about men. I didn't even miss the sex. I was certain that I'd accomplished the task of becoming a non-sexual being as I had during previous dry spells—but this time for good.

So I couldn't have been more surprised when my body betrayed me. It happened during my run along the trail that led through the forest in my D.C. neighborhood. When I saw him jogging toward me. Shirtless. That perfect upper body with its hard planes and grooves covered in a sheen of perspiration. Good Lord, what a body! It looked as though it had been sculpted from the finest milk chocolate. Behind my sunglasses, I ogled him. Ogled him without shame.

And as he neared me, my pulse tripped—as though it had been the one running and had stumbled. After six weeks of hating men, my sleeping sexual being was suddenly jarred fully awake.

And then like my pulse, *I* tripped. Damn! I caught myself before I fell on my face, which would have left me mortally embarrassed. Righting myself, I stopped and drew in several deep breaths, wondering what was wrong with me.

Okay, so I knew the answer to that. Obviously, I wasn't totally immune to the opposite sex. I was still a woman. Still totally heterosexual. And like every other heterosexual woman on the planet, I can certainly appreciate a fine man.

And there was no doubt that Andre Moore was fine—a fact I had known for a couple of years. Yes, the man I'd damn near fallen on my face over was one I'd lusted after before, as he was one of my neighbors. Andre lived about five houses down on my street, and I often saw him in the distance. Occasionally, our paths actually crossed and we exchanged verbal pleasantries. I'd always thought the man was hot. And off limits.

As he neared me, I couldn't help eyeing his naked chest. The hard wall of muscles, those perfectly sculpted abs. No wonder he had been a professional athlete. Although he'd retired from the NFL a year ago, he still kept his body in pristine shape.

Something else I had come to know—and appreciate from afar—in the last couple of years.

But I thought I was immune to a gorgeous man at this point in my life. Apparently I wasn't.

As my eyes ventured to his strong, lean thighs, I told myself that there was no harm in looking. If I got too hot and bothered, that's where the toys came in.

As he reached me, Andre waved at me and offered me a small smile. I did the same. Two neighbors being polite. Although I was strangely aroused. I might just have to head to a sex shop after my run and find something new ….

I began jogging in the opposite direction, and that was that.

Until moments later when I felt a hand touch my arm. Startled, I jerked my gaze to the left and saw him there, now jogging beside me.

If he had called out to me, I hadn't heard because I had ear buds in my ears. I took them out now, stopping my forward motion but continuing to jog on the spot. "Yes?" I asked.

"You okay?"

"Huh?"

"I saw you stumble. Did you hurt your ankle?"

"Oh." I waved a dismissive hand. "I'm fine."

I thought he would continue on, but he didn't. "I see you around, but we've never formally met." He extended a hand. "I'm Andre."

Didn't he see that I was trying to get back to my workout? Now wasn't the time for a formal introduction.

I continued to jog on the spot, hoping he would get the hint. "Yes, I know who you are."

One of his eyebrows shot up as he looked at me, but there was a expression of humor on his face. "Is that a bad thing?"

"Why would you ask that?" I came to a stop, since I felt silly jogging on the spot, while he wasn't moving.

"Because you didn't shake my hand," he pointed out.

"Oh. Sorry." I took his offered hand and shook it. And damn if I didn't feel a sexual charge electrify my body. It left me flustered—and apparently deaf, because I saw his lips move, but didn't hear what he said.

You know how sometimes when you look at a picture up close, you see the imperfections? Well, being this close to Andre, I saw no imperfections at all. In fact, he looked even sexier up close. He had to be at least six-foot-two or six-foot-three, which was a huge plus. His rounded face was clean-shaven, as was his head. And I could only imagine that with those thick lips, his kisses would be sensational ….

"You don't want to tell me your name?" he said.

I blinked, mentally falling back down to earth with a thud. "Um, sorry." What was wrong with me? "I'm Bella."

"Bella." Andre said my name as though he was sampling the way it sounded on his lips. "You don't really look like a Bella."

"No?"

"I hear Bella, I think Italian."

"My mother's Italian," I explained. "Well, part Italian. My father's American. They agreed to name me after my maternal grandmother … which is more information than you ever wanted to know."

Andre nodded. "No, it's cool. I like the name."

His eyes wandered from my face to my body, leaving me wondering if he liked something else …. A current of heat shot through my veins.

You don't care what he thinks, I reminded myself. *What the heck is wrong with you?*

I put my ear buds back in my ears and placed my finger on my MP3 player's PLAY button, which was conveniently strapped to my wrist. It was time to get on with my day. "Well, nice to officially meet you. Of course, like everyone in the neighborhood, I know you used to play professional football. That's why I already knew your name."

"And now I know yours."

"All right. See you around."

I started to press the PLAY button when he said, "Don't go running off just yet."

"Pardon me?" I asked, stopping my music again.

He gave me an odd look. One that was a little charming, and perhaps also a little flirtatious. Certainly he couldn't be hitting on me?

"I was wondering …. I've noticed you before. Quite a bit, actually. And now …" His voice trailing off, he looked at a loss for words.

"And now what?" I prompted.

"Sorry," he said, and smiled. A full-blown, radiant smile. And my goodness, did he ever have a set of dimples. They made him all the more endearing. "I was wondering if I could take you out to dinner."

"Dinner?" I nearly choked on the word. That was the last thing I'd expected him to say.

"You do do dinner, don't you?"

"Yes—yes. I—I do," I stammered. "But—"

"But?" Andre raised his eyebrows expectantly.

I didn't even know what to say. I was certain that this was some sort of joke. He had to be kidding. This was the first time we were talking beyond pleasantries, and he wanted to take me to dinner? Why?

"I—I tend to be really busy," I said. "I have a horribly demanding work schedule, and in all honesty, dinner probably isn't the best idea."

"Oh." He looked disappointed.

"I just don't have a lot of time for—for socializing," I said, not wanting to mention the word *dating,* in case he was simply offering to get a neighborly bite together. "But I do appreciate you asking." I offered him an apologetic smile. "Sorry."

"I understand," he said.

Did he? "I mean, it's nothing personal," I went on. "It's just … timing."

"Sure." Andre raised a hand as if to say *Hey, it's all right.* "You enjoy the rest of your day."

And then he began to run again, continuing on in the original direction he'd been going.

I stared after him for a long while, wondering why, although I had turned him down, my heart was racing so fast.

Dinner …. Had he really just asked me to dinner? A guy I had secretly lusted over for two years?

And I'd actually said no?

Maybe if we'd had this conversation a year ago. Hell, even the day before I'd met Steven. But now ….

Now, I was a changed woman. A woman who no longer believed in love. Sure, I was flattered. And even a little turned on. But I'd been right to turn him down.

That's what I told myself. Yet as I started to jog again, I couldn't help thinking that perhaps after Steven, a man like Andre was exactly what I needed. Someone to make me feel good, to make me forget my pain.

The only thing I knew for sure was that I was going to go shopping for a new toy. Because after weeks of not being aroused at all, talking to Andre had left me hot and bothered.

And considering I'd given up men, a toy would have to suffice.

CHAPTER TWO

"You're not actually serious?" Holly asked, staring at me as if I had grown a third eye smack in the middle of my forehead. "I mean, how old is he?"

"You mean how *young*," Vivica interjected, chuckling softly.

I fiddled with the stem of my wine glass, not making eye contact with either of my two dearest friends. I was out with Holly and Vivica for dinner, something we didn't do nearly as often as I would like. We had finished off a half-carafe of red wine and had ordered another—which we could do without guilt because we were cabbing it home. It was the first time we'd been together for a meal since my Steven meltdown, and when they'd asked what was new in my life, I had dared to mention the fact that Andre Moore had asked me to dinner.

"I didn't say I was interested," I said, a tad defensive. What I had hoped—by telling my friends that I'd felt a spark of attraction for a man after weeks—was that they would pat me on the back and tell me that I was finally on the road to healing. Being shot down by both of them now didn't feel good. "I'm just saying he's easy to look at. And it was … *nice* … getting a bit of attention. It's not wrong to find him attractive, is it?"

"He's a hot guy," Vivica said. "We all know that. But one—he's at least ten years younger than you. And two, he's a retired ball player. You know he's got at least thirty women on speed dial. Hell, Craig was an accountant and he had about five women on speed dial. Stupid prick."

"Ah, you said Craig!" Holly slapped the table, victorious. "Drink up."

"Shit," Vivica muttered, then drank a good mouthful of her red wine.

I chuckled, then took a sip of my wine as well. Vivica, only divorced for six months now, had a habit of badmouthing her ex. We totally understood—the passive-aggressive jerk had screwed her over—but we were still doing everything in our power to help her forget him once and for all. Tonight, we'd warned her that every time she uttered Craig's name, she would have to drink wine.

"My point, Bella," Vivica said to me, "is that you're asking for trouble if you get involved with someone like Andre Moore. Heck, even his name screams player."

I finished off my glass of wine. I was feeling a little deflated. I'm not exactly sure what I'd wanted from my friends. Perhaps a little encouragement? An unabashed *go for it* where Andre was concerned?

Because let's face it—I imagined he would be a pretty good palate cleanser. One night in bed with him, and I was sure I would no longer be remembering Steven. It was a thought I'd had over and over again in the week since he'd asked me out.

Now, I was glad that I'd never told my friends about my secret crush on him. It wasn't super serious or anything, which is why I'd never mentioned it. But he was the kind of guy who left me breathless just looking at him. I responded to him on a purely sexual level.

Now, don't get me wrong. I held no illusions that anything would ever happen between us. But that doesn't mean a woman can't fantasize, does it? And after he'd asked me out last weekend—let's just say my libido was in overdrive. All week, I had daydreamed about what it would be like to make love to him.

Tall, dark and fine. Six-foot-threeish. He would be taller than me, even if I wore my highest heels. That was a definite plus. Not to mention his beautifully sculpted body. Dimples that would make any woman blush. And that smile—the first time he'd actually leveled it on me, I'd felt an electric charge like nothing else in my life. But I'd been able to keep my inappropriate feelings under control … until he'd asked me out.

"The man's fine as hell," Holly conceded. "But Viv's right. Football player? You know the man has tons of women. I'm shocked he would even ask you out. Not that you're not beautiful, but I'm sure the guy is just looking for another notch on his bedpost."

I scowled. "Gee, thanks."

The waitress arrived then with our second carafe of wine. "Have you decided on any dessert?" she asked.

"You just brought it," I said, smiling sweetly.

"Nothing for me," Holly said.

"Nor me," Vivica added.

As the waitress walked off, Holly picked up where she'd left off. "I'm not putting you down.

Just keeping it real. Besides, I don't even think Andre's thirty yet. And you're turning forty in a couple of weeks."

"Thanks for that reminder." I made a sour face, then reached for the carafe of wine. I filled my glass.

"Of course, you don't look a day over twenty-eight," Vivica said. "God knows, if you weren't so awesome, I'd hate you."

"I'm sure he has no clue how old you really are," Holly said. "He's probably gone through the rest of the women in the neighborhood and is now turning his sights on you."

"Can we change the subject?" I asked. With both of my friends sitting across the booth from me, I felt like I was in the proverbial hot seat. I didn't want to defend an attraction that I felt was perfectly okay. I hadn't jumped into bed with Andre. And I certainly hadn't said that I was planning to. And I didn't particularly like the way Holly was demeaning Andre's interest in me. I didn't keep dibs on him, but I hadn't noticed a steady stream of different women entering his home. He didn't strike me as a player. "You told us that we should have spoken up about not liking Steven," Holly went on, undeterred. "Remember? I'm not trying to be hard on you. I'm trying to stop you from doing something you'll regret."

"Exactly," Vivica agreed. "Look, I'd be tempted too. Lord knows, any woman would be tempted to jump into bed with a guy like that. But what will it get you? You're not the casual sex kind."

"I got it," I said testily. "Now *please* can we change the subject?"

Vivica turned to Holly. "How's Mike?"

Currently, Holly was the only one of us who was involved with a man. She was married, had been for ten years. The passion had died years ago, something Holly often complained about. But she seemed content. She put all of her efforts into being a great mother, which she was.

"Mike's great," Holly said. "He's been super busy since he made partner, but I can't complain. I've got a big house, two wonderful kids. My health."

It almost sounded like Holly was trying to convince herself that all was okay in her world.

"And your fortieth?" I asked. "Has he said yes to the cruise?"

Holly's nose wrinkled as she shook her head. "He's working on this huge litigation case. You remember the one. So it isn't likely he can take the time off."

"You're saying he can't plan for four months from now?" I asked.

"He can't be sure he won't be in court then," Holly explained.

"Oh, that's too bad." I knew how much Holly was looking forward to doing something special for her fortieth birthday in September.

"Don't worry," Vivica said, patting Holly's hand. "We'll make sure you celebrate in grand style."

Holly smiled, her expression saying that she was grateful for her friends. "I know you will."

Celebrating a fortieth birthday with your girlfriends was nice, but I couldn't imagine anything better than spending alone time with your man as you hit that milestone. Being somewhere—anywhere—to enjoy some seriously hot sex.

That's what I wanted. But with my birthday coming up in exactly two weeks tomorrow, I knew that wasn't an option. Not now that Steven had gotten married.

For some reason, Andre popped into my mind. His naked chest covered with sweat as he'd been running along the trail. The fact that he'd stopped to chat with me, ask me if I would like to go to dinner some time ....

Was Holly right? Did he simply want a roll in the hay? And if that *was* all he wanted, did I even care?

Heck, if Shemar Moore or Dwayne "The Rock" Johnson want to take you to bed, do you say no? You know it'll just be sex, but a chance to bed a hot guy you've admired ... I know women would be seriously tempted.

And because of Andre, I was suddenly back to feeling sexually alive. No matter Andre's end goal, I had learned that my attraction to him hadn't been one-sided, and that was exciting.

A fortieth birthday celebration with a man like Andre ... how hot would that be?

"Earth to Bella." Holly snapped her fingers in front of my face.

"Oh," I said. "Sorry."

"Where'd you go?" Vivica asked, looking at me with a curious expression.

I'd zoned out, thinking of the impossible and the ridiculous. Even if the option of sex with Andre had existed before, I'd most definitely shot the idea down by how quickly I had rejected him.

"I'm just thinking that it's gonna suck being in Paris on my birthday without both of you," I said.

"I know." Vivica sighed softly. "If not for the divorce which cost me a fortune, I'd head there to spend a few days with you. I hate that your business trip is scheduled for then."

"But don't worry," Holly said. "We'll plan something special for when you get home. You're turning forty. It's a big occasion."

I waved a dismissive hand. "It's not really a big deal. I don't want some huge to-do." I wasn't looking forward to marking this milestone. Heck, I was still in denial that I was this old. "We can just as easily pretend I'm turning thirty-five. We'll just get together for a drink."

"It is a big deal," Vivica insisted. "And considering I was an emotional basket-case when my fortieth rolled around because of Cra—" She caught herself, then cursed. "Damn."

"Drink up," I told her. "You know the rules."

Vivica drank more wine, then continued. "As I was saying, my fortieth sucked because I was totally depressed. So we *have* to do something special for your day."

"All right," I conceded. I knew they'd plan something, despite my protests. "Just don't put a dinosaur on my lawn or take out the front page of USA Today announcing that I'm forty." I gave them a look, a warning.

"Leave it to us," Holly said. "We'll make sure you have a birthday celebration you won't forget."

"And it wouldn't kill you to check your inbox for that dating site," Vivica said. "Are you still paying for the service?"

"Oh, shit. That's right. I keep forgetting to cancel it."

"Don't cancel," Vivica said. "I've gone on two dates. No potential, but it was nice to get out there. I think that'd be good for you, too."

I simply nodded. Because I knew that I couldn't share my thoughts on what *would* be good for me. Andre. In my bed. Rocking my world.

Oh yeah, I knew my friends wouldn't approve.

❖

I went home from dinner with my friends and promptly turned on my computer. Until Vivica had mentioned the dating site, I'd forgotten that I'd even signed up for it. Which pretty much tells you how I feel about the whole concept.

Maybe I was too old … and old-fashioned. But I thought online dating was stupid.

You fill out a profile, put up pictures you think will draw attention, and then say things about yourself that are meant to entice. About a year ago, I'd gone on a few dates with guys I met online—and not one of them was in real life the person they'd portrayed themselves to be online.

No, I preferred meeting men the traditional way. At an event. In a coffee shop. Heck, even encountering men at a bar was preferable to dating online.

That said, I hadn't done a good job of meeting men. When you work fifty to sixty hours a week and travel for weeks at a time, there isn't much time to try to find love.

Before Steven, my last boyfriend had been over two years ago. I don't even count him as a boyfriend because we never really dated. We'd had a couple of dinners over the span of two months, then he told me he couldn't get seriously involved with me because I didn't have enough time for him. Despite that, from time to time we got together for a booty call. Sex and nothing more. It had left me feeling empty and cold. And that's when I realized that I was better off alone, as I had been for years. What was the point in screwing a man I knew would not be in my life in a permanent way? Vivica was right when she'd said that I wasn't a casual sex kind of person.

And maybe that was a character flaw on my part. Maybe I needed to be willing to fill my sexual needs and not worry about a relationship.

I opened up my account for the dating service. When I'd filled out the online profile a year ago, my girlfriends and I had gotten together to get the task done. A bottle of wine, a lot of giggling, and I'd put up something I wasn't thrilled with—but they'd assured me it would find me a man. They'd taken pictures of me, forced me to smile and pose in a sexy way. They'd made sure to ply me with alcohol so that I would not be scowling and looking skeptical in all of the photos. And then my profile had gone live.

And here's the thing. I'm five-foot-nine. Not that I have a problem with short men, but I just don't like dating them. I'm not gonna say that if the perfect guy came into my life and he offered me everything I wanted and he happened to be five-foot-six that I would turn him away. But when you see an online profile and the guy is five-foot-six …? Yeah, that holds me back from even wanting to get to know them.

Call me shallow.

Anyway, I had gone on three dreadful dates after joining the dating site, which had only confirmed that online dating wasn't for me. So why was I now going back online to see if anyone had reached out to me?

My inbox was overflowing. And I had several "winks"—ice breakers sent by men to let you know that they were interested in you. Perusing the small photos of my potential suitors, I more than once had to do a double take to make sure that the person in the picture was in fact a man. One of them, with long stringy blond hair, actually looked female. I shuddered.

"Boring. No. Oh, *hell no.*" I scanned through the photos of all the men on the first page, my feelings about online dating confirmed. Why was it so hard to find a decent man this way?

"Because the decent men aren't online," I told myself. "They don't have to be."

The decent men are in your neighborhood, talking to you as you're doing your morning run ….

Maybe it was Holly and Vivica's vehement disapproval of me even finding Andre attractive that had me feeling even more drawn to him. Was it really so wrong for me to go on a date with him? It wasn't like he was barely out of diapers. He was well past the legal age.

Vivica and Holly had scoffed at the idea of me dating a younger man. I had male colleagues who dated women ten to twenty years their junior and no one batted an eye. Why was it that people frowned when women did it?

I closed off the dating website. One of these days, I would have to find a way to take down my profile.

Before I knew what I was doing, I found myself looking up the name *Andre Moore.*

As his website loaded, my heart beat a little harder. I sighed. The picture that came on the screen was

a shot of him from the mid chest up, his hands clasped around a football, a big smile on his face. And those dimples … why did I find those dimples so damn sexy?

A wave of disappointment washed over me when I saw his age. Twenty-nine. He was a decade younger than I was.

I scanned through the gallery nonetheless, because it certainly didn't hurt to look. I checked out the various poses of him on the football field, at press events. In two of the photos of him at a couple different charity events, he was pictured with a stunningly beautiful woman, the one I used to see going into his house sometimes. The articles said that her name was Clarissa Evans, and she was labeled as his girlfriend. That fact caused my stomach to tighten.

Even his name screams player ….

The thing was, I hadn't seen Clarissa around in a long time. And unlike what my friends believed, I didn't see any evidence to support the fact that Andre was a player. Not that I had to know, of course. But I never saw tons of different cars coming and going from his house—not that I was checking.

I looked at his face again, at that smile, those dimples, and those thick lips. God, what could he do with those lips?

A surge of lust shot through me. I couldn't stop my naughty thoughts. Andre's lips tantalizing all of my erogenous zones ….

My body on fire, I turned off my computer. Then I went to my bedroom, where I could allow myself to indulge in my erotic thoughts … and have Andre, if only in my dreams.

CHAPTER THREE

The smoke alarm began to wail, instantly reminding me that I had forgotten the oatmeal I was making on the stove.

"Shit, shit, *shit!*" I jumped out of the bath and grabbed my robe from the hook behind the door. I ran from upstairs where I had been luxuriating in a rare bath, wondering what the hell had happened to my brain. I'd put the oatmeal on the stove … then had forgotten all about it.

Actually, I'd put the oatmeal on the stove … then had gotten distracted with thoughts of Andre. I'd gone into the bath with my toy, my body needing release.

Now, I charged into the kitchen, seeing the smoke. I waved my arms through it as I made my way to the stove, as if that would make a difference. I quickly grabbed the pot by the handle, then dumped it into the sink and turned on the tap. The cold water sizzled against the heat of the pan and caused more plumes of smoke to billow.

"Bella, how could you have been so stupid?" I chastised myself.

I rarely cooked. I ordered out a lot because I worked so many late hours as an auditor. But surely I could make a breakfast of oatmeal without burning the house down.

Apparently not, I thought sourly.

There was too much smoke in the house. I tied the knot around my robe, then dumped the water out of the pan. I needed to get this pot outside. Carrying it, I headed to the front door, where I proceeded to put it outside on my front step.

"Good morning."

The pot fell from my hand at the unexpected sound of a voice, and my head jerked up. Seeing who was standing at the end of my walkway, my eyes bulged. I quickly stood upright, holding the folds of my robe together over my chest, making sure that I was showing no skin.

Smiling, Andre raised a hand in greeting. He was dressed in black sport shorts and a white t-shirt. Sweat glistened on his arms and face, and a pair of Beats Audio headphones were over his ears.

I waved back, wondering if when I had been bending over, my robe had been hanging low and revealed more than I would've wanted. I couldn't tell by the way he was looking at me.

"You have a mishap?" Andre asked, his gaze going to my stainless steel pot as he dragged the earphones down around his neck. "That's a lot of smoke."

"Stupid me. I left the pot on the stove and then went upstairs into the bath, completely forgetting about it. I guess I'm getting old and senile," I added with a laugh. Was this what happened when a person approached forty?

"Old?" Andre made a face as though that was hard to believe. And then, instead of jogging on down the street, he made his way up my driveway. I held the flaps of my robe even tighter, making sure that he could see nothing beneath.

"I haven't heard from you."

He smiled, and God those dimples. I wanted to rip my robe open and invite him in. And that was so unlike me.

"Hear from me?" I asked. "I wasn't aware I was supposed to contact you …"

"I was kind of hoping you'd changed your mind about dinner."

"Oh." I swallowed. "And I pretty much figured that you'd forgotten you'd even asked."

"Why would I forget that I'd asked?"

"Because surely you had to be kidding …"

His eyes crinkled as his smile widened. "Kidding? Why would I ask if I wasn't serious?"

"Because." I knew that response sounded stupid. "Because … don't you have a girlfriend?"

Andre chuckled softly. "No. If I had a girlfriend, I wouldn't have asked you to dinner."

"You're not dating Clarissa?" Before he could ask how I knew her name, I said, "I saw something in the paper about you two once."

"That's been over for a few months," Andre explained.

"Oh," I said lamely.

"Is that why you didn't say yes to dinner?" Andre asked. "Although, maybe I should make it a breakfast offer." His eyes gestured to the burned pot. "Since you apparently could use a meal right now."

"Despite how it looks, I'm not totally pathetic in the kitchen." I made a face. "Maybe I am."

"I'd be happy to take you out now, if that would work for you."

Saturday morning. There was no reason I couldn't go for breakfast with him. No reason other than my self-respect and sanity. "I … I really need to get back inside and tend to the alarm. It's driving me nuts."

"After that," Andre said. "Can I take you out?" His voice ended on a hopeful note.

"Uh … well, there's some work I have to get caught up on …" My voice trailed off when I saw the look of disappointment in his eyes. Actual disappointment.

Was he really looking forward to going out with me? Maybe Holly was wrong. Maybe Andre didn't see me as simply another conquest.

"But," I quickly stated. "I think I can spare some time. All work and no play makes for a grumpy person." What was I doing? "Where did you have in mind?"

"Anything you like. There's that new restaurant a couple of miles away that serves breakfast all day. Or … if you're adventurous, I could make you breakfast."

A zap of heat charged my nether region. Was he suggesting … did he want to get me alone in his place so that we could have sex? Was Holly right, after all?

"Nope. Forget I suggested that," Andre quickly said. "I don't want you getting the wrong impression."

His words were like a pinprick on my balloon of hope, irrational as it was. Did I actually want to hear him say that he wanted me alone? That he wanted to ravage my body?

All I knew for sure was that as I stood there, naked beneath my robe, my body was alive in a purely sexual way. And then I felt ashamed at the feeling. What would my friends think of me, lusting after a man a decade younger than I was?

"I've been itching to try that new breakfast spot, actually," I found myself saying. I wasn't ready to be alone in a room with him. I wasn't naïve. I knew where it could lead. And I didn't want to fall into bed with him, just because he turned me on. Unlike a lot of men and some women, I wasn't a slave to my sexual feelings. I could have them and not act on them.

Besides, I'd never dated a younger man. And casual sex with a neighbor … talk about a recipe for disaster.

I didn't imagine anything would come of this breakfast with Andre, so what would it hurt to have a meal with him? We could get to know each other. Become friends.

It was a win-win situation.

"How about you meet me at my place," Andre suggested. "Gimme about half an hour to take a quick shower and get dressed."

"Sure thing."

❖

I put on jeans and a t-shirt. Nothing fancy. In fact, I deliberately dressed down, not trying to come off as a horny female who could use a good time in bed.

Andre's eyes lit up in a smile when he opened the door and saw me. "Gimme a second," he said.

I was in the process of saying "Okay" when he closed the door.

I made a face. That was awkward. Was I supposed to stand here? Go inside?

As I waited on his porch, I glanced around the neighborhood. Across the street, I saw a curtain quickly shut. Or was that my imagination?

Was I already giving the neighborhood gossips fodder for the rumor mill?

Moments later, the garage door began to open. Of course. I hopped down the steps to meet Andre.

His car, a sleek black BMW, started to reverse out of his driveway. He had dark shades on now, and looked every bit the star he was.

The car came to a stop, and I went around to the passenger side. I quickly opened the door and got in.

"Nice ride," I said. "Top of the line Beemer. Is that standard issue for all athletes?"

"I'm not like other ball players. You'll learn that soon enough."

I nodded, but my gaze began to wander toward the house where I'd seen the curtain fall. Even though I didn't socialize in the neighborhood much, I'd heard that Janelle, who lived in that house with her parents, was interested in Andre. And at twenty-something, she was an appropriate age to be dating him.

Once we were out of the neighborhood, I looked at Andre again. He was wearing a cream-colored, short-sleeved dress shirt and black slacks. He was decidedly better dressed for breakfast than I was.

"I feel under-dressed," I said. "Maybe I should change."

"You look great just the way you are." Andre held my gaze for a long moment before turning his attention back to the road.

It didn't take more than seven minutes to get to the restaurant, seven minutes in which my pulse was racing faster than normal. The heavy bass of hip-hop played over the stereo's speakers, and we didn't really talk during the drive.

When we got to EggsCeptional, Andre backed into an available parking space on the street. He put his arm across the back of my seat as he maneuvered, and I couldn't help thinking about what it would be like to have his arms wrapped around *me* ….

The car parked, Andre turned to me and said, "Now I know that you're perfectly capable of opening a car door yourself, but will you be upset if I open it for you?"

"Upset? No."

"Good. Because some women get all bent out of shape when a man does something like that for them. I hate that."

He exited the car and came around to the passenger door. Then he opened it, and offered me a hand to help me out onto the sidewalk.

I wondered who Andre had been dating, because I couldn't imagine women objecting to a little chivalry. Perhaps, on the verge of forty, I was too old to understand the younger generation of women who would balk at a man holding a door for them or offering to carry a heavy box to their car.

"Thank you," I said, stepping onto the sidewalk. Andre then placed a hand on the small of my back and walked with me to the restaurant.

As I entered EggsCeptional with him, I wished that I had put on something sexier. In part because people seemed as though they had dressed to impress this morning, and also because I saw eyes all over the restaurant turning in our direction. It didn't take me more than a few moments to realize that people recognized Andre. Former star wide receiver for the Redskins. Suddenly, I felt woefully inadequate on his arm.

"I really should have changed," I muttered. But given that I dressed up every day of the week, I enjoyed being casual on the weekends.

"You look beautiful." He whispered the words in my ear, and my body felt a thrill of desire. I no longer cared what I was wearing, as long as I had Andre's approval.

As we were ushered to a table, I took stock of the people around us. The eyes still looking in our direction. It was a little overwhelming. "Is this what it's like with you all the time? Everywhere you go?"

"Yeah. And it gets old. Ever since I caught the winning touchdown in the last seconds of that Super Bowl game … well, you can imagine that people have loved me ever since."

"That must be nice. To be admired and respected like that."

"It is. I've got a buddy in Arizona who missed a crucial pass in a playoff game. His team lost. He got death threats."

"You're kidding." I looked at him, appalled. "Over a game?"

"People take their sports seriously. So yeah, I consider myself fortunate that people don't look at me and feel the desire to plunge a knife in my heart."

I chuckled, finding the idea absurd. But Andre raised his eyebrows and nodded, letting me know that he wasn't exaggerating.

Still, I could never imagine anyone wanting to hurt Andre, even if he'd made a bad play. He was the kind of guy that men wanted to emulate, and women wanted to be with.

I lifted my menu. "Do you already know what you'll—" My words stopped abruptly when I noticed two men in their twenties heading over to the table. They had a look of awe on their faces. My gaze went to Andre, and he looked to his left, now seeing the men. Instantly, his back straightened and a smile graced his lips.

"Sorry to disturb you," one of the men began. "But that play. That catch in the end zone. I know the way you landed you broke your ankle and that ended your career, but man, you're my hero. Can we get a picture?"

"Sure."

Andre stood and took photos with both guys. I smiled at them too, but secretly hoped that there wouldn't be more of this. I already felt out of place. Walking into a restaurant like this, even though it was a casual breakfast spot, I felt that I should have made myself look like the kind of woman who should be on Andre's arm.

But I had to wait even longer. Because those two men opened the proverbial flood gates. Others approached the table for autographs and photos.

"You're very gracious," I said after the last person left. Andre had spent several minutes engaging with his fans.

"You've got to appreciate the fans," he said. "That said, I didn't expect that attention here. I really wanted to spend my time getting to know you."

The waitress arrived then and smiled at Andre. "I take it you're someone famous."

"I played football," he told her with a shrug. "No big deal."

"Well, welcome to EggsCeptional. Have you had a chance to look at the menu?"

"I'll start off with a cappuccino," I said.

"I'll have the same." Andre opened the menu. "We haven't really had a chance to decide what we want. Can you give us a few more minutes?"

She did that, and when she returned a few minutes later, I'd decided on an omelet with mushrooms and cheese, and fresh-roasted potatoes. Andre opted for the steak and eggs.

Putting my elbows on the table, I rested my chin atop my joined hands. "Is that true? You broke your ankle and that ended your career? Sorry—I don't really watch sports."

"That's okay. And yep. Ironic, isn't it? I make the play of my career, and then it's game over for me."

"But I see you jogging …" My eyes narrowed in confusion.

"Which I can do. I just can't put my ankle through the rigorous kind of activity that football requires. So I retired. Went out on a high, which was nice."

"I like your positive attitude," I told him.

"A broken ankle ends a great career? Sure, I would have loved to play five more years. But in the grand scheme of things, what do I really have to complain about?"

I loved that he was grateful. I'd met far too many spoiled, entitled people with money. "So," I went on, "what's it like being a star?"

"I don't see myself as a star. I'm a guy who can catch a ball. I got paid very well to do it. I see myself as blessed."

He was incredibly down to earth. "You mean your success never got to your head?" I asked, a little skeptical.

"You don't feel particularly special when you realize that your mother has stage four breast cancer and there's not a damn thing you can do about it. All the money and success in the world means nothing then."

I drew in a sharp breath. "No …"

Andre pursed his lips as pain streaked across his face. Glancing down, he drew in an audible breath. "I'm a human being, just like everyone else. I've got different skills, and that afforded me a good life. I'm not perfect, but I try not to take anything for granted."

"I'm sorry about your mother," I said. "Did she …?" I couldn't say the word.

Andre nodded. "It's been seven years. She lived long enough to see me drafted into the NFL. I was able to buy her the home of her dreams, and she got to enjoy it for about two years. Then came the cancer … it took her quickly. And …" His voice trailed off. "And that's that."

And that's that. I knew it was anything but. "It sounds like you really loved your mother."

"She was my world. It was just me and her growing up. I never knew my dad."

"And now? Do the two of you talk?"

"I have no clue where he is, and that's fine with me. I have no desire to connect with the man. In fact, if he were to try to come into my life now, I would never trust that it was for the right reasons. He's just not a part of my life, and that's okay. I've made peace with that."

The waitress arrived with our coffee then, and I couldn't help thinking that Andre's life hadn't been so rosy. Raised by a single mother, no father in the picture. I could understand why he wouldn't want a relationship with his father, even though I'd had both of my parents in my life while growing up. Holly's father had walked out on the family when she was ten, and she'd never forgiven him. In recent years, her father had tried to connect with her, but she had flat out refused to have anything to do with him.

"What about you?" Andre asked after he sipped his coffee. "What's your family like?"

"My parents are still together. They moved to Phoenix about six years ago for better weather. I have one brother, who lives in Seattle with his wife. They've got a two-year-old little boy."

"So your family's spread out all over the country."

"Pretty much, yeah. This is where we all started. In Maryland, actually. Then Michael was offered a job with Amazon, and my parents decided that they were done with winter …. But I've got great friends here in D.C. So life is good."

"Why are you single?" Andre went on. "You're beautiful. I can't understand why some man hasn't snatched you up."

I sipped my coffee, considering what I should tell him. "I *was* married," I admitted, surprising myself. I usually leave out that fact unless I know someone very well.

His eyebrows rose. "You were?"

"Officially, yes. But really truly in my heart? No. I met the guy in Vegas … it was a bad situation that started with loneliness and lust and ended in disaster."

"You got married in Vegas?" Andre sounded amused.

"No, we didn't want to do the cliché. We wanted to prove that our love was real. Which sounds incredibly stupid, but it is what it is. We got married three weeks later in Miami, and six weeks after that, I was filing for divorce. No doubt the single biggest regret in my life, but I rectified it." I paused, saw that Andre was still looking at me, raptly waiting for me to go on.

But before I could speak, the waitress arrived with our meals. Intermittently, while we ate, I filled Andre in on the rest. My broken heart in college. My long years of not dating anyone. Then, finally, Steven's betrayal only a couple of months before.

"My mother thinks I'm unlucky in love. And I guess I'm starting to believe her."

"Don't say that." Andre held my eyes for a long beat. "Obviously, you've met idiots and jerks … but that doesn't mean the right guy isn't out there for you."

I made a sound of derision, then felt an odd tingle as I met Andre's eyes again and saw that he was still looking at me. As if he was trying to tell me something.

Suddenly, I was uncomfortable. My meal finished, I pushed my plate away from me. "Thank you for breakfast," I told him.

"You're welcome."

"I hate to eat and run, but I really do need to get back home."

"No problem."

He was gorgeous … and agreeable. And I could easily imagine myself getting naked with him.

Which was why I needed to get away from him as soon as possible.

Andre motioned for the waitress, and she brought the bill, which he promptly paid. Then I began to rise, and he did too.

In the car, I said, "Thanks again. Sorry to rush you out of there."

"Don't apologize. I'm just glad I was finally able to take you out for a meal." He paused. "And I'd like to do it again."

I chuckled. "I'm flattered, Andre. I really am."

"But … you still have feelings for your ex," he supplied.

I thought about it. "No. He hurt me, yes. But for him to be engaged to someone else while dating me? I'd be a fool to still have feelings for him. However, trusting another man … that's the issue."

"We're not all jerks, Bella."

Damn, I loved the way my name sounded on his lips. "I want to believe that."

A few beats passed. Then Andre asked, "Are you going to the Summer Kickoff barbecue?"

"Oh, that's right." I'd forgotten all about the annual neighborhood barbecue to celebrate the start of the summer season. "When is it? Next weekend?"

"Yes," Andre replied. "You'll be around?"

"I'll be in town, yes."

"But you're not planning to go to the barbecue?" he surmised.

"Honestly … I'm not sure. It's Saturday?"

"Yeah. Starts at three."

"I may have to head into the office. I'm not sure."

"Try and come," Andre told me. "Should be a good time."

"I'll try," I told him honestly. "If I'm at home, and I don't forget, I'll make an appearance."

"Good."

His lips held a hint of a smile, and I wondered what he was thinking. Perhaps that with a little bit of charm, he could sway me into dating again? Or did he simply want to be friendly, even if I wanted nothing more?

But it wasn't so much Andre's feelings I was considering, as my own. It was as if my brain and heart refused to cooperate with each other. My brain was telling me to remember to be cautious, that spending more time with Andre would only lead to heartbreak. But my heart … my heart was telling me to jump first and indulge, the consequences be damned.

CHAPTER FOUR

The doorbell rang as I was sweeping my kitchen floor. I rested the broom handle against the counter, then made my way to the door and swung it open. My stomach fluttered when I saw Andre standing there.

"Hey," I said.

"Afternoon."

As his eyes roamed over me, my stomach plummeted. I knew I looked a mess. My hair was in a sloppy bun atop my head. I was wearing cut off jeans and an over-sized t-shirt.

"Sorry," I said, suddenly very aware of just how undesirable I looked. "I was cleaning."

"Good. You're not at work."

"Good? Why?"

He gave me an odd look. "Did you forget …?"

I narrowed my eyes, confused. "Forget what?"

"The neighborhood barbecue …. We talked about it last weekend."

"Oh. That's right." I made a face.

"You weren't joking when you said that you might forget."

"I also didn't say that I'd be going."

"I'm pretty sure you said that if you were at home, you'd drop by. Are you actually planning to head into the office?"

That's right. I had said that. But attending the barbecue was not on the top of my priority list. "Actually," I began, "I'm trying to purge and clean up before I head out of town next weekend."

The last couple of years, I'd been out of town when the Summer Welcome barbecue took place. Some years, I'd been home but had kept my car in the garage and not ventured out. It wasn't that I was antisocial. It was that I always had work to do and didn't necessarily feel like going out to hang with my neighbors—most of whom were coupled off. The few times I had attended the barbecue, I had always gotten questions about why I was single. *You're such a beautiful woman. I can't believe there isn't a man out there for you.*

"You'd rather clean toilets than enjoy this beautiful day?" Andre gestured to the sky.

"It's not that I'd *rather* clean toilets. It's more like I finally have to do all the cleaning I've been putting off for far too long."

"It starts in a couple of hours. Surely you can spare a bit of time. Take a break. Someone once said, all work and no play makes for a grumpy Bella."

I smiled. "Touché. But I didn't prepare anything. I can't attend the barbecue empty-handed."

"That's okay. I ordered a ton of food and drinks. I'll say it's from the both of us."

"You don't have to do that."

Andre held my gaze for a beat before speaking. "In case you haven't figured it out, I want to spend more time with you."

Again, my stomach fluttered. Then, giving him a wary look, I asked, "Why?"

"You're a beautiful woman. Why not?"

It was time I shoot down this thing—whatever it was—once and for all. Like my friends had said, he was too young. I'd enjoyed our breakfast last week, but I had come to realize that I didn't fit into his glitzy world.

"I realize that I look younger than I actually am," I began. "And while I'm flattered by your interest, you need to know that I'm thirty-nine years old. In fact, I'll be forty next weekend."

"So?" Andre didn't even hesitate, as if I'd what I'd told him didn't matter in the least.

"You're not serious." I made a face. "I'm about to turn forty. You're gonna turn thirty either this year or next. Obviously, I'm too old for you."

"So that's what's holding you back?"

"Did you hear what I just said?"

"I heard you."

"Then you must understand."

"Understand what? That we have to be the same age in order to date?"

"No, I'm not saying that."

"Men date younger women all the time and no one makes a big deal about it. Why can't a woman date a younger man? My last coach was fifteen years older than his wife. All I see when I look at you is a beautiful woman. One I very much would like to get to know better. What does age matter? It's just a number."

Andre's comment struck a chord. I had often felt that way myself. And I'd felt that way when my friends had so strongly objected to me having anything to do with him. Men dated younger women. Why couldn't I date a younger man?

"Now that that issue's been put to rest," Andre went on, "will you come to the street barbecue? I'll feel much better with you there."

Damn it, my heart began to flutter a little. Why was I drawn to this man?

Because he's gorgeous, and sexy as hell. A trained psychologist wasn't needed to make me understand that I was a woman who was lusting after a seriously fine man.

And so what if there was an age difference between us? I didn't need to be thinking about planning a life with him. He was young enough that he would no doubt want children, and I was embarking on forty. My eggs were soon going to be drying up.

But that didn't mean that I couldn't have some fun with him, did it?

"So?" he asked, his expression charming as he looked down at me.

I began to nod, despite my reservations. Maybe this was about sex, a primal attraction. And so what if it was? We were both consenting adults.

"Okay. I guess it won't kill me to go to the street social."

Andre chuckled. "Don't sound so enthusiastic."

"I'm only going because of you."

His eyes held mine. "That's fine with me."

I spent a good hour trying on and taking off outfits before deciding on a simple summer dress. I showered and washed my hair, and let my naturally curly locks hang down past my shoulders instead of pulling it back into a bun, as I typically did. That was the way I wore it at the office, to look more professional and downplay my sexuality. But today I wanted to look casual and cute.

I applied light makeup. Just a bit of eyeliner and lip gloss. Then I smiled at my reflection in the mirror. I actually looked fresher-faced and younger this way.

The dress I was wearing showed just enough cleavage without being too much. Only after I checked out my complete appearance did I admit to myself that I was hoping to impress Andre. Unlike the first time we'd gone out.

Why are you trying to impress that man? I asked myself, noting that I looked sexier than I had in a long time.

You know why, a little voice whispered in my head.

When I exited my house, my heart was beating fast. I could hear the music and chatter at the end of the cul-de-sac, and I started in that direction.

I was at the end of my driveway when I saw him. Wearing khaki pants and a white shirt, glimpsing him even from this distance made my body come

alive. I had totally loved being with Steven, but there was something about Andre that excited me in an even more intense way.

He saw me as I was making my way toward the group of happy neighbors, and his lips curled in a smile. God, I loved that. It made me feel giddy to know that just seeing me brightened his day.

He started toward me immediately, meeting me before I reached everybody else. Giving me a once-over, he let out a low whistle. "Wow. You look stunning."

I blushed. Actually blushed like a tenth-grader getting a compliment from a guy she liked. But what hot-blooded woman wouldn't be affected by that kind of reaction from a man?

"Thank you," I said.

Andre continued to look at me, as if he couldn't get enough. His eyes warmed my skin, making it tingle. After what I'd gone through with Steven, was it wrong for me to indulge in the attention?

"I'm really glad you didn't bail," he said.

"Me too," I told him. It was good for me to get out. To enjoy some camaraderie with the neighbors, while getting to know Andre better.

He placed his hand on the small of my back and led me toward the rest of the crowd. I felt a little uncomfortable, but I didn't pull away. He was giving people the impression that we were together, but I played it cool, not trying to make a big deal out of anything.

Susie, my next-door neighbor, beamed at me. She came right over to me and gave me a hug. "I didn't think you'd be here. You're usually out of town."

I returned her smile. "This year I'm not away on business, so why not?"

Susie was the perfect suburbanite. She was the kind of woman who would greet newcomers to the neighborhood with an apple pie or other baked treat. Which is exactly what she'd done with me. When I'd moved to the neighborhood six years earlier, she had arrived at my door a few days later with a fresh-baked pie and a warm smile. She had two kids, a boy and a girl, and she appeared to be perpetually happy. Her blonde bob was cut to perfection, and she never seemed to leave the house without being perfectly put together. She was a stay-at-home mom whose husband was an executive. She liked her life, and it showed.

I greeted other people, neighbors I had seen but not really gotten to know. Most of them I at least had a passing acquaintance with, but some who lived down the street I didn't even recognize. I didn't tend see them when they drove by and vice versa.

I shook hands and exchanged names with those that I wasn't familiar with. Then I met the new family that had moved into one of the houses on the cul-de-sac just two months earlier, after the couple that used to live there split.

"I'm Joanne," the woman said, shaking my hand.

"And I'm Jeff," her husband told me.

"We've been married for five years now. And I'm three months pregnant." Joanne beamed, pressing her left hand over her flat belly, which displayed her large engagement ring and diamond-filled wedding band. "And oh, that must be your husband."

"My h—"

The question died on my lips when I felt the hand gently slip around my waist from my left side.

Andre.

"Hey. What can I get you to drink?"

"You don't have to get me anything," I told him. "I can do that."

"I want to," Andre told me, and I remembered what he'd said about some women getting bent out of shape when a man did the little things for them. I was so used to doing for myself, but I didn't want that independence to come off as off-putting.

So I said, "Sure. If there's a cola, I'll take one. No," I quickly corrected. "Make that a juice. Cranberry, orange—whatever's there. I should be cutting soda out of my diet."

"He seems like a really doting husband," Joanne said. "Wish my husband waited on me like that."

"He's not my husband," I told her.

"Ahhh. That explains it."

Stifling a chuckle, I wandered a few feet away, watching as Andre strolled the rest of the way to the table where the beverages were laid out. I took the opportunity to check him out. Seriously, how sexy could one person be?

"He's so easy on the eyes, isn't he?"

Turning, I saw Susie standing beside me, her eyes following Andre's movements as mine had been. She sighed dreamily.

"Yes," I agreed. "Very easy to look at."

"Not that I'm not happy with Doug, but it doesn't hurt to look, right?"

"Of course not."

I wandered over to the food tables. There were pastries, platters of fresh fruit, veggies and dip. Two of the neighbors who lived beside each other were on a grill cooking up burgers and hotdogs and chicken kebabs. Kids ran around in the street, giggling. It was a festive atmosphere.

Andre came back over to me with a bottle of cranberry juice. "Here you go."

"Thank you."

He gestured toward his house, where there were two Adirondack chairs on the sidewalk. "You wanna have a seat?"

"Okay." I preferred sitting with him anyway, the only person I had so far even built much of a relationship with. Yes, I knew my other neighbors, but didn't hang out with them. I just didn't have the time to spend Sunday afternoons chatting mindlessly. The time I did have, I preferred to spend with the friends I knew and loved.

"So," Andre began as he sank onto one of the chairs, "you asked if I was involved with anyone. But I didn't ask you the same question." He met my gaze. "Are you?"

"I thought we did have this conversation. I told you about my failed marriage, about Steven …"

"You did. But that doesn't mean there isn't anybody you're seeing now in a casual way. Someone who's standing in the way of me getting to know you better."

I took a sip of my cranberry juice before answering. "No. There's no one."

"Good."

I looked at him from behind my sunglasses, wondering if he could see my narrowed eyes. "Why do you say good?"

"Because if you're not dating anyone, then that means I have a shot."

"Is that what your interest is?" I asked. "You want to date me?"

"Why do you think I keep asking you out?"

I looked away. I couldn't tell him the thought that had been in my mind.

That he probably was attracted to me and wanted a little action. You start with dinner, of course … then jump to what you really want. Sex.

"Ahhh," he said. "So you figured that I asked you out—to be polite, of course—but my real goal was to get you into bed."

I said nothing, but I'm sure he could read in my eyes the truth that that was exactly what I'd suspected.

"Didn't I tell you that I wasn't your typical ball player?" he went on. "I'm not after only one thing."

"Look, I appreciate the fact that you seem like a good guy. You don't want to just take advantage of me … that's good to know. But although you blew off the age difference, if you're really serious about dating me, there are things to consider. Like that fact that you'll likely want kids one day."

"You have no clue what I want."

He gave me a long look, and I was the first to turn away. Damn it. How was it that this man made me feel so tingly inside? Wasn't I beyond this sort of teenage lustful feeling?

As my eyes wandered toward the left, I saw Janelle, the neighbor I'd suspected had seen us through her window last week, sauntering toward us. She had a smile on her face, but a skeptical look in her eyes. She was wondering what was going on between the two of us.

"Hey," Janelle practically sang. She was trying to be overly pleasant. "How y'all doing?"

"I'm fine," I told her.

"I'm good, Janelle." Andre offered her a polite smile.

Janelle continued to grin, her gaze flitting between the both of us. "Is there something going on that I don't know about?" she asked, her tone playful.

"You mean between us?" I quickly said.

"You two are looking mighty cozy. But I don't want to jump to any conclusions now." She chortled.

"Please, don't," I told her. "We're just two neighbors, enjoying the Summer Kick Off barbecue."

"Of course." Janelle waved a dismissive hand. "I should've known better. You're way too old for Andre."

Ouch. That stung. Suddenly, I felt as though I were back in high school with a mean girl. Janelle's comment had been deliberate. Either she'd wanted to out my age, or make Andre feel bad for being interested in an older woman.

I almost wanted to ram my tongue down his throat just to piss her off.

Obviously, Andre was thinking along the same lines. Because the next thing I knew, he took my hand in his, leaned across the armrest of his chair to get closer to me, and slipped his fingers into my hair. And before I realized just how far he was going with this, he urged my face to his and kissed me.

As my eyes widened, my body flooded with sensation. Slow, sweet, and too long to be appropriate on a street where kids were playing, the kiss woke up every nerve ending in my body. My reaction to him was visceral.

When he pulled his lips from mine, I remembered Janelle. Looking up at her, I saw that her eyes were wide with horror. I knew she was around twenty-seven or twenty-eight, still living at home with her parents. Hoping to snag a man like Andre with fat pockets to take care of her desire for Louis Vuitton and Gucci and all of the other designer labels I saw her sporting.

"Oh." Janelle looked uncomfortable. "Um …"

She quickly shuffled off and I couldn't help but laugh. Andre did too. When the laughter died down, I said. "You're still holding my hand."

"Your point?"

"Janelle is gone."

"I don't see what one thing has to do with the other." His eyes held mine, and I didn't look away this time. I wondered if his heart was tripping in his chest as mine was. The man was certainly sexy, and he was making me feel beautiful and desirable.

"You're really not joking, are you?" I asked.

"About wanting to get to know you better? Date you? Nope."

"And what do you see coming of this?" I asked. "If I say yes to going on a real date with you?"

"What does anyone hope for when they start a relationship with someone?"

"Whoa whoa whoa whoa." I pulled my hand from his. "Start a relationship? Don't you think you're putting the cart before the horse?"

"One step at a time. I like you. I like what I see so far. And that kiss …? Damn." He sank his teeth into his bottom lip. "Damn."

Heat washed over me, leaving me flushed. I allowed my mind to go there, where it had been in my recent fantasies. I pictured Andre kissing not only my lips, but other parts of my body that craved a man's touch. And God help me, I began to get aroused right there on the street.

Someone else came over then, a neighbor named Bob. I almost expected him to comment on our inappropriate public display of affection, but he started to talk about football, asking whether Andre thought he might play again. The conversation evolved from there to Andre sharing his desire to one day go into coaching. Leaving the two of them to talk, I got up and made the rounds, noticing that Janelle was eyeing me with a dirty look. I didn't care. I spoke to the other women, made idle chatter, listened to them talk about their kids in soccer, who had done well in the recent high school track and field meet, and who was heading off to college.

"Come August, we'll be empty nesters," Diana, a neighbor at the end of the cul-de-sac was saying, "and I can't wait. John and I will finally get to do all the traveling we've wanted to do."

I lived in this neighborhood with mostly traditional families, and these were the moments when I was painfully aware of the fact that I was almost forty, with one failed marriage behind me, and no kids. It wasn't that I dwelt on that fact, nor that it particularly bothered me. But there were times when I couldn't help thinking about the fact that life doesn't always end up the way you planned for it to be. When I was eighteen, I was certain that I was going to marry Jeremy, my high school boyfriend I'd dated for two years. But he was the first man to break my heart when he went off to another state for college.

I looked at Andre, smiling that infectious smile of his as he spoke to the neighbor. After he'd asked me out, I'd become hot and bothered. I had started to contemplate the idea of having sex with him.

But he was talking relationship. About liking me, and hoping for more.

Did I dare let down my emotional wall and allow him into my life?

CHAPTER FIVE

I thought about Andre all night. I did more than think about him, actually. I imagined the two of us having wild, sweaty, mind-blowing sex. I woke up in a state of arousal. The kind of arousal for which you need release.

Andre had walked me to my door after the party was over, and had kissed me again. The second kiss had been to prove that the first one hadn't been for Janelle's benefit.

Then he'd reiterated his desire to take me out for dinner. A real date. "We'll get dressed up, go somewhere nice."

"I'm sure you'll come to your senses by morning," I'd told him, trying to sound as if I were joking.

"Are you putting yourself down?" he asked. "Or playing hard to get?"

Those had been his parting words, and they'd left me thinking. I was, on some level, unable to accept the idea that Andre really wanted to date me. Especially now that he knew about our age difference. Not that it had to be a deal breaker, but in terms of a guy planning his future … if he wanted kids, I wouldn't be the best woman to get involved with.

It was only after Andre had left that I'd realized he hadn't given me his number, nor asked for mine. Which meant that if I was going to say yes to dinner, I had to go to his door and tell him so.

Maybe that had been his plan. To make me mean it when I said yes.

Likewise, if I never showed up at his door, then he would have his answer.

The thing was, I didn't know if I had the guts to follow up and go out on a real date with him. Sex I could handle. But the idea of a relationship with a man like Andre … that I wasn't sure about.

Maybe he was simply good material to fantasize about, to get me through the nights when I missed having a man in my bed.

Later that morning, as I was backing out of my driveway, I noticed the small bouquet of flowers outside my door. Stopping the car, I got out and trotted up my front steps. With growing excitement, I picked up the bouquet. There had to be at least two dozen red roses. The bouquet was wrapped in cellophane, the package completed with a large red bow.

I was grinning now, downright elated.

Tucked into the bouquet a small envelope. I quickly opened the cellophane so I could get at the card. Several seconds later, I began to read.

I'm very much serious about getting to know you better. Let me know when I can take you out.

As my heart began to beat hard, I whipped my gaze down the street in the direction of Andre's house, expecting to see him standing there on his walkway, smiling and waving at me. But he wasn't there.

When had he even gotten to purchase this bouquet? It wasn't even eight in the morning. The fact that he'd been thinking of me and wanted to get these flowers on my doorstep before I went to work made me feel ….

Well, made me feel special.

I sighed happily. I wanted to say yes. Yes to dinner … and to a whole lot more than that.

As I unlocked my front door to bring the flowers inside, my excitement was tampered by the memory of how Vivica and Holly had reacted to me telling them about Andre. They'd found his proposal of dinner ridiculous. Holly believed he simply wanted another notch on his bedpost. Not to mention that she thought I was way too old for him. Vivica believed that if I got involved with Andre, I was headed for more heartbreak. In her eyes, Andre was a player.

Was he? And even if he was, did I care?

All I knew for sure was that as I went to work, I had a smile on my face. One that lasted all day. A smile because of Andre.

Even my colleagues noticed. One of them, a gay male who was always interested in my sex life—or lack thereof—went as far as to ask if I'd gotten laid this weekend because I certainly looked like it.

"Brian!" I chastised him. "Please. Get your mind out of the gutter."

"Girl, with that expression on your face. It looks to me like you got some, honey. And good for you."

I did my work for the day, and now I understood what it meant to have a spring in your step. I was practically floating on cloud nine because of Andre's interest in me.

Not to mention I felt far less stressed than I often did while performing my duties. And several times throughout the day, I actually stopped to daydream and think about Andre and how amazing his lips had felt on mine.

Hours later, I was going through my agenda. I was a little disappointed that I wouldn't be able to go for breakfast or dinner with Andre this weekend, because I left for Paris in four days.

Unless ….

No, I couldn't.

I bit down on my fingernail as the thought flirted at the edge of my mind. Could I?

I didn't let myself fully consider the thought. I stopped it, because it was ridiculous.

I could *not* invite Andre to Paris.

"He barely asked you out to dinner, and now you're thinking of inviting him on a business trip? Are you insane?"

But a part of me did feel insane. Insane in the most vibrant and electrifying way. I knew what I wanted from him. My body knew. And I was too old to deny it. Hell, I would be forty this very weekend. Why shouldn't I celebrate in grand style?

That is, if Andre was willing. I'd often heard that the older woman younger man combination actually made the most that sense. Women in their late thirties and forties finally know what they want sexually. Younger men want it all the time. It was the perfect scenario.

I didn't hold any illusions that Andre and I were going to sail off into the sunset together. But one night together? One hot, scandalous, fantasy-fulfilling night in Paris? My body became flushed just thinking about it. My panties were starting to get moist.

Did I dare ask him?

Why not? a voice in my head asked me.

I was tempted, but unsure. Throughout the last hour of my workday I contemplated, *should I, shouldn't I?* I weighed the pros and cons of inviting Andre to Paris.

One very big potential con was that he could reject the idea. Which would leave my ego a little bruised.

He'd already asked me out, making his interest clear. But he'd also stressed that he wasn't interested in only sex. My inviting him to Paris might be construed as an invitation for a sexual romp with no expectations.

I frowned. And then I thought of a fact that couldn't be denied. The sexual tension between us was hot. God, the memory of that first kiss had left my body flushed several times during the day as I recalled it.

If he was feeling what I was feeling, why wouldn't he say yes to Paris this weekend? We were both adults. There was no rule that said we had to date for months before getting physical. My inviting him to Paris didn't have to be construed as *only* an opportunity for sex.

He wanted to get to know me. And that wasn't something I necessarily wanted to do under the watchful eye of our neighbors. If I explained that to him, surely he might say yes to Paris. Besides, it was my birthday this weekend. Why should I spend it alone? I'd originally planned and hoped that Steven would be with me in the city of lights. But now that he wouldn't, why shouldn't I be with someone else?

My decision was made. I decided that I would ask Andre. I would ask him before I lost my nerve.

I braced myself my entire drive home to go to his door and ask that he go to Paris with me. Being almost forty, surely I could just ask for what I wanted. I went to his door, prepared for either rejection or elation. But he wasn't there.

And I couldn't text him. We hadn't even exchanged numbers, which seemed really silly at this point.

"Besides, you can't ask a man to go to Paris with you via text," I said to myself. But since I didn't want my nerves to get cold, I decided that I would write him a note thanking him for the flowers, and ask him if he was busy this weekend. I wrote out the words on a blank card I had at home, but paused when I wanted to get to the gist of my note.

Just do it.

And so I did. I wrote the words I knew I wouldn't be able to take back.

I'm going to be in Paris this weekend for business. Want to join me?

To give him an easy escape clause, I added:

If you don't, don't acknowledge this question at all. We can pretend it never happened. Again, thank you for the beautiful flowers.

Then, even though the insecure part of me didn't want to follow through with leaving the card at Andre's doorstep, I took a chance and did. And then I went home, certain that I was never going to hear from him again. Which was better, if he was going to turn me down. No point in any awkwardness. Just cut anything off before it even started.

But I heard the knock on my door later that evening. Around eight o'clock. As I opened the door, I began to hold my breath. Waiting.

Andre looked down at me with a question in his eyes and said, "Just don't talk to you again? Pretend it never happened?"

I breathed. Swallowed. "I just … I know I was being very presumptuous by even suggesting it, so—"

"Yes."

"—so I figured if you felt awkward, you didn't ever have to—"

"*Yes,*" Andre repeated, firmly, and the word finally registered.

"You—yes?"

"Yes." Andre's full lips curled in a smile. "I'd love to go to Paris."

My body began to throb. And my pussy began to get moist. He wanted to go with me. Oh my God ….

"I can't let you spend your birthday alone."

"How did you know it was my birthday?"

"You told me. You said you were going to be forty this weekend."

"Right." And talk about extra brownie points for remembering.

"Are you going to invite me in?" Andre asked, his voice sultry. "So we can discuss the particulars?"

"Oh. Right. Of course." Lord, I could barely think straight. I stepped back and gestured for him to enter my foyer.

His large frame seemed to fill my home. And in a way that made it all the more obvious what was missing from my life.

I crossed my arms over my chest, saying, "So you'll come. That's great. I have to be in Paris for business, and I was thinking how much it would suck to have to spend my birthday there alone."

"I'll be there."

I wasn't meeting his eyes. "Here's the thing. I know you said you're not after only one thing. And I respect that. But if you come all the way to Paris—"

"Please don't tell me you want me to keep my hands off of you."

My body flushed. "No. That's not what I was going to say. That's not what I want." I paused, still not looking up at him. "I'm not exactly sure what's happening between us—where this will lead. So this weekend, why don't we … why don't we leave it to spending one glorious night in Paris together and see where it goes from there?" Finally, I looked up at him, ready for his rejection.

"One night?" he asked. "That's what you're suggesting?"

"Yes," I told him, sounding decisive now. I knew he wasn't going to go for it. He was going to tell me that he didn't want to head all the way to Paris for one night, that I was being unreasonable.

Maybe I was. Maybe my unfair suggestion was a way to force him to say no ….

"Okay."

"Okay?" My eyes bulged. I wasn't sure I'd heard him correctly.

"Did you expect me to say no? Did you *want* me to say no?"

"I—I'm not even—I don't—" I stammered, making no sense at all.

And then he stepped forward and placed his hands on my arms, forcing me to unfold them from their closed-off position. Then he slipped a hand around my waist and drew me close.

A little sigh escaped me as my breasts pressed against his chest. His eyes locked on mine, and my heart began to thump wildly.

"I am mad attracted to you," he rasped, reaching for the hairpins holding my bun in place. He made quick work of taking them out. "I think you don't realize how much."

"I …" I couldn't even form a sentence.

The hairpins removed, he placed them in one of my palms. Then, framing my face with both hands, he lowered his lips to mine.

And that first glorious touch of his lips against mine … oh baby!

His lips moved over mine with slow sensuality as his hands slipped into my hair. He suckled my top lip, then my bottom lip, before adding a flick of his tongue.

My mouth opened on a heavenly sigh. Urging my head closer with his fingers, Andre deepened the kiss. His tongue swept over mine, and my eyes fluttered shut. Then, finally realizing that I was standing there like a helpless fawn, I flattened my hands against his chest. Feeling the hard pecs, I sighed again, then snaked my arms around his neck, pressing my body closer to his.

I surrendered fully and completely to his kiss. And I was ready to surrender completely to him ….

With what sounded like a groan of protest, Andre broke the kiss. I felt almost disoriented, having been on cloud nine one second, and now jarringly back on solid ground.

"If one night in Paris is all I can have with you, I'll take it."

I was breathless, unable to utter a word. Because if I spoke, I would surely beg him to take me to bed.

"I know that if I ask you for more time than that, you'll tell me that you have business to do. That you don't want the distraction. Am I right?"

I nodded.

"I know what it's like to be on the road. And I don't want to get in your way. I'll take the one night. Gladly." His voice was husky now, backing up the promise his kiss had started. "Because after that one night, I know you'll want more."

I swallowed again. My body was on fire. I knew he would be great in bed. There was no question. The chemistry between us was off the charts.

But I would wait. I would wait until Paris. Make my birthday truly special.

"So you'll really come?" I asked.

"I know you didn't mean that how it sounded … but yes, I intend to."

I blushed furiously.

Andre chuckled softly as he stroked my cheek. "I think I'd better leave. Because … well, I can't ensure I'll remain a perfect gentleman if I stay."

"Yes, I think that's wise."

"In all this time, we haven't exchanged numbers. I'm going to need that to get the details from you regarding the trip. The hotel, the dates."

"Of course." I recited my phone number.

"Hold on," he told me, then pulled his phone from a leather holder on his waist. Once he did, I repeated the number. He read it back to me from his screen.

"Yes," I told him. "That's it."

"All right, I'm going to send you a text so that you have my phone number."

"Or to make sure that I didn't give you a fake number?" I offered, adding a little smile to let him know that I was joking.

"I think we're past the point of playing games."

In his eyes, I saw the promise that this weekend would be the best sexual experience of my life.

I couldn't wait.

CHAPTER SIX

I didn't tell my girlfriends. Some things, you don't have to tell everyone. This would be my delicious secret. My time with Andre to celebrate my birthday the way I wanted to.

The way I deserved.

I didn't need my friends being skeptical. I didn't need them putting a damper on my actions by giving me lectures about how I was going to do something stupid. I needed one night of pleasure. One night where I didn't second-guess myself or question what I was doing. One night where I simply indulged.

I arrived in Paris on Friday night, and Andre was due to arrive Saturday. Saturday was my actual birthday, so that was good. I would have time to rest and recover from the jet lag before he arrived. Then we would do the things in Paris that I had always wanted to do with a lover. Climbing the Eiffel Tower. Going for a cruise on the Seine. Dining at exquisite restaurants.

And Saturday night …. Quite bluntly, I expected Andre to rock my world.

By Sunday, he would be leaving and that was fine. I had to get ready for business on Monday morning. I would take this little bit of excitement and indulgence and then continue with my life.

Hotel Fouquet's Barrière in Paris was the epitome of luxury. Ideally situated at the corner of Avenue George V and the Champs-Elyses, it was in the heart of the city and close to many Parisian attractions. The exterior of the building was like a piece of art, with lights on the second level lit up and casting a gold-colored glow over the upper portion of the building in the night. It reminded me a lot of the Flatiron building in New York with how the two sides of the building came together at a sharp angle at the juncture of two streets.

Hanging over the first level was a red awning that read *Fouquet's*, beneath which was a restaurant patio that I recognized from some popular movies filmed in France. Despite the slight chill in the air, there were several guests dining outside. I'd heard that the food at the restaurant was delectable, and I couldn't wait to eat there.

I expected luxury from how the building looked outside, but when I stepped into the lobby, my lips parted. My expectations were exceeded. The lobby was chic and stylish, with classic touches. The French Provincial furniture added an element of sophistication, with gold-colored Queen Anne chaise lounges set up along the wall around a semi-circular lobby. The lounges, as well as regal high-backed chaises, made me feel as though I had entered a palace.

It was the perfect place for a romantic tryst.

Opposite the lounges were seating areas by the windows, each with its own comfy chairs surrounding a small table. The drapery that hung from the ceiling to the floors was also gold in color, and square-shaped lamps offered low lighting to help the setting seem even more intimate. There were several of these seating areas, with walls interspersed between them to make the areas seem like little oases unto themselves. The chandeliers were stunning, with touches of gold. They were more modern as opposed to antique in their design. So were the mirrors that hung along the walls in the seating areas.

The floor was a polished white marble with intermittent stripes of mahogany brown. That brown matched the color of the walls around the front desk, and the desk itself. Along the curved wall with chaise lounges opposite the front desk, I saw black and white photos of celebrities, including Marilyn Monroe. The hotel had the ambience of what fairytales were made of, and I was certain that I would experience some of that here.

"Bon soir, good evening," a young man greeted me warmly.

"Good evening."

"Welcome to Fouquet's Barrière," he continued in English, now that my language had been determined.

"Thank you," I said, noting that the French accent made him sound decidedly sexier.

I placed my purse on the counter top. The reception desk structure was like a modern piece of art. Made of dark mahogany, it was multi-curved. There were long, thin panes of glass alternating with the mahogany on the front portion where the desk went from the counter to the floor, almost resembling keys on a piano.

"You have a reservation?" the man asked.

"Yes." I reached into my purse for my passport.

"Thank you," he said as he accepted it. "Is this your first time in Paris?"

"No," I told him. "I've been once before."

The last time I had been in Paris, I had stayed at the Four Seasons. I remembered how lonely I'd felt entering such a beautiful and grand hotel without someone on my arm. Being in town for business, as opposed to exploring Paris with a lover.

But this time, I had something to look forward to. Andre.

My heart fluttered as I thought of him.

"One moment, Ms. Sinclair," the clerk said, his eyes on the computer screen. "I have a package for you."

"Oh," I said. "Okay."

The clerk disappeared into a room behind the reception desk. Less than a minute later, he came out with a small, bright silver gift bag. White tissue paper resembling a rose was protruding from the top of the bag, and curly strings of silver ribbon tied the bag's handles together.

"Voila," the man said, smiling warmly.

As he handed me the gift bag, I realized that he was also giving me a card envelope. "Thank you," I said. "This is a very nice touch from the hotel."

"It is not from the hotel, Mademoiselle."

"It's not?"

"It's a gift. From a secret admirer, I'm sure."

My eyes widened slightly, then a sense of excitement began to build inside of me. A gift … it had to be from Andre!

Or one of my girlfriends, I quickly thought. Maybe they'd sent a gift for my fortieth birthday.

I could hardly wait to open it, but forced myself to do just that. My room key in hand, I followed the bellman to the elevators.

On the fourth floor, I opened the door … then gasped. "Oh, my. I think there must be a mistake."

"Is there a problem?" the man asked. Just like the clerk downstairs, this man sounded incredibly sexy. I loved the French accent.

But the accent I was looking forward to hearing whisper in my ear was undoubtedly the slight southern drawl that belonged to Andre Moore ….

"The room." I gestured to it. "This is a huge suite. I think I've been given the wrong room."

"I'm sure there is no mistake, Mademoiselle."

I was sure that there had been. This wasn't the kind of accommodation I was typically given when traveling for work. "Just give me a moment to call down and confirm with the front desk."

I hustled into the room and picked up the phone, which was near the posh-looking sofa by the window. Through the open curtains, I could see the Arc de Triomphe in the distance, and the many lights adorning the trees on the Champs-Elyses. Talk about a spectacular view.

I pressed the button to call the front desk, and a pleasant-sounding female answered the phone. "Good evening, Ms. Sinclair."

"Good evening. I'm just calling about my room."

"Is there a problem?" The woman sounded concerned.

"No. The room's lovely. But this is a suite. I was booked in regular room."

"One moment." I heard clicks on a keyboard. "Ahh, there is no mistake. Your room has been upgraded."

I gazed around the suite, which was comfortable and luxurious. "I don't understand."

"Somebody upgraded the room for you. All the extra charges are taken care of. So please, enjoy."

Tingles of excitement spread over my body. Andre? I went back to the front door where the bellman had been patiently waiting. "Apparently I'm in the right room," I told him.

He nodded. "Excellent. I'm sure you will love this suite." He offloaded my luggage from the cart. "If you find something that does not meet your satisfaction, please do not hesitate to call the front desk."

I gave the bellman a healthy tip, which he took without even glancing at the bill. Then he disappeared quietly, closing the door behind him.

With him gone, I went to the left, where the open bedroom door showcased a king-sized bed adorned elegantly yet simply with an array of pillows. Behind the bed was a gold-colored headboard that spanned over much of the wall. A white terrycloth robe lay on the bed, with a folded card beside it.

I knew that it would tell me to feel free to use the robe, so I ignored it. Instead, I put my travel bag down on the floor, then sank onto the softness of the down-filled comforter, placing the gift bag and card on my lap as I did. I quickly opened the envelope and pulled out the card.

Open the present at midnight.

Love Andre.

So it *was* from him! Holding the card against my chest, I fell backward on the bed, sighing dreamily. The way a seventeen-year-old girl getting a letter from a boy she had a crush on would.

I was alone in Paris, but I didn't feel alone.

I sat up, rereading the card. Then I glanced at the bedside's digital clock. I still had four hours until midnight. How was I going to hold off opening the present until then?

Here I was, thirty-nine on the precipice of forty. And the despair I'd felt weeks ago over Steven had completely dissipated. The fact that I had even hoped to go to Paris with Steven was no longer on my mind. I had something newer and better to look forward to.

Andre, a man ten years my junior, was making my heart flutter like a schoolgirl.

We would have one night in Paris. No expectations.

I was tired, but also alive with excitement. There was no way I could nap for a bit, despite my jet lag. So I called the front desk to inquire about the pool and spa. I learned it was open for two more hours, so I grabbed my bathing suit and left the room.

The spa pool … talk about divine! Just like the lobby, the pool was a curving structure, giving it a modern and chic look. Two large silver-looking taps protruded from the pool on opposite ends, pouring water. The pool was illuminated, and looked downright decadent.

I spent an hour luxuriating there, then another twenty minutes in the wet sauna.

I felt rejuvenated when I left the spa. But I was all too aware that I still had over two hours left before I could open my gift.

Back up in my room, I ordered a light room service meal since it was late. Then I turned on the television and flipped through the channels until I found an English version of Law and Order.

More than once, my eyes wandered to the gift bag. I was oh-so-tempted to just open it already.

But I refrained. Andre had gone to the lengths of having a gift delivered for me all the way from the U.S., and the least I could do was wait until midnight as he'd requested.

But I would have to do something special for him. Tomorrow, as I waited for him to arrive, I would go shopping. I'd find a boutique with some racy lingerie and buy some stuff. The French were renowned for their lingerie, so the task wouldn't be hard. Edible undies, flavored lubricant …. Everything to make our night unforgettable.

In fact, I regretted not asking him to come to Paris tonight. I'd had this big elaborate plan. My fortieth birthday. That was the night for wild, unabashed sex. Not the night before. It seemed so silly now. Because as the clock finally neared midnight, I found myself wishing that Andre was here to truly ring in my birthday with me.

I was in the bed beneath the down covers, waiting out the clock. I reached for the gift bag, which I'd placed on the night table. I loved that Andre had told me to open this at midnight. There was something extra special and spectacular about the anticipation that came from waiting to open the gift. I imagined him looking at the clock from across the pond, waiting for six p.m. to hit. Then smiling as he thought of me opening his present.

Finally, the digital clock changed from 11:59 to midnight. I pulled out the delicately configured tissue paper with little finesse. Inside the bag was a long, rectangular box—wrapped in silver foil—which I opened a little more gently. My pulse was racing with excitement and delight.

Beneath the wrapped foil, I found a Cartier box.

I gasped. Cartier was one of the world's premier jewelers.

Then I opened the box. Inside was a stunning bracelet. It appeared to be white gold, with orchid after orchid forming the entire bracelet. Within the petals of each orchid and its center were tiny diamonds.

"Oh my God," I uttered. Could this be true? Had Andre actually gotten me something so spectacular, or had I fallen asleep and was dreaming?

I lifted the bracelet from its box and placed the cool metal against my skin.

Nope. I was definitely not dreaming.

"Andre … why?" I asked aloud.

Because he really likes me, was the thought that popped into my head. And he wanted to make that fact perfectly clear.

Honestly, I couldn't remember ever feeling this excited. Squealing in delight, I began to put the bracelet on my left wrist. And once it was on, I held my wrist up high, looking at the sparkling orchids with admiration.

Glancing at the box, I noticed the small white envelope that had been tucked into the top of it. I hadn't noticed it before because it hadn't fallen out. Now, I pulled it out from the box.

Written on the small piece of card stock inside the envelope were the words, *HAPPY BIRTH-DAY, BELLA.*

I knew that Andre was coming to Paris to woo me, seduce me, make scorching hot love to me. But this … this was taking my birthday fantasies beyond where I'd ever expected them to go.

This felt … special.

It hit me then, that I'd just turned forty. A milestone most women dreaded.

I started to giggle. Because at the moment that the clock had struck midnight, I hadn't been thinking about turning forty. I'd simply been feeling special.

And I had Andre to thank for that.

I called his number, but it went to voicemail. I frowned, disappointed. I'd wanted to thank him for the beautiful gift. God only knew what the hefty price tag had been.

I didn't bother to leave a message for him. I would just wait until tomorrow and thank him when he arrived.

But before he got here, I was definitely going to pick up something exquisitely racy at a lingerie shop. That way, I could thank him in grand style.

CHAPTER SEVEN

The next morning, the blaring alarm on my cell phone woke me up at eight a.m. Still tired, I was tempted to turn off the alarm and go back to bed for a few more hours. Instead, I sat up, groaning as I did. I was going to be in Paris for a few weeks, and I may as well start getting my body adjusted to the time zone.

Last night, I'd left the breakfast card outside my door, asking for an eight-thirty breakfast. That would leave me time to get up and shower, and be ready when room service arrived. Later, I would head back to the spectacular spa for another swim. If they could fit me in for a mani-pedi and a massage some time during the day, I would do that too. Might as well pamper myself for my birthday.

But I was definitely going to make sure that I had time carved out to do a little lingerie shopping. Andre's flight was due to arrive just after six, so by the time he got through customs and headed into the city, I expected him at the hotel no sooner than seven-thirty.

Minutes after getting out of bed, I was in the bathroom brushing my teeth when I heard the doorbell. Frowning, I quickly exited the bathroom and glanced at the bedside clock. It was only eight-thirteen. Room service was early.

I grabbed the robe I'd laid on a chaise, and slipped my arms through it while en route to the door. As I was knotting the tie on it, the doorbell rang a second time.

"Coming," I called, then trotted the rest of the way. "Sorry," I began without preamble as I swung the door open. "I wasn't exp—"

The words died on my lips as reality hit me like a Mac truck, causing me to sway. It wasn't someone from room service at my door.

"Andre," I said, my voice barely above a whisper. I could hardly believe my eyes.

A slow smile crept on his sexy lips as I stared at him in shock. "Hey," he said. Casually. As though he hadn't just surprised the heck out of me.

"B-but—I—I thought," I sputtered. I knew my eyes had to be as wide as saucers. "I— your flight—"

"I took a red-eye last night," he explained. "I wanted to be here to greet you at the start of your birthday." His grin widened. "Happy birthday, babe."

My heart melted. Was it possible that I had the world's sweetest man right here at my hotel room door? "Thank you," I said, my voice soft and fluttery. "But you were already with me for the start of my birthday." I held up my wrist, displaying the delicate bracelet. "This is so lovely. Thank you for the gift … and for helping me to not feel alone."

"A beautiful woman deserves something pretty. It pales in comparison to your beauty, but it was the best I could do."

"I'm not sure if I can handle your silver tongue."

"We'll see about that," Andre said, his eyebrows shooting up and a playful smile dancing on his lips. Instantly, I realized my faux pas. I began to blush.

"And on that note, may I come in?" Andre asked.

I stepped backward, my gaze not meeting his. "Of course." Sheesh, when was I going to stop making him stand at my door like a stranger? "Of course."

He strolled casually into my room, all six-foot-three inches of him. Broad shoulders. Incredibly fine physique. I swallowed—hard. Heat swept over my body as the reality that we were behind closed doors hit me. We were behind closed doors, and I was extremely turned on.

Andre looked around the room. "This place is beautiful. I hope you like the upgrade."

By now, you'd think that I'd start realizing Andre's surprises were endless. While I'd considered that my employer could have provided the upgrade, I had suspected that Andre was the one behind it. Now I had confirmation.

"It's lovely." I paused as I faced him. "And it totally wasn't necessary."

"Yes, it was." He dropped the bag that was slung over his shoulder and walked toward me. I drew in a breath, holding it until his arms slipped around my waist. "I wanted you to have the most incredible birthday ever."

"So far, it's been off to a great start," I told him. "The gift, the room … everything has been incredible. A week ago, I thought I'd be spending a lonely birthday in Paris. Now, I couldn't be more excited."

I eased up on my toes, my lips seeking his. He lowered his head and gave me what I wanted, putting his mouth on mine. Heat erupted. I moaned, he groaned—as if we had both been waiting eons for this moment. His tongue urged my lips open and swept over mine, seeming to reach for every recess of my mouth with its broad strokes.

I dug my fingers into his wide shoulders. He tightened his hands on my waist, pulling me close as his mouth and tongue became more urgent. My head swooned, the sensations from the kiss making me delirious with need. Never before had I so badly

wanted to take my clothes off and get naked for a man. My desire for him was overpowering.

I lowered my hands and began to undo the tie on my robe. I was ready. But Andre's hands went onto mine, holding them in place as he broke the kiss.

My eyes shot to his. I saw the undeniable heat in his expression, felt it in his kiss … which left me confused as to why he was stopping me from opening my robe.

"What is it?" I asked.

"One hot night," he said in a raspy voice. "That's what you asked me for, and that's what I'm going to give you."

"Night … as in later?" I quickly figured out what he was saying. "You're going to make me wait?" My voice sounded high-strung, almost like a desperate plea.

He chuckled softly. "I'm going to be a good boy and stay away from you during the day."

"What?" I protested. "They why did you get here early?"

"No, that came out wrong. I don't mean I'm going to stay away from you. I mean that I'm going to keep my hands off of you. Until later. So I can deliver on giving you that one hot night you requested."

I whimpered. My body was already on fire. I wasn't sure I could make it through the day without getting some. "Seriously?"

"Seriously." He kissed my cheek, a slow, lingering kiss that was doing nothing to quell my fire. "Besides, I want to show you that I'm not just here for what you think I'm here for. I didn't get on a plane and fly to Paris just for a piece of ass."

The bracelet he'd given me had already showed me that … though I could practically hear Holly telling me that Andre could afford to lavish plenty of women with stunning gifts, so I shouldn't think that his present signified anything important.

"Me and my big mouth." I pouted, lowering my head.

"No need to look disappointed." Gently, he stroked my cheek, and I looked up at him again. "I promise I'll make it all up to you later."

My body trembled at his lowly uttered words, and my nipples actually hardened. God, I yearned for his touch. My lips parted, and I almost pointed out that we could save the sex for later, but indulge in foreplay now.

But I decided not to. For one thing, the nightie I was wearing beneath my robe wasn't near the kind of sexy I wanted it to be. Besides, his words … his promise … had been deliciously seductive. My body was in sexual overdrive. Waiting for it would only make tonight that much more explosive.

"Mind if I take a shower?" he asked.

"Of course not."

I led the way into the bedroom, where I pointed him in the direction of the bathroom. He went in with his travel bag and closed the door. When, moments later, I heard the shower start, I fell backward onto the bed, splaying my arms above my head. My body was throbbing, my pussy already moist. I wanted to lie there and spread my body for him, be irresistible to him when he got out of the shower.

Heck, maybe I should go into the bathroom and surprise him. Start some hot foreplay beneath the steady stream of hot water ….

I wanted sex all day long. Forget the sightseeing. This was my fortieth birthday!

Groaning, I got up from the bed as Andre's words sounded in my mind again. *I didn't get on a plane and fly to Paris just for a piece of ass.*

Those were words I appreciated, but they also scared me. Because I could so easily fall for Andre.

And yet, I didn't want to allow that to happen. I didn't want to think about tomorrow, didn't want to allow myself to be vulnerable. Being vulnerable led to being hurt.

"Stop it, Bella," I told myself. "Stop over thinking everything."

I got off of the bed and got dressed, putting all thoughts of tomorrow and where this fling with Andre might lead firmly on the back burner. All that mattered was right now.

A short while later, Andre exited the bathroom. If the man expected me to keep my hands off of him, he wasn't doing a good job of not tempting me. Sans a shirt, and wearing only denim jeans slung low on his hips, he looked far too enticing.

I took in the hard planes and ridges of what was more than a six-pack. Quickly counting, I determined that there were eight clearly developed muscular sections on his abdomen. I let out a low whistle.

Smirking—as though he knew just how badly he was tempting me—he pulled a cotton t-shirt over his head. The shirt hugged his impeccable upper body, and he made it look like a million dollar garment.

"You changed," he said, speaking of the summery pink dress with white polka dots that I'd put on.

"I figured it was best. Given that you're going to make me wait until tonight," I added, sulking. My eyes stayed on his magnificent upper body, then went lower, to his strong thighs. Did I really have to wait until tonight to get some?

"It's going to be a great day," he said. "And an even better night."

I walked toward him and slipped my arms around his waist. "It's already an amazing day, and you just got here." Then, remembering that room service was supposed to have arrived for eight-thirty, I uttered, "Breakfast! Room service was supposed to be here twenty minutes ago. I can't believe they're late."

"Actually …" Andre's voice trailed off, and the corners of his mouth curled in a smile. "I canceled it."

"How did you even know?" I asked. "And why?"

"I figured you would order room service. So I checked, and you did. Then I canceled it. And why did I cancel? Because I knew I would be here to surprise you. So why would we have breakfast in here when there are so many amazing restaurants and cafés in Paris? I want to take you out for your birthday."

Again, his words tickled my heart. I was going with the flow, but there was a part of my brain that was reminding me, even now, to keep my heart closed. It would be dangerous to expect anything more than today.

"All right. I'm not against that. Did you already have a place in mind—since you seem to have done so much of the planning already?"

"No. I figured we would ask downstairs."

Letting my arms fall from around his body, I extended my hand. He took it in his. "That sounds like a plan."

Hand in hand, we went downstairs to the lobby, where we spoke with the concierge and learned that Le Diane, one of the hotel's restaurants, was a great spot for breakfast. The ambience of the place didn't disappoint, with its aesthetically pleasing décor, not to mention the aromas filling the space. But even as we looked at the menu, I leaned close and said into Andre's ear, "Why don't we head outside? Stroll around and see what strikes our fancy?"

"Whatever the birthday girl wants."

Warmth tickled my insides. Here I was in Paris with a man who was not only stunning to look at, but he seemed to have a heart of gold. Add to that fact that he was what most would consider a seriously eligible bachelor, and I couldn't imagine why he wasn't in a relationship.

"Why are you single?" I asked him as we casually walked along the Champs-Elyses, which was bustling with people.

"I haven't found the right woman."

"Are you that picky? Because from what you've shown me … I just can't see many women running from that. You're gorgeous, and sweet."

Andre stopped and pulled me into his arms, right in the middle of the sidewalk. "You think I'm gorgeous?"

"Duh. Of course."

"It's nice to hear you say that." And then he kissed me, a sweet kiss that lingered.

Blushing, I pulled away. "There are people everywhere."

"We're in Paris," he said. "The city of love. It's to be expected."

Taking his hand again, we continued to walk. "I thought it was the city of lights," I said.

"Paris is a romantic city."

"Have you been here before?" I asked, feeling an irrational spurt of jealousy at the idea that he had already christened this city with a lover.

Looking down at me, he said, "Nope. It's always been on my to-do list." He winked. "And now I'm here."

A niggle of excitement, mixed with desire, shot down my spine. "So, back to why you're single …"

"I've had to be careful about the women I date. Having been a pro football player, a lot of women look at me and see big houses, fancy cars, and vacations made for royalty. They're not in it for me."

How could they not be in it for him? Have all of the luxury, *plus* an incredible man? "And your last girlfriend? The stunning one that I used to see coming in and out of your house?"

"Wanted my money."

"Are you sure?" I asked. "It seemed that the two of you were dating for quite a while. Not that I was paying any specific attention," I quickly said.

"Trust me, I'm sure. And I gave her a lot of what she wanted. I have no problem with that. I'm here with you, and you're going to see just how well I can treat a woman. But all I ask is that you're in it for me."

"I'm not the type to go after man for his money. I've always been able to take care of myself, and that's not going to change."

"I hope that you can allow yourself to be pampered." He paused and looked at me. "Can you?"

My heart fluttered, and a sensation of warmth spread through me. I wasn't sure what was happening between us, but I reminded myself that I wasn't going to question it. Not today. In fact, having Andre here hours before he was scheduled to arrive had lifted my spirits. It was nice to know that someone cared enough about me to not have me spending my birthday alone.

"I think I can," I told him. Our gazes held, and I felt my body becoming hot in all of my erogenous zones. "Um … maybe we should just go back to Le Diane, the restaurant at the hotel."

"Whatever you desire."

Andre's words seemed to hold more meaning than just for the specific situation of eating breakfast.

As we got to the restaurant's entrance, his hand went to the small of my back and he guided me inside. It was the little things like this that I missed, I realized. Even with Steven, there wasn't this level of intimacy. How had I not realized that until now? I almost felt stupid for having pined over Steven, when he didn't make me feel even half as special as Andre made me feel.

Our breakfast was delectable. I had freshly-made crepes with whipped cream and cherries, while Andre opted for an omelet with ham, cheese and vegetables. We sat inside by a window, where we could look out and enjoy all the charm of Paris.

And practically every time our eyes met, all I kept thinking about was later. Being naked. In bed with Andre. It was the subtext of our every interaction. *I can't wait to do you later ….*

When the waitress brought our bill to the table, Andre reached for his wallet in the back pocket of his jeans. "I'll just charge it to the room," I told him.

"This is your birthday. You are going to be treated and spoiled. When are you going to start understanding that?"

"Okay." I smiled. "I hear you."

The bill paid, we rose from the table. I saw the way some women looked in our direction, checking out Andre. Unlike in D.C., the women weren't looking at him because of his football player status. They were ogling him because he was a gorgeous specimen of a man. It made me feel a sense of pride. He was here with me.

"Where to now?" he asked once we were out of the restaurant, and back in the hotel lobby.

"You mean other than going upstairs?" I said, my tone hopefully optimistic that he would change his mind about waiting until later.

"Yeah. Other than that."

I wrinkled my nose as I frowned at him. "Actually, I was planning to do some shopping. There are some things I'd hoped to pick up before you arrived." I gave him a pointed look.

His eyebrows rising, he regarded me curiously. "Things like …?"

"Things that are appropriate for a fortieth birthday celebration with a guy I want to impress," I went on. "I'm sure that will be boring for you, tagging along with me as I try on outfit after outfit."

"If you're talking about what I think you're talking about, then I'll gladly shop you with." He flashed me a devilish grin.

"Most guys would rather slit their wrists than go shopping with a woman."

"Are you kidding? The kind of shopping you have in mind?" Those dimples appeared as his smile widened. "Who better to tell you what looks good on you than me?"

The look he was giving me caused another surge of heat to electrify my body. Damn, how was I supposed to walk around today in this state of heightened arousal?

"Maybe we should save the shopping for … later." I needed to take the focus off of my body's primal needs, or Lord knew, one touch from him in public and I might end up climaxing. "We're in Paris. There's the Eiffel Tower, the Louvre. And I've always wanted to do a boat cruise along the Seine."

"As I said, whatever you want to do."

"Except …" I gave him a long look, followed by a pout.

He chuckled. "That's dessert. And trust me, it'll be decadent."

We went to the concierge, where we got information about times for the various tourist attractions. There was an evening boat tour along the river, which we thought would be a great idea. Keeping it simple, we made dinner reservations at Le Diane—which we would do after my lingerie shopping. We would travel from dinner to the boat for the night tour.

Then, finally, it would be back to the hotel. Where, at last, we could get naked and do what we both desperately wanted to do.

Paris was vibrantly alive for me in a way it hadn't been the last time I'd been here. And there was no question as to why. Seeing Paris from the top of the Eiffel Tower with Andre by my side was exhilarating.

We realized we wouldn't really have time for the Louvre if I was going to get my shopping done, so decided to pass on that.

"We definitely can't miss the shopping trip," Andre said after I'd finished buying miniature Eiffel Tower souvenirs from a vendor.

"Actually, I've been thinking about the shopping excursion." I waved a hand at a vendor who wanted me to look at his trinkets, letting him know I wasn't interested. "I think that what I buy should be a surprise. If you're going to make me suffer—"

"You think you're the only one who's suffering?" Leaning close, he whispered in my ear, "I've been trying to hide a hard-on for much of the day."

That made me throw my head back and laugh—and Andre promptly placed his lips along my neck.

Gripping his arms, I righted myself. "Damn you," I muttered. "That's exactly why I can't go lingerie shopping with you. Because I don't want to get arrested for sex in a department store change room."

"I'm sure it won't be the first time it's happened. We're in Paris, and the French are very liberal-minded when it comes to sex."

"Well, it won't be happening today. Since you have so insistently told me that I have to wait until tonight for some action." I took a step backward, my stomach fluttering. "You've given me a lot of surprises. Tonight, I want to surprise you."

Andre drew his bottom lips between his teeth, and I couldn't help thinking of him doing that to my—

I promptly shut the thought down. I didn't want to have a public orgasm.

"Okay?" I asked, shifting from one foot to the other.

"Sure." He nodded. "I like surprises. And in the meantime, I can take a nap. Make sure I'm good and energized for later."

"I'd say that's a priority," I told him, knowing that no one who overheard any snippet of our conversation would get what we were talking about.

"That means you plan to work me hard."

"Oh, you'd better count on it."

CHAPTER EIGHT

Back at the hotel, Andre went upstairs. I went to the concierge to conspicuously ask about the shops that sold lingerie.

"Yes, of course," the man said, speaking to me in the same tone he had when discussing making dinner reservations. "There are many wonderful shops for you to choose from."

After giving me the list, I searched some images on my smart phone and decided on La Perla over Rien of France. La Perla was a huge name in French lingerie, and offered a variety from classic designs to lingerie with an edge.

The French were renowned for their lingerie, and that fact truly hit home as I perused the boutique. From lacy bras and frilly thongs, to see-through slips with elegant embroidery covering the delicate parts, to edgy bodysuits, this place had it all.

My first thought was a bra and panty set, because they were so damn sexy. I could see Andre going crazy over any of the items. But, I wanted to draw out the teasing a little more … make him work a bit harder for it, as he had made me wait all day … so I opted for a bodysuit over one of the baby dolls that had caught my eye. I chose a bodysuit made of sheer mesh with lace accents that covered the nipples and pubic area. Trying it on, I knew that not having Andre come with me to shop had been the best idea. Wearing this piece of stunning lingerie, I looked the sexiest I'd ever been. I bought a pair of black

stockings to complete the outfit, because what French lingerie would be complete without stockings?

The one-piece bodysuit would require some time to remove … allowing Andre to tease and please me until he got to the juicy bits.

I grinned at my corny thought, but knew that at least one bit of me would be good and juicy by the time he got to it.

Damn, the man wasn't even with me right now and I was still getting so turned on by him. I couldn't wait until later.

Back in my hotel room, I found Andre sleeping. A wave of desire swept over me as I checked him out, lying on the king-sized bed. If I'd entered a lottery for men, I couldn't have won a better prize.

Quietly, I headed into the bathroom to shower, then change into my purchase. But before doing so, I took a slinky black dress from my suitcase. I was going to wear my new lingerie under my outfit for dinner, so that when we got back to the room, we could get straight to dessert.

I showered. Once I'd dried off, I dabbed some perfume on my wrists and behind my ears. Then I put on the bodysuit.

It's amazing how a piece of lingerie can make a woman feel beautiful. Checking out my body in the mirror, I didn't see a forty-year-old woman whose best years were behind her. I saw a sexy, curvaceous woman whose body was firm where it needed to be, and luscious where required. My large bosom damn near exploded from the lacy cups. Even with my hair pulled up in a lose bun to avoid getting it wet in the shower, I looked incredible.

Maybe I would do a strip tease for Andre later. A sort of burlesque act. Bending over and seductively taking off the stockings, and seeing how long he could resist me ….

Dressed, I exited the bathroom to get my flatiron and makeup bag from my suitcase. Seeing Andre sitting up on the bed, I gasped, startled.

"Oh. You're awake."

"Hey, babe." He extended his hand.

I walked over to him and gave him my hand. With a gentle tug, he pulled me onto the bed beside him. "You look freakin' incredible."

"I'm not even ready yet. I still have to do my make-up and my hair."

"You're beautiful," he rasped, and slipped his hands into my thick mane. And then he was pulling me close and covering my lips with his.

Unlike the last ones, this kiss didn't start off slow and teasing. It went from zero to extreme heat in a nanosecond. My breasts pressed against his chest as our bodies instinctively edged closer still. I opened my mouth wide, allowing Andre's tongue the access it sought. With a soft groan, his tongue swept through my mouth with broad, delicious strokes.

I gripped his shoulders, then broke the kiss and eased back to look at him. "We're not going to make it for dinner if we keep this up."

"I'm thinking I'm ready to skip to dessert."

My eyes searched his, trying to determine if he was simply teasing me. All I saw was heat and lust and a good helping of desire. "Are you sure?"

"I've never been more sure about anything," he rasped.

I beamed. "It's about time."

His lips came down on my mouth again, his tongue mating with mine with a sense of urgency. And then he began to stroke my face, his fingers tantalizing my skin as his mouth worked magic.

My entire body erupted in flames. Damn, this man was thrilling me like no other.

I had to break the kiss to adjust my body so that I positioned my legs on either side of his body. But as though he couldn't stand to be parted from me, he quickly slipped a hand into my hair and urged me down so that my mouth was on his once more.

The kiss grew more intense, our heated sighs filling the silence in the moments we had to gasp in breath.

Andre smoothed his flat palm down my back, then over the curve of my ass, which he paused to squeeze. His hand continued its slow journey, moving past my behind and down the back of my leg. When he reached the hem of my skirt, his fingers inched beneath the fabric and ventured up. Reaching the lacy, elastic hem of the stocking, he paused his hand and groaned into my mouth.

"Garters?" he rasped.

"You'll have to take a look."

With a growl of sexual hunger, he claimed my lips again while moving his hands higher. He flirted with the mesh and lace of the bodysuit. My chest was heaving with my labored breaths as his fingers heated my skin. He was probing, searching for access. Finally, he eased back and looked at me. "What *is* this thing you're wearing? It's like your body is more tightly guarded than Fort Knox."

Pulling my bottom lip between my teeth, I gave him a sly smile. Then I eased off the bed and stood. Lifting the hem of my dress upward, I shimmied my hips in a flirtatious manner, giving him a glimpse of my stocking here, then a glimpse of the top of the stocking on the other side. Turning slowly, I lifted my dress and continued dancing to the rhythm of lust beating through my veins, showing—then promptly hiding—my behind.

I looked over my shoulder at him, saw that his eyes were wide with intrigue. He was rooted to the spot on the bed, as though transfixed. Here was my chance. My opportunity to do that little burlesque strip tease I'd imagined earlier.

So, keeping my back to him, and my head perched over my shoulder, I slowly and sexily swayed my hips. Then began to bend over with deliberate slowness. I stroked my legs with gentle flicks of my fingertips, then caught the hem of my dress and lifted it upward to reveal my entire ass. Lowering the dress, I turned to give him a side-view of my body. I continued to dance, lifting my hands high while swaying my hips. I was going on instinct, and hearing Andre's moans told me that I had his undivided attention.

Bending forward, I lifted the dress high above my right leg, then slipped my fingers beneath the hem of the stocking.

"No," Andre said quickly. "Leave them on."

Flashing him a little smile, I turned toward him. Then, crisscrossing my arms over my belly, I reached for the sides of my dress and pulled it upward, giving him a tempting glimpse of the sheer lace. His mouth was ajar, his lust-filled expression saying I had his attention for as long as I wanted it. I turned again, shaking my booty a little, then bent over, knowing that I was giving him a delicious view. Hearing him growl, I angled my head in his direction and saw him grabbing his erect shaft through his jeans, as if to control it.

I had waited so long for this. Ever since arriving in Paris last night, the one thing on my mind had been having sex with Andre. Now, facing him again,

I pulled the dress over my head and tossed it onto the carpeted floor.

I heard his audible breath. "*Wow.*"

One word, but it made me heady with a desire that could only be quenched by his touch.

Then he was moving his body to the edge of the bed. He extended his hand to me. "Come."

It was a command I obeyed without hesitation. I walked toward him—strutted, really—my pulse racing madly. His eyes held mine as he took both of my hands in his. Damn, I liked that. The way he was looking at me. Connecting with me intimately with his eyes before the moment when he would ravage my body.

Slowly, his eyes went lower, taking in every inch of the expensive piece of lingerie I had purchased. He released my hands and put one palm against my belly. My stomach flinched at his touch. Then he smoothed his hand around from the center of my belly to the small of my back. Again, his fingers searched, and then he said, "How do you get this off?"

"Do I have you stumped? Surely, you've seen women in bodysuits before."

Both of his hands were smoothing over my torso, his eyes tracking their movements. "This is one sexy piece of lingerie. I've had women wear baby dolls, edible undies—the kind of thing that's easy to rip off in the heat of the moment. But this? This speaks of the kind of constraint I've tried to have with you since we met. This speaks of the art of the tease." He placed both his hands on my hips and jerked my pelvic bone toward him. Then his mouth pressed against my belly through the sheer fabric. "And oh boy, am I going to tease you."

No one had ever uttered such a hot promise before. Absolutely no one. Taking my hands in his, he moved them behind my back. Then he continued to kiss my skin, his thick lips trailing a path from my navel upward. As his lips went higher, he began to rise from the bed. By the time his lips reached my bosom, he was standing, still holding my arms behind my back as though to keep me his prisoner.

"Damn. You have one amazing body. I felt the kind sexual confidence that I supposed only age could bring. I was ready to take what I wanted, claim it without any shame.

His lips suckled the flesh of one breast, then the other. And suddenly, I wondered if I was actually teasing him, or myself. Because what I wanted more than anything was for him to take the lacy fabric and rip it out of the way and taste the first heated morsel of my body that desired and craved him so badly.

But he didn't. Instead, he released my arms and turned me around so that my back was to him. Then his hands were smoothing over my shoulders, his fingertips dancing down the length of my arms. When he reached my hands, he linked fingers with mine and put both of our hands on the front of my body, mine beneath his.

I sighed softly. The sigh turned to a moan when he brought my hand down to cup my pussy.

I was wet, I could feel it through the material. But with his hand on top of mine, he couldn't. And I wanted him to feel it. Wanted him to feel how hot and wet he'd gotten me.

"Feel me," I said, taking his two digits in my hand and rubbing them over the moist fabric at my center.

Behind me, I felt the growl that emanated from his chest.

"That's how much I want you," I told him.

"I want you too, baby."

His hand still on mine over my pussy, he used his left hand to pull the hair band out of my thick mane. Then he gently nudged my head downward. From there, his lips found the back of my neck. Soft, fluttery kisses made my skin tingle. Then came his tongue. It trailed from my mid-neck down my spine, stopping when he got to between my shoulder blades. Then his mouth moved to the right, and he kissed my shoulder blade before gently easing the strap of my bodysuit down. He did the same thing with the left side.

I mewled, wanting so badly for my body to be rid of this lovely piece of lingerie. I wanted to stand naked in front of him, offering him all of me.

Behind me, Andre pressed his groin against my body. I could feel his rock hard shaft against the top of my butt. He trailed the fabric of my bodysuit down my arms, and I lifted my shoulders to help make the task of disrobing me easier for him. The bodysuit snagged at my bust, not peeling off easily—an idea I had relished when I'd bought this particular item so that we could draw out the teasing. Andre moved his hands from my arms to my ribcage and upward, his fingers delicately searching for the top lacy frills of the bodice. Then, gently slipping his fingers beneath the fabric and my flesh, he peeled the bust down.

My breasts spilled free. Gripping his upper thighs, I eased my head back against his chest, moaning with pleasure as I did. I wanted him to turn me in his arms. Taste my breasts. But his hands did the work, tweaking my nipples, tugging them into taut peaks. As his fingers teased my breasts, he kissed the side of my face. Then his lips found my earlobe and he nibbled on it as he played with my nipples. God, the sensation!

Finally, his hands went lower. Slipping them underneath the mesh of my bodysuit now, he pushed the fabric down while smoothing his warm palms over my naked torso. He got to my hips, where I did a little shimmy as his hands pushed the material over my curves.

With the bodysuit now bunched at the top of my thighs, both of Andre's hands went back to my center, searching for my pussy. His moans of delight mixed with my own as he fondled my folds.

"Yes, baby," I uttered when he slipped a finger inside of me.

I placed my hand over his, pushing on it so that his finger would reach farther into me. He added another digit, and my breathing grew more ragged. The sensations were making me deliciously delirious.

With his free hand, Andre framed my chin and angled my face over my shoulder so that he could kiss me as he stood behind me. His tongue plunged into my mouth, matching the rhythm of his fingers plunging into my sweet spot.

I could hardly focus on the kiss. My lips kept pausing as rapturous moans escaped my mouth. I was ripe. I had been ready for his touch all day. I could feel my climax building.

Andre tore his lips from mine, and before I knew what was happening, he was whirling me around. Seating me on the bed. Hastily dragging the lingerie down my legs and over my feet.

"Damn, do you know how sexy you are wearing only these stockings? I'm so hard, I could come without you putting your hands on me."

I mewled.

His eyes darkened with even more lust as his eyes settled on the center of my femininity. "I wanted to take my time with you. To tease you until you begged me to make you come. But if I draw this out any longer, I might just die. Looking at your beautiful pussy … I have to taste it. It's time you had your first birthday orgasm."

Sighing in delight, I braced my hands on the bed to keep my body upright. Andre spread my legs. I looked down at him. I wanted to see this. I wanted to see this gorgeous man work his mouth and tongue over me until I climaxed.

His eyes met mine. And a devious little smile came on his lips, as if to say that I had no clue what I was about to get into.

Still looking at me, his lips parted. The tip of his tongue twirled out. I held my breath. And that first flick … that first glorious sensation that came from the moist heat of his tongue—I nearly died from the pleasure.

My head lolled backward, and I closed my eyes and shut out everything but the feeling of my pussy in his mouth.

"Oh, baby …. Oh, God."

I forced my head back up. Watched more of his lusciously erotic actions. Slow. Sensual. Perfect. A suckle here, gentle nibbles there. And when he added his fingers ….

My head fell backward as my body weakened from the exquisite feelings. My breathing started leaving my body in quick, staccato bursts. And as his fingers moved up and down inside me, matching the rhythm of his tongue moving up and down on my nub, I came. Violently. I clamped my lips tightly together to stop the scream that had bubbled up from my throat. It escaped on a raspy breath, low enough so as not to attract the attention of anyone on the other side of the wall.

"Oh, baby. Oh my *goodness.*"

My whole body was thrumming from the most glorious orgasm I'd ever experienced. And Andre didn't stop. His mouth continued to move tenderly over me … *oh God* … drawing out my pleasure to the absolute fullest.

"Andre … *ohhhh* …" My moans intensified, growing louder. And then Andre was devouring me, as though he needed to fill himself of my nectar in order to survive. I fell backward on the bed, my strength gone as he continued to give me the sweetest pleasure.

"Andre, I can't … oh baby …"

Finally, his lips stopped their merciless onslaught. He kissed my inner thighs, then moved his mouth to my belly. His lips were wet from my essence. Moving his way upward, he suckled one nipple, then the other, before finding my mouth. He kissed me deeply, the taste of my own body passing from his tongue to mine.

"Your pussy's beautiful, baby. Damn, I could eat it all night."

A shiver of delight passed through my body. Though my climax had left my arms feeling like jello, I mustered the strength to place my hands on his hips. I slipped my fingers beneath the fabric of his jeans. "This is what I want," I rasped. "You. Inside of me."

Andre eased up and unbuttoned the clasp of his jeans. Gripping his jeans and the waist of his briefs in my hands, I pushed both items of clothing down over his hips. Then I squeezed his butt with one hand while reaching for his shaft with the other. I stroked him, and he kissed my lips, breathing heavily into my mouth as my hand worked his member.

Unexpectedly, he tore his lips from mine and stood tall. As he began to drag his jeans and white briefs down his legs so he could completely disrobe, my eyes roamed over his body. Those wide shoulders and strong arms. His muscular chest and well-defined torso. He looked as though he had been sculpted from granite.

My gaze went lower, and I sucked in a sharp breath at the sight of his rock-hard erection. He was large, both his girth and length. And damn, I wanted him so badly.

I looked up. Saw that he was watching me as I'd checked him out. "You're perfect," I said in a soft voice. I got onto my knees and moved toward the edge of the bed. "All these muscles." I smoothed my hands over his shoulders, then down his abdomen. "And this …"

My hands went lower. With one hand, I circled my palm around his aroused member. With the other, I cradled his sac. Then I bent forward and kissed the tip of his shaft. Feeling him shudder, a surge of feminine power shot through me. I swirled my tongue over the tip of him, stroking him as I did.

Andre gripped my shoulders and stepped back. "No … I need to be inside you. *Now.* Get on your back."

"Mmmm." I purred. "Okay."

I did as he instructed, and watched with wicked satisfaction as he went over to his suitcase. He bent over to search through his luggage, and I shamelessly enjoyed the view.

Moments later, I heard the sound of a package tearing. He kept his back to me as he slipped the condom on. Then he turned and stalked toward me, and I drew in a breath at the look of heated determination in his eyes.

Reaching me, he grabbed my legs and pulled me forward so that my butt was at the edge of the bed. Securing an arm behind one of my knees, he reached for my pussy while positioning himself between my thighs. Making sure I was ready, he guided his erection inside of me with a strong thrust.

I moaned, he groaned. Exquisite sensations exploded inside of me.

"Oh my God, Bella," he rasped. Lowering his head, he sucked on one of my nipples, and heated tingles of pleasure spread through my body. Then he brought his mouth to mine again and kissed me. Kissed me slowly as he moved gently inside of me. As my moans deepened, he began to pick up speed. Easing back, pushing deep. I lifted my butt to meet each delicious thrust, moving faster to urge him on. We found our rhythm, steady and intense. Jerking my head to the side, I gasped in air, the luscious vibrations inside of me already building to a fever pitch.

He withdrew, then plunged deep, and I screamed. He did it again, and I had to stuff my fist in my mouth to keep my scream contained. But my cries became harder to stifle when he twirled his tongue around one of my nipples.

"Yes, baby," I whimpered, digging my nails into his back.

He grazed my nipple with his teeth, and I pushed my chest up, wanting more. He obliged, covering my nipple with his lips and drawing it deep into his mouth.

My center pulsed, and another orgasm rippled through me. I arched my back as it spread through all of me like molten lava. I screamed, then bit down on the side of my hand to stifle my rapturous moans.

"That's it, sweetheart …" Andre's thrusts went into overdrive, matching each of his quick, grunt-like breaths.

"Yes," I rasped, still coming. "Andre …"

He ground into me hard and deep, then collapsed on top of me with a loud growl. I felt his shaft twitching as he came inside of me, and as weak as I was, I tightened my vaginal walls around him to help add to his pleasure.

"Baby," he said, his voice husky as he framed my face. I looked into his eyes, and he held my gaze as we lay, our bodies still joined, our chests rising and falling against each other's.

Then his lips curled in a smile, and I found myself wondering how I was so incredibly lucky to be here with him, lying naked, making love with this incredible man.

I stroked his faced. "What an amazing birthday present!"

He chuckled softly. "I guess you liked it."

"Liked it?" My eyes bulged. Then my eyes searched his. "I loved it."

He gave me a quick peck. "Good. Because there's more where that came from tonight. A lot more."

Purring, I slipped my hand around his head and urged his face down until his lips met mine. And as we kissed slowly, and deeply, his body still inside of mine, I couldn't help thinking that nothing had ever felt this good.

This right.

We ordered room service, which we ate while naked in bed. I put on my robe only to answer the door to receive the food and the wine, then promptly took it off when the door was locked and Andre and I were alone.

We dined on the main course, while indulging in erotic foreplay in between. And by the time he began consuming the whipped cream and strawberries from my body, we were both ready for round two.

Doggy-style. Sixty-nine. In the living room. In the oversized tub. Our sexual appetite was fierce, and we spent the night making love, resting a bit, then getting up to do it again.

By the time the morning came around, my nub was swollen, and I was tired … but never had I felt so exhilarated and alive.

When I woke up, I was on my back and Andre was on his side. His arm was stretched across my abdomen. I liked that even when we weren't making love, we were still close.

Already, I was beginning to dread him leaving. He'd delivered on his promise to give me a night of pure pleasure, and soon he would be on his way. I wasn't ready for him to go.

Easing my body upward to look at the digital clock which was on his side of the bed, I saw that it was eleven minutes after nine.

Andre's arm tightened around me, forcing me to lie back down. "Hey," he said softly.

"Morning." I sighed. "I didn't mean to wake you."

"What time is it?"

"About ten after nine," I told him.

Andre groaned. "Damn. I'm gonna have to get up soon."

"I didn't even ask. What time's your flight?"

"Two-thirty."

"Oh."

Leaning forward, he kissed me on the forehead. "Don't worry. You'll see me back at home."

"Or …" I hesitated, then continued. "You don't have to go. Not quite yet."

His eyebrows rose as he looked at me. "You want me to stay."

"I …" Was that what I wanted? "I guess so, yeah."

"And I'd love to stay, too. But you know you've got business, and with me here, I'll end up in your way."

"But I—" I what? I wanted to be thinking about rushing back to the hotel to make love to him, rather than focus on my work?

"You know you can't have me sticking around," Andre persisted. His hand ventured to my breast, and he cupped it. "Right now, your mind is clouded by … well, by this." The tip of his finger circled my nipple.

"Which you'd better stop doing if you're going to be leaving." I sighed, pouting. "Really, you don't have to. Maybe stay another couple of days."

"Trust me, I want to. But I don't want to get in your way. You told me you wanted one night, and that's what we had. When we see each other again in D.C., it'll be worth the wait. Like last night was."

I whimpered. Did he always follow rules to the T like this? "Do we have time for breakfast?"

"In the room, or downstairs?" Before I could give an answer, Andre continued. "Better make it downstairs. We might be tempted to do what we did with dinner if we eat in the room."

Playing with our food and eating parts of it off of each other had been a highlight of the night, one I wouldn't soon forget.

"You're right," I said, unable to hide the sadness from my voice.

"Hey." Andre maneuvered my body so that I was on top of him. "Don't be so glum. Because then I'm gonna start wondering if you don't want to see me again when you're back home. I didn't come here for this to be a one-time thing."

"Of course I want to see you again." Even lying on him right now, though my body was sore from our vigorous lovemaking, I was already getting aroused. "It's just … I don't return to the States for three weeks."

He kissed me softly. "Wasn't last night worth the wait?"

"Yes. God, yes."

"Then it will be worth the wait until I see you again. When you're back in D.C. Back at home … and we'll have more than just one night."

And damn, when he kissed me again, slowly and sweetly, all I could wish was that the three weeks I was in Paris were ending, rather than beginning.

And that I would be the one getting on a plane in a few hours and heading home.

Heading back to Andre.

After receiving her MBA from Cornell University, Tonya D. Price worked for over fifteen years as an executive in the internet industry and at universities before becoming a full-time writer. She has published numerous short stories in magazines and anthologies. Her thriller short story "Payback," first published in Fiction River's Hard Choices, *will appear in* The Best Mystery Stories of 2019. *Tonya also writes the non-fiction series,* Business Books for Writers. *You can follow Tonya at: www.TonyaDPrice.com or connect with her on twitter @TonyaDPrice2.*

IN TUSCAN TWILIGHT

by Tonya D. Price

Beatrice Kunst could finally relax. Everything had gone according to plan. Her flights from Cleveland to Munich and then to Pisa had been on time despite a narrow connecting window. Her taxi driver had arrived late, but he gotten her to the station just as the Pisa to Lucca train was scheduled to arrive.

No one would suspect she hadn't been on the train.

She stood in front of the nineteenth century station portico listening to the honking cars she couldn't see. Her smart watch buzzed three times. Three o'clock. The head of the art conservation firm that had hired her as a consultant to restore the newly discovered oil painting by the artist, Pompeo Batoni, should arrive soon, although this was Italy and Italian time did not adhere to the mechanical accuracy of a clock.

The roar of an approaching car caught her attention. She turned in the direction of the noise. With the dim gray haze that comprised most of her vision, she noted in her remaining small circle of sight a cute medium blue Fiat Barchetta.

The man who got out of the convertible sports car stood about six inches taller than Beatrice who stood at five-foot-ten herself. The man's thick black hair speckled with a few gray hairs hung a bit long in the fashion favored by many Italian men.

As he approached with an outstretched hand, he appeared a few years older than her. Thirty-nine, perhaps? Maybe forty.

Removing his sunglasses, the man gave her a wide smile and she noticed his dimpled chin.

"Beatrice Kunst?" His voice was a deep baritone colored by the rhythm of a Tuscan accent with a softness that struck Beatrice as genuine. But what stood out was those gorgeous chestnut brown eyes. She had trouble looking away from those eyes. A warmth of embarrassment much hotter than the Tuscan sun crept over her face.

Taking a deep breath, she forced her pulse to slow down and tried to ignore that he was the kind of handsome she had only encountered in her beloved Batoni paintings of idealized Italian gods.

She took him for an athlete. Perhaps a bicyclist. His tieless white shirt and pale-yellow jacket showed he had the style sense common among Italian men. He wore the white pants favored these days. He looked as if he should be on a photo shoot as he stood beside the sports car of Beatrice's dreams.

She smiled, remembered he was asking if she was, in fact, herself. "Si, I'm Beatrice Kunst." She offered her hand, following the Italian custom of a woman doing so before the man.

"Welcome to Tuscany." He took her hand in his. A long-forgotten rush of sensual longing left Beatrice struggling to stand. "Raphael Cana, we talked on the phone. I am looking forward to working with you on the Batoni. How was your trip?"

"Uneventful. The best kind."

He struggled to fit Beatrice's suitcase in the Barretta's small trunk. When he succeeded, he opened the passenger door. "Per favore."

Exhausted from the fourteen-hour trip from Cleveland to Pisa and then the drive to Lucca, Beatrice ran a hand over the matching blue leather seat. In an unguarded moment she said, "I think I'm in love."

"Oh, really?" The dimple in his chin deepened as he shot her a deadly grin.

Beatrice was always a sucker for a dimpled chin. She laughed a bit too loud, as she tended to do in front of handsome men. "I have always wanted a Barretta. They are hard to find in the States, and this color is so rich. Is this a 2003?"

"You know your cars. What do you own now?" Raphael went around to his side of the car and hopped in. He started it and pulled out into traffic.

Beatrice looked away. "I don't drive anymore. It doesn't fit my current lifestyle." Giving up driving had been for the best. She lived a five-minute walk from her job at the Cleveland Art Museum. Life had been a series of adjustment since her vision diagnosis. Not driving had been one of the small accommodations she had made and not one she minded. "Living in a big city, a car eats up money. Gas is more expensive, as is insurance and parking."

"I understand." Raphael took a right turn through a large archway marked, Porta S. Pietro. Saint Peter Gate. "Having a car in Lucca is not easy either, but a Barchetta is small, which makes navigating the narrow streets in the old town easier."

He slowed as a young mother pushing a baby carriage crossed before him. Then he sped up again passing pedestrians with no more than a foot between the car and the people.

Beatrice noted, with some misgivings, there were no traffic lights at the many plazas where the little streets crossed each other. Walking on the uneven cobblestones would be difficult.

Raphael stopped in front of a building five stories high, painted in faded yellow. Old arches from prior medieval structures embedded in the stucco façade reminded Beatrice that these houses dated back to medieval times.

As Raphael removed her luggage, he said, "The art conservation team hoped you might join us tonight for dinner at eight o'clock. If you are not too tired."

Walking the streets at night posed a problem. "How far away is the restaurant?"

"Not far from here. It is behind the old Roman amphitheater. A five-minute walk. Nothing is far in Lucca."

Beatrice couldn't see how she could decline even though all she wanted to do was go to sleep. "I'm not very good at directions. Especially at night."

Raphael regarded her before answering, "No problem. I can be back here at seven forty-five, and we can walk together."

"Will it be dark by then?"

"No, the sun sets around nine this time of year."

Beatrice had forgotten Italians ate late. Restaurants didn't open for dinner until seven. If she refused, she would have to go without eating until the morning. "Great. I'll see you then."

Raphael got back in the Barretta. "Ciao. Bring a jacket, eh? Our table is outside. In June it still gets a bit cool in the evenings."

Three hours later, when Beatrice opened the heavy iron door and stepped out into the small street, she found Raphael waiting for her. The sun still shone, although it hung low in the sky. By nine, the sky would be turning dark. Hopefully, Raphael would be willing to walk her home as well.

When they reached the restaurant, the conservation team sat at four round tables gathered together to the left of the quaint arched door under a large umbrella.

Raphael introduced Beatrice to the team as the lead project conservator. She already knew a wealthy Lucchese businessman was the owner of the Batoni, although how it came into his possession, she did not know. Imelda, a young woman Beatrice guessed to be in her early thirties, was the Assistant Conservator. Imelda's expertise lay in the restoration of cultural heritage, a valued role on such an important project.

Diego was the chemistry expert, joined by Florio, the work supervisor. A material technician and a records technician rounded out the all Italian team.

The company website listed Raphael as the digital expert and President, which struck Beatrice as odd, but she expected to gain more insight into his role on the team over time.

While waiting for dinner, the group shared an excellent Palistort red, an excellent local Lucchese wine. When the waiter came to fill her glass, Beatrice raised her hand. "No, grazie."

"What?" Imelda tossed her long black hair behind her left shoulder. "You must drink wine with an Italian meal."

Imelda's comment didn't surprise Beatrice. Everyone drank wine in Italy. She tried to explain. "I have not slept for over twenty-four hours. If I drink wine tonight, I am likely to fall asleep at this table. I hope you don't mind if I pass. The San Benedetto is fine." She tapped the side of the mineral water bottle for emphasis and refilled her glass.

Raphael placed his hand over his heart and bowed his head. "I would be happy to walk you back to where you are staying."

"Thank you. I would be happy to take you up on that offer." Beatrice raised her water glass, "but I am still forgoing the wine tonight."

Imelda's eyes narrowed, and she raised her chin up to indicate her displeasure. "Then, more for us."

Raphael gave Imelda a disapproving look. Then turned to Beatrice. "I understand. You have had a long day."

Beatrice had never meant to insult anyone. More likely than not Imelda now took Beatrice for a teetotaler, which she certainly was not. She loved local Tuscany wines as much as anyone, but she couldn't risk alcohol when she had to walk home in the dark.

By the time the sun set the discussion around the tables focused on Batoni's painting of the Last Supper. The discovery of one of Batoni's last works found hidden behind a wall in one of the town's palaces had the entire populace guessing as to why and when the painting had been concealed.

Since the palace dated back to the 1600's, Raphael speculated the owners might have wanted to protect the painting from Napoleon. Imelda theorized someone may have stashed the canvas inside the palace walls in the thirties or forties figuring that Mussolini or the Nazis would not destroy the palace but use the grounds for themselves. Such a strategy would protect the painting from vandalism and theft.

As the evening wore on a single lamp by the restaurant door gave off a faint light, and a candle on each table added a romantic glow to the dinner, but neither helped Beatrice. Night blindness had been the first symptom of her eye disorder.

At home, she avoided problems by never going out after sunset. Now she faced a dilemma. She couldn't negotiate her way home when she couldn't see. The scuffling of chairs told her the team must be standing up to leave.

She rose and tried to follow the team's footsteps.

"Beatrice, did you need something?" Raphael's voice came from behind her.

A voice she didn't recognize said in English, "Excuse me, Miss, may I get by?"

Beatrice guessed she had headed for the restaurant entrance rather than follow her group out into the street. "I'm sorry."

She felt Raphael lock his arm in hers. Using gentle pressure on her elbow, he turned her around. In a low voice only she could hear, he said," I did promise to escort you home."

Although Beatrice had no idea how she would get home by herself, she was so embarrassed she declined his offer. "You don't have to do that."

Luckily, he insisted. The walk was not as difficult as Beatrice feared. Under the bright shop lights her vision improved.

Things worsened when they reached her building.

Raphael pulled her to a stop. "Here we are. I know these streets are confusing when you first arrive in Lucca, but after a day or so you will find your way around with no problem."

Beatrice knew she would take much longer than a few days to learn to negotiate the town. After a group of jovial tourists speaking English passed by, she said, "Thank you so much for walking me back."

"Are you okay?" His voice sounded close to her.

"Yes, thank you. I'm just tired." She waited for him to leave, not wanting him to see her fumbling with her key.

"Do you need help?" He seemed to be waiting for her to go inside.

Beatrice found the large, old-fashioned key to her room. She held it up. "Here it is. Thank you so much for a lovely night. I'll see you tomorrow."

"See you then. Ciao."

"Ciao." Beatrice waited until she couldn't hear Raphael's footsteps any longer. Then she felt for the lock with her fingers and located the large side plate. She found the top and bottom of the plate and, moving her right hand upward, found the keyhole. The key slid in with no problem. Once inside motion detectors set off several bright lights. She had no issues seeing the stairs to her rented room.

The next morning Beatrice woke up to bright sunlight breaking through the space between the two wooden shutters on the French doors leading to her small balcony. Today, she needed to find her way to the restoration lab using the map her landlord had given her.

To avoid bikes, pedestrians, and cars, she walked close to the medieval buildings. On the way to the lab, the aroma of a small bakery lured her inside where she ordered an expresso and warm croissant, the breakfast of busy Italian professionals.

Her walk turned out to be easy. She continued down Via Fillungo until she came to a large square plaza dominated by the massive Church of Saint Michael. On the rooftop, she spotted the famed statue of the Archangel Michael, the cathedral's namesake. She could use the landmark for finding her way to the office each day.

Revived from having eaten, she continued coming to the intersection of Via Roman and the Via Saint Croce. She turned left, arriving a few minutes later at what looked from the outside to be an old, run-down building.

Inside the white marble tiled entryway, Beatrice found a directory with the firm name: "Art Conservation and Preservation, S.R.L., Fourth Floor."

The company had a state-of-the-art door security system. Beatrice rang the bell, standing so she could be identified. Raphael opened the door and spread his arms wide when he saw her "Beatrice! Buongiorno. You found us!"

"Buongiorno, Raphael." Beatrice never expected to find such a modern open space lab inside what looked on the outside to be about a fifteenth-century building. Looking up at the ceiling, she gasped at the array of large skylights overhead. As she walked into the large room, she spun around to admire the walls of windows. "I love this space."

Raphael shook his head in agreement. "We have the entire top two floors in this building for our laboratories. We have four main labs for paintings, mount making, scientific research, and our tech lab. I can give you a more complete tour later but come with me. We are just about to unveil the Batoni."

Beatrice had no idea the company had such money behind it. Obviously, they were doing quite well for themselves.

To her surprise, the team already sat in a small area on chairs arranged around a conference table. Apparently, they didn't follow the standard nine am to one and two-thirty to six pm work schedules common in most Italian companies.

Raphael raised a flat screen display from the floor and began talking through a slide show depicting the environmental conditions inside the wall where the painting had been discovered.

"So," Raphael rubbed his hands together as he sat down the projector control. "Now you have the history of what we know about the discovery of the Last Supper, let's go take a look at the real thing."

Everyone filed into a conservation lab with the latest instruments and materials. It seemed no expense had been spared in outfitting the labs.

"Here is what everyone has been waiting to see." Raphael took a position on one side of a preservation box set on a long table with a wooden top. Imelda walked over to the other side. Together they lifted the lid off a preservation box. Beatrice joined the others crowded around the Batoni.

A gasp rose among the team members who had not seen the painting before.

Beatrice had seen oil paintings in worse shape, but not by much. "We certainly have our work cut out for us." The Batoni had suffered from over two hundred centuries of neglect. Lucca's annual humidity hovered around seventy-two percent throughout the year.

Tucked between two walls, some mold had accumulated. Beatrice noted a small piece of canvas missing in one corner of the painting. Possibly insect or rodent damage. Minor, but in need of repair. Some of the oil paint had cracked, and there was one place where it appeared to Beatrice's trained eye that paint might have fallen off.

Imelda turned to Raphael. "We will take a minimalist approach of course."

He turned to Beatrice. "That is up to Dr. Kunst."

This could be a test. The cleaning of a such a painting often resulted in horrendous disagreements within art conservation teams. "We haven't even examined the painting yet. Let's take things one step at a time and base our decisions on our scientific investigation. First, we need to assess the damage. Then we can begin to discuss our approach. We will must confer with the owner. Also,"

Imelda cut Beatrice off. "Great words, but I heard you removed all the varnish and lightened up the colors so much on a Batoni portrait that the painting doesn't reflect Batoni's original intentions at all." Imelda took a step toward Beatrice. She spread her feet apart, her chin jutted upward, and her hands tightened into fists as if she might throw an upper jab at any moment.

Raphael waited for Imelda to finish before commenting. "The goals of restoration are always a delicate balance between whether the painting should be restored to resemble the work the moment the artist completed the art or if the piece should be cleaned minimally, allowing the impact of history to be revealed." He looked straight at Beatrice. "What we want to know is your philosophy."

Beatrice tried to avoid an argument. "We have just had our first look at the painting. As you know, we need to do a lot more research and investigation before we choose the best approach for conservation."

Imelda interrupted. "Raphael, are you going to let this American, this drunk, ruin our Batoni?"

This wasn't the first time someone assumed Beatrice's stumbling and disorientation was due to excessive drinking or drugs. But Imelda's direct attack struck Beatrice as odd. She seemed to want to provoke a fight. "I was not drunk."

Raphael turned on the younger woman. "Imelda, remember you are the Assistant Conservator. The owner hired Dr. Kunst as a consultant because she is the world's authority on Batoni." Once again, he redirected the conversation toward Beatrice. "We are interested though in where you stand on the debate as to how much intervention is appropriate."

Beatrice caught the reference to "the owner hired Dr. Kunst." Apparently, the team did not approve. Her work on a Batoni portrait had been the subject of an intense debate, even getting her on the cover of a leading art conservation journal. What the journal had not emphasized was the poor condition of the painting and canvas, which had been in better condition than the oil painting in front of them. "Batoni's technique and materials evolved over his lifetime. It is too early at this stage to be arguing over our approach until we assess the painting's condition."

Raphael nodded. "I agree. Let's start our investigation as to the condition of the work. We are assuming there was no previous work done on the piece. We do not know that."

"Imelda bit her lip, turned and without a word walked away and out of the office.

Beatrice spent the morning talking to individual members of the team and inspecting the facility. During her meeting with Raphael she asked him about the company. "Your equipment and resources far exceed that of any small firm I have encountered. Your lab could compete with the resources of some of the best equipped museums."

He studied her with those brown eyes for a few seconds as if debating what to say. "I sold a high-tech firm and used the proceeds to follow my passion for art conservation. I have a strong relationship with an art museum in Florence and often work with them. They would have handled this project but the owner, a prominent Lucca resident, insisted that our firm lead the project." Raphael shrugged, "We may be one Italy, but for some, old resentments linger."

"What resentments?"

"Florence and Lucca were only united 1860 when Italy became a country." He gave her a wry smile. "Florence was our enemy for many centuries."

Beatrice swallowed hard, trying to concentrate on the conversation. He really did look like some Roman god.

At eleven-thirty Raphael entered the chemistry lab where Beatrice, Diego, and Florio sat together in front of a computer working on a project plan for examining the Batoni.

"Ciao, everyone. Are you breaking for lunch soon?"

"Ciao, Raphael. You are reading my mind." Diego was the youngest of the team and, from what Beatrice could tell, never stopped eating.

Raphael waited until Diego walked away. "Would you like to visit the Botanical Garden? I know a good street café nearby that makes great panini—roast pork, rolled bacon, scamorza cheese, truffle cream, aubergines."

Beatrice hadn't adjusted to the time difference yet. Her stomach rumbled just at the mention of food. By her calculations, it was approaching breakfast time in the States. "Absolutely. Lead the way."

The fastest route, it turned out, was to climb up a short path to the top of the city wall. Beatrice knew Lucca's fame in part came from the fact it was one of the few medieval cities with a defensive wall that was never breached. When she and Raphael reached the top, she stopped in surprise.

Elderly couples and mothers pushing baby carriages walked a path at least fifteen or twenty feet wide. Large green lawns abutted the pathway.

Raphael led her to the ramparts where she could view the rest of the city. "This is one of three walls in Lucca. You can see parts of the Roman wall in the foundation of the Church of Santa Maria della Rosa. The second is the medieval wall. In the bastion of Santa Croce below the wall, you will see some of those ruins. We will walk along the site of the medieval wall to get to the Botanical Garden. We are on top of the third wall, built between the thirteenth and fifteenth centuries."

Unlike below, in the town, pedestrians stuck to the left and right on the smooth gravel path. Everyone walked in the same direction, unlike down in the city. Bikers stayed in the middle and used bells to warn of their approach. Best of all, Beatrice didn't see a single car. "Is this a pedestrian zone?"

"Well," Raphael laughed, "You won't see any cars, if that is what you mean, but as you can tell, you will see bikes, foot-pedaled vehicles propelled by four people, and you might even see a horse at times."

From the top of the wall, Beatrice could see the rooftops of the city. Several houses beside the wall had rooftop gardens. Her impaired depth perception threw things off a bit but not so much it bothered her. On the other side of the path, she could see small grassy areas with swing sets for children and one field was large enough for a group of girls to play soccer.

"See that salmon-colored house?" Raphael pointed at a wheat colored building. "That is where Batoni was born. It is a museum now."

"Oh," Beatrice tried to memorize the location. "I must go there sometime."

Trees lined both sides of the pathway, and a breeze took the edge off of the hot Tuscan sun. After a little more than a half mile, Raphael pointed to a path from the top of the wall to the street. "We can follow this to the street café and then walk over to the garden."

As a student in Rome on a small scholarship, Beatrice lived on cheap but delicious street food. She looked forward to the Pucce Salentine bread made from pizza dough. They had the sandwich wrapped up to eat at the garden.

Raphael paid for two tickets, despite Beatrice's offer to buy her own ticket. "No, I invited you. There is something I want to show you."

They passed numerous varieties of rhododendron, each carefully labeled as they walked to an iron bench beside an American Redwood tree. The giant tree provided plenty of shade.

The roast pork sandwich was every bit as good as Raphael promised. Beatrice was almost finished with her lunch when she realized Raphael wasn't saying anything. His sandwich sat on his lap, untouched.

Concerned, she asked, "Is something wrong."

"If I ask you a question, will you tell me the truth?"

That sounded ominous. "I'm not in the habit of lying."

Raphael began to unwrap his sandwich. "You didn't take the train to Lucca. I know because the train was delayed the day you arrived."

Beatrice feared she knew where this conversation was headed. "I never said I rode the train. I agreed to meet at the time the train was scheduled to arrive. I took a taxi from the Pisa airport."

"Something is wrong. I can tell. At dinner, you didn't seem to realize you were entering the restaurant when we went to leave. You had trouble walking in a straight line."

"I wasn't drunk."

"I know. You didn't have any wine, but you stumbled twice on our walk to your building."

Beatrice didn't like where the conversation was going. "I am clumsy."

"When I dropped you off at your building, you found your key but had to feel the wall to find the lock."

She felt betrayed. "What did you do? Stand and watch me?"

"I wasn't spying. I wanted to make sure you got inside your building."

Unable to look at him she stared at the ground. "What are you accusing me of, Raphael?"

"I am not accusing you of anything, but I'm worried about you. I can tell something is wrong. Maybe I can help."

"I was tired last night and had a headache, that is all." There, she had told a lie, just what she said she wouldn't do.

They sat in silence for several minutes.

Raphael said "I shouldn't pry," at the same time Beatrice said, "I was tired, but that is only partly true. But you are right, there is something wrong."

Raphael turned to face her and took her hands in his. "Tell me." His concern sounded sincere.

She didn't want to have this conversation. Certainly not this soon. She had just started work on the Batoni project. This was the project of a lifetime. She had devoted her career to studying Batoni and wanted nothing more than this chance to be a part of preserving one of his greatest works for future generations.

Raphael looked at her with those brown eyes of his. She gathered her courage. What the hell, she would tell the truth. "I have a degenerative eye condition. It's called retinitis pigmentosa."

She could hear the concern in Raphael's voice when he squeezed her hand. "I never heard of this."

"I'm not surprised. It's rare. Both of my parents had the recessive gene, and I hit the jackpot." What could she do but shrug? "R.P. is unpredictable. Basically, my peripheral vision is getting smaller, but I have good days like today when my vision is not good but not so bad."

"How bad is not good?"

Beatrice couldn't help but laugh at that one. "Well, most of the time, I see a kind of gray fog around a clear circle of sight. When I look at you, for instance, I can see your face, not much more."

"You poor thing."

Pity was the one thing Beatrice couldn't stand. "I don't want pity. My situation is not sad or tragic. I have adjusted. Everyone ages day by day and then one day you realize you look different than you did when you were younger. That is what is happening to my vision. It is going a little bit, day by day. I was diagnosed nine years ago. I'm not some invalid."

Raphael edged closer to Beatrice. "I only meant you poor thing having to look at my face." He leaned forward and her breathing quickened. "I do so like looking at your beautiful face."

Okay, now she was seriously flustered.

Then reality struck. What if Raphael told someone? The art world could be cruel. They would all be talking about the art conservationist who couldn't see the paintings. Every conservation project she had supervised would be analyzed and criticized.

"Please don't tell anyone. If word gets out I have vision problems, no one will hire me. I can still see well enough to work."

"You should tell people. They will understand and then they won't make assumptions like Imelda did."

Beatrice pulled her hand out of Raphael's grip. "R.P. is unpredictable. I might never go blind. There is no need to tell anyone yet. I will never have perfect vision, but I can still see. Just not at night."

"Why not at night?"

Beatrice never liked talking about her condition with people, but she had decided to be honest, so she admitted, "Night blindness is the first sign of R.P. It is how I was diagnosed."

"You could use a cane. Then you could go out at night, and it would make walking the streets safer for you. People in cars and on bikes will be more careful when they passed."

Why was everyone trying to get her to use a cane? Her mother. Her doctor. Now Raphael, who hardly knew her. "I don't need a cane. *I'm not blind.*" She hadn't meant to shout.

Raphael raised his hands. "I'm sorry, eh?"

Beatrice stood up. "I think we should go back now."

He wrapped up the sandwich he hadn't touched. "Of course."

As Beatrice stood, she saw the plaque beside the bench. "What is that?" She pointed at the salmon-colored relief mounted on a pole and the braille above it.

Raphael lowered his head as he confessed. "That is one of the plaques I made for the garden so blind people can read about the plants."

"Blind people?"

Now Raphael looked embarrassed. "Please, Beatrice. Lower your voice."

A woman with a cane walked by them.

Beatrice did lower her voice, but she couldn't hide her anger. "You brought me here because you knew I had trouble seeing."

"Honestly, I didn't know. I just knew something was wrong."

"I don't believe you." Beatrice turned and began running down the path in what she thought was the entrance. As she rounded a turn, her foot hit a stone and she fell forward. She picked herself up,

certain Raphael would be behind her, but when she looked around, he wasn't there.

Beatrice thought about going straight back to her room, but she had a job to do, and until Raphael fired her, damn it, she would finish her work.

For the next two hours, Beatrice stumbled through Lucca's maze of streets. In the tourist areas where she had walked in the morning the street signs had been posted eye level and on metal signs with a border of medium blue. Each sign bore the street name in large, medium blue letters too, so the tourists didn't get lost.

The Botanical Garden didn't lie in the tourist area. Beatrice struggled to read the faded lettering of street names painted high on ancient buildings.

As she wandered around lost, the sky grew dark. A front of gray and black storm clouds appeared over the town on fast moving winds. The temperature dropped.

Beatrice went from shop to shop asking for directions, only to discover not all the streets people told her to take appeared on her map.

She fell more than once after misjudging the height of the curbs. As she stepped out into an intersection, the sudden screech of brakes startled her. She looked up and found herself staring at the ashen face of a teenage boy. She had walked right in front of the poor kid's car.

By the time she reached the office, the time app on her smart watch had buzzed four times. She had been lost for three hours. As she opened the door, a loud clap of thunder startled her. Heavy rain poured from the sky.

Raphael saw her before anyone else. He rushed to her side. "Beatrice, are you all right?"

Too tired to be mad at him, she shook her head. "It seems you are always asking me that question. I am fine."

Diego came out of the digital lab. Seeing Beatrice, he waved. "Raphael, it is working. Beatrice, come see what Raphael and I have created."

Raphael held up a hand. "Diego, this is not a good time."

The younger man ignored Raphael. Taking Beatrice's hand, he pulled her along. "Come see."

Beatrice allowed Diego to guide her into the lab. Beside a 3D printer was a model of "The Calling of St Matthew" by the Italian artist, Caravaggio.

Beatrice knew that there were those in the art world working with 3D imaging of paintings and had read that some were creating sculptures of artwork for the blind. Suspicious, she asked, "What is this?"

Diego laughed. "Raphael and I have been working on making models of artwork for the blind using a 3D printer so they can interpret the work for themselves. Put your hand here."

Before Beatrice could object, Diego placed her right hand on the model. The different ridges were various degrees of warm and cold.

The young project leader looked like a proud father. "Every brush stroke is represented in 3D. The temperature translates into color. The warmer the ridge, the warmer the color, and we are designing an app that will announce the color you touch. Here," he moved her hand over the ridges. See? Dark red is warmer than salmon. Cornflower blue is cooler. Isn't it wonderful? Raphael designed the computer interface, and I am helping him with the temperature program. What do you think?"

"Very impressive, Diego. How long have you and Raphael been working on this?"

"Two years. We got the idea from the plaques Raphael designed for the blind at the Botanical Gardens."

Now Beatrice understood Raphael had taken her to the garden to show her his work.

Beatrice put a hand on Diego's arm. "Thank you for sharing this with me."

She found Raphael in a windowless conference room designed for private meetings. They stood side by side.

Beatrice broke the silence. "You were right. I do need help. I got lost after I left you. I walked in front of a car. I fell. I just have not been ready to admit that I might be at the point where a cane would be helpful."

Raphael reached out to push a lock of her hair off her face. "I didn't know about your," he hesitated, "situation." I took you to the garden to show you the plaque, not because I knew you had trouble seeing."

"I realize that now. You were right. The truth is I have been adjusting for a long time by cutting more and more out of my life. In Cleveland, I chose an apartment a short walk from my office down a street with no crosswalks. I never went out after sunset. The only people in the States who know I have a vision problem are my parents and my doctor. Everyone else either thinks I'm just a recluse or the clumsiest person they ever met."

She thought about all the times her doctor and parents tried to talk to her about utilizing technology for the visually impaired and how hard she had resisted. "People who worked with me probably suspected, as you did, that something was wrong and just got tired of me refusing to tell them what was going on. Plenty asked, but I pushed them away out of fear I wouldn't be able to continue working."

"I wish you had told me earlier."

Beatrice knew the honest thing would have been to tell Raphael before she took the job. But how could she admit to him her vision had become so limited when she had refused to admit the truth to herself. "I'll resign from the project."

"No." Raphael shook his head. "We need you on this project."

"I don't want to be a burden to the team, and especially not to you. Coming to Lucca was a mistake." She remembered the look of horror on the young boy's face who almost hit her. "I can't live here. It isn't fair for me to put others in danger. I can't see the cars or bikes. There are no traffic lights to tell me when to cross the street, and the little streets are a maze I can't decode."

Raphael took Beatrice's hand. "You won't be a burden to the team. And I think you are wrong. You can be more independent within Lucca's walls than you ever were in Cleveland. If you learn to use a cane, you will find the drivers patient. They are used to clueless tourists who don't look where they are going. When they see your cane, they will stop for you. Pedestrians too."

Beatrice remained skeptical. "But the streets themselves are confusing."

Raphael tapped on the computer. "No, no. The streets are easy to learn because they are laid out in the old Roman grid of wide streets running north-south and east-west. The main north-south street are the pedestrian zones where the tourists roam.

These streets cross the main east-west street at the big squares."

He pulled up a map of Lucca on the computer screen. "See? Once you understand the layout, getting around is a matter of learning the street names. Besides, you can use a navigation app to get around."

Now Beatrice really felt like a fool. She always used a navigation app in Cleveland. Why hadn't she thought to use it in Lucca? "You can get reception between these high buildings?"

"But of course. There are cell towers placed all over the town. We might be a medieval city, but we are a twenty-first century medieval city."

"Well," Beatrice gazed into Raphael's brown eyes. She found his enthusiasm hard to resist. "I would love to work on the Batoni."

Raphael leaned forward, taking her hands in his, again. "And I would love to collaborate with you … on the Batoni and …."

When he smiled, that damn cute dimple deepened. Beatrice caved, her heart finishing his sentence: Work together. *Be* together.

They looked at each other for what seemed like an eternity until Beatrice, unable to resist any longer, whispered the words she had been thinking whenever he'd not annoyed the hell out of her: "kiss me." Then she repeated, "Baciami."

Little by little, he drew closer until his lips touched hers. She closed her eyes, his kiss everything she had dreamed it would be. Another clap of thunder shook the building.

Beatrice drew back and opened her eyes but couldn't see anything. The electricity had gone out, but she wasn't scared. She could still feel Raphael next to her and hear his breathing. She hesitated, then confessed, "I can't see you."

Raphael held his palm against her cheek. In that low baritone that sent shivers down her spine, he said, "If you let me, I can be your eyes. You've got this. And when you haven't, I've got you."

He wrapped his arms around her and pulled her closer to him. She closed her eyes as he kissed her again. She believed this collaboration could last a lifetime.

Copyright © 2019 by Tonya D. Price.

D. H. Hendrickson has published two hockey romance novels, Body Check *and* No Defense, *as well as four other novels (writing as David H. Hendrickson). His novel* Offside *has been adopted for high school student required reading. His short fiction has appeared in* Ellery Queen's Mystery Magazine, Pulphouse, *and numerous anthologies, including multiple issues of* Fiction River. *His story "Death in the Serengeti" has been selected for* Best American Mystery Stories 2018. *Hendrickson has published over fifteen hundred works of nonfiction, most recently* Travis Roy: Quadriplegia and a Life of Purpose. *He has been honored with the Joe Concannon Hockey East Media Award and the Murray Kramer Scarlet Quill Award. Follow him at www.hendricksonwriter.com.*

THE BOY IN THE BOXERS

by D. H. Hendrickson

Julia Johansson backed her fifteen-year-old Hyundai out of the Karlson driveway, heater blasting, headlights on, and Bruce Springsteen on the radio singing "Santa Claus is Coming to Town." She turned onto the main road, or what amounted to a main road in this succession of one-stoplight and no-stoplight towns north of Boston. She switched her high beams on to pierce the pitch-black darkness on the empty, unlit road. When a few snowflakes fell on the windshield, Julia turned on the wipers only to turn them quickly off when the rubber squeaked across the mostly dry surface.

The car was filled with the familiar, comforting smells of pastries, cookies, cakes, Swedish meatballs, potato pancakes, and sweet lingonberry crepes. The *sill*—pickled herring with onions, cloves, and peppercorns—was in the trunk. She had banished it in part because it was served cold, but also because no one wanted the odor of *sill* on their *vitabra*, the Swedish coffee cake made with raisins, cinnamon, and sugar that was the specialty of her parents' shop, Johansson's Bakery.

Sometimes back in the shop, Julia grew jaded at the smells, barely noticing them, but in the close confines of the car, they made her smile. Even now, with only one delivery remaining and only three stacks of white boxes left rising halfway up the back seat, the pleasing smells lingered.

In fact, she could go for a piece of *vitabra* right now. She realized that she was *starving*. She'd been going non-stop since nine that morning, and it was now past seven-thirty, Christmas Eve. Her promotion had been a roaring success. Even her stuck-in-the-mud parents had grudgingly agreed.

They weren't Old School. They were Ancient Relics and Fossils School. They'd had her late in life, and she'd had to drag them kicking and screaming into the twenty-first century. What do we need a website for? None of our customers follow social media. Promotions will only cost money!

She loved them to death, but some of their arguments made about as much sense as, well, a Swedish bakery in a part of the country where there weren't hardly any Swedes. Did they get their M's mixed up and back before she was born meant to set up shop in Minnesota—where the customers were!—instead of Massachusetts?

So, she'd set up a website for the bakery, and put Johansson's Bakery on all the social media platforms, and regularly posted pictures of the Mouth-Watering Delicacy of the Week. And she'd come up with a special Christmas promotion that wouldn't cost her tight-fisted parents a penny. All customers making sufficiently large, pre-paid orders would get their deliveries made while she serenaded them with their choice of two *a cappella* Christmas carols.

The promotion also tossed a bone to her artistic soul. What she wanted more than anything was to sing. Music was her passion. Performing songs that made people smile or cry or sometimes laugh. Songs that moved emotions. She'd fronted several bands that played in Boston clubs, but they never went anywhere. She wasn't going anywhere. Twenty-three years old and not even a hint of a breakthrough.

Was it her fault? Was she just not good enough? Or was she too much of a hard-ass, as her last lead guitarist claimed, unwilling to "play the game" and wear skirts that barely covered her ass and low-cut tops that revealed almost everything up there when she bent over to sing parts of songs with extra emotion.

"You've got the bod. Use it!" he'd said. "Shake that sexy long brown hair. Then shake that nice cute ass!"

But that wasn't music! Or was it these days?

And so, she'd flitted from one band to another until right now she was … between bands. It was hard. Except for Sundays when the bakery was closed, and days she had to leave early for a gig, she worked twelve hours a day, six days a week. Without her, the bakery certainly would have failed during the last big economic free fall.

Her parents needed her. But she was also leaving her dreams stuck in neutral. And if you stay stuck in neutral long enough, you find you've gotten nowhere and you're out of gas.

She'd even tried going into Boston on Sundays for a while, taking the T into the busiest subway stop at Government Center, and performed there, her back to the grimy T-stop walls, subway cars screeching while she sang *a cappella*. Most people ignored her. Many complimented her and tossed change or dollar bills into a hat she left on the ground.

But there were a few pervs, too, who'd leer and suggest how she could make some serious money, or pretended they weren't looking where they were going and "accidentally" brushed up against her.

Julia had heard you had to take a lot of shit to make it in the music world, especially if you were a woman, but the degradation of her subway performances was more than she could stomach. So for now, it was singing Christmas carols to build her parents' business and also collect a few tips.

But, man, was she worn out. Just one more delivery tonight, then a quiet Christmas with her parents tomorrow, who she'd convinced to switch from celebrating on Christmas Eve night, the usual Swedish tradition, to Christmas Day like most Americans, so they could squeeze a little more business out of today.

She pulled into the driveway of the Anderssons, right up to the two-car garage on the left side of the house and texted her mother that she was there. Her mother, always a worrier, had been nervous about Julia doing deliveries and had insisted on this safety scheme. If Julia didn't text again within twenty minutes that she was back in her car and leaving—"it really shouldn't take that long to deliver the packages and sing two carols!"—then she'd be getting a call from Mom, and if Julia still didn't answer, the police were getting called.

Her mom replied with a "K." Funny how her parents could go from seeing no need for websites and smart phones—"what's so smart about it?"—to using "K" and "ur" and all the other shortcuts.

Julia took her pointed elf's cap of green with wide strips of red off the front seat, settled it on her head, tucked her long, brown hair behind her ears, and opened the door. The cold air struck her first—a bit above freezing, not really that bad, but still a stiff blast compared to the warm, toasty air inside the car, designed to keep the pastries warm. The second thing she noticed were the shrieks of laughter and hilarity coming from the back of the house.

For Ryan Andersson, the best part about their extended family's Christmas Eve tradition wasn't the big meal or even the exchanging of presents, much as he enjoyed them both. What he loved most of all was getting together with his five cousins and playing hockey on the backyard rink. The "boards" were only a foot high to hold the freezing water in, and the ice was subject to the vagaries of December weather, but it wasn't a fully satisfying Christmas Eve without it.

Over the years, the rink had grown from twenty feet by forty feet when they were little to its current size of sixty by a hundred, the longer dimension extending further away from the house. Floodlights illuminated both ends. The boards still rose just a foot high, all of them a succession of 16-foot planks put down on top of plastic and held together by joining pieces. As the rink had grown, the surrounding wooded area had gotten closer, but a gap of fifty feet of brown grass remained on all sides, still awaiting the first snowfall.

He and the cousins had always been his best hockey buds, four of them boys, one a girl, all within three years of each other. The six of them had been nuts about hockey almost from birth, perhaps even conception. His dad, having watched the old movie, *The Three Amigos*, had dubbed them The Six Amigos and it stuck even to this day. On Christmas Eve, if the Amigos weren't playing out here on the rink, they were playing floor hockey with an orange rubber ball down in the basement, always setting the stage with, "It's the seventh game of the Stanley Cup finals, and we're going into overtime," and then whenever one of them put the game-winner in the net, it was, *"He shoots! He scores! The Bruins have won the Stanley Cup!"* Unless, of course, it was Cherie who scored in which case the gender of the pronoun changed.

That was Christmas Eve for Ryan.

Tonight, it would only be four of the Six Amigos. The two oldest ones, Cherie and Donnie, were studying abroad in Europe and wouldn't be making it back for the holidays. It would only be Connor, Taylor, and Aiden joining Ryan. Warm weather had threatened even that, turning the surface of the rink into a soupy mess as of just two weeks ago, but a cold spell had hit just in time to freeze the ice solid, and now it was a few degrees above freezing, making it about as perfect weather as possible for the best of all Christmas Eve traditions.

And Ryan needed it more than ever.

Halfway through his freshman year, an hour away at Boston College, it had been his first year without competitive hockey since he was a five-year-old in the Learn to Skate program. For as far back as he could recall, he'd been competing on teams, enjoying the sport itself and the camaraderie of friends. He'd always been pretty good, all the way up through high school. But there was a Grand Canyon-sized gap between being pretty good in high school and making a college team, much less one at a Division I school that regularly challenged for the national championship. At the age of nineteen, his competitive hockey career was over.

And he missed it. Man, how he missed it.

So Ryan felt a special glow as he and the other three Amigos on his left headed from the back door, suited up with all their pads and jerseys except for their skates. He'd been looking forward to this day all semester long.

Behind them, the back door opened and Ryan's father, a short, stocky man with graying hair, called after him.

"I know you're a mostly an adult and all that, and you're used to making your own decisions now."

Ryan turned to the other three Amigos and said with a smirk, "But…"

"But I don't want you taking your helmet off," his father said. "Concussions are a big deal these days and besides, your mother and I didn't pay thousands of dollars for your orthodontics only to have those pearly whites knocked out by one high stick."

"Yes, Dad," Ryan said over his shoulder.

"I'm serious!" his father called out.

"I won't," Ryan called back as he kept walking. "I promise."

"Okay, have fun!"

As the back door from the house closed and the four Amigos were once again by themselves, an impish impulse struck Ryan.

It was crazy. Outright lunacy. In fact, more like *looooon-acy*. How could he resist?

"Watch this," he said.

While the other three laced up their skates on the bench just outside the foot-high "boards" at center ice, Ryan began striping off his clothes and pads. Jersey, Shoulder pads. Elbow pads. Pants.

By the time he was done, he was wearing only his skates, gloves, the all-important helmet, and his boxers.

The other three were laughing so hard, they could barely stand up.

"Keep the sticks down!" Ryan said, as he hopped onto the ice, cradled a puck on his stick, and flew across the smooth surface, the cold air rushing over his bare skin. Did it get any better than this? He didn't think so. He was going to have to keep moving or he'd freeze his nuts off. Almost literally. But as insane ideas went, this was one of his best.

It took three trips for Julia to get all the stacks of white boxes into the Andersson kitchen. From the oven on the right to the sink on the left, they filled the counter. Their smells mingled with those of lasagna and ham on the counter on the other side of the sink, along with cheese and crackers on the kitchen table. It made for a mouth-watering cloud.

Three middle-aged couples ringed the kitchen. Inside the adjoining front room, three girls about Julia's age laughed hilariously. Julia stood beside the stacks of boxes, still wearing her dark blue, unzipped coat over a bright red sweater and bright green slacks.

"What would you like me to sing?" she asked.

Mr. Andersson, who had let her in, introduced her to the rest of the group, and asked, "Any suggestions? I'll only veto 'Rudolph, the Red Nosed Reindeer.'" He poked his head toward the front room. "Girls, would you like to hear a Christmas carol?"

"How about Silent Night?" Mrs. Andersson, a slender woman wearing a bright red and green dress, asked.

"My pleasure," Julia said. "One of my favorites."

She began to sing and all about the room eyes widened and heads nodded in appreciation. The three girls in the front room emerged to listen.

When Julia finished, they all clapped with gusto, Mr. Andersson even calling out, "Bravo!"

Julia beamed. It wasn't Carnegie Hall, but it was always nice to have an appreciative audience.

"Are you a professional singer?" Mrs. Andersson asked.

"I wish!" Julia said. "Maybe someday, but for now I just work in my parents' bakery."

"What a sweet voice!" Mrs. Andersson said, to murmurs of agreement and similar compliments from the rest.

"Thank you, everyone," Julia said. "What's the other carol you'd like me to sing?"

Muffled cries of delight sounded from the back yard.

"Why don't you perform one of your songs for the boys?" Mrs. Andersson said. "They've been out back playing hockey for Lord knows how long. I'm sure they could use a break. Maybe they'll even stand at the blue line and have you sing the national anthem."

Julia agreed, and the others grabbed their coats and headed for the back door.

"If they ask for both the US and Canadian national anthems, we'll tell them they can only choose one," Mr. Andersson said with a chuckle. He opened the back door and motioned for her to go first.

At first, all Julia saw were the two floodlights brightly illuminating both ends of a large skating surface, the near one about fifty feet away and the other about two hundred feet in the distance. Then she saw the four hockey players. And then she saw—

Her jaw dropped.

"Ryan Andersson, what are you doing?" Mrs. Andersson shrieked. And then in a softer voice, but still

with urgency, "Ma'am?" and then again "Ma'am?" And then finally, "Pastry girl!"

Julia supposed this was meant for her, but her eyes were fixed on the most astonishing thing she'd ever seen. A boy about her age was playing hockey wearing nothing but his boxers! A man, to be technical about it. He was fully grown, to be sure. No mere teenager. Probably in college. But he radiated such a powerful boyish exuberance she couldn't help but think of him as a boy. A boy in his boxers. And not just any boy.

An Adonis!

Not to be superficial, but holy shinola, when the word chiseled had been invented to describe a man's physique, surely this was what the inventor had mind. Rock-solid, muscled shoulders, chest, and legs. The flattest of flat washboard abs.

The key to staying warm when playing hockey outdoors in nothing but your boxers was to keep moving. And that's what Ryan had been doing, joyously racing up and down the ice, playing two-on-two with the other Amigos, the nets facing backwards so you couldn't score from a distance, you had to skate the full distance and score from behind what would usually be the end line.

Up and back. Up and back. Trash talking. Whooping it up. Just like old times.

God, he had missed this! This was as perfect of a Christmas Eve as possible, aside from Cherie and Donnie not being here to fill out the full complement of Amigos.

Perfect until he heard his mother's unmistakable shriek just as he was crossing center ice on a breakaway, Connor a stride and a half behind him and Taylor loafing way behind.

"Ryan Andersson, what are you doing?"

Ryan glanced toward the back of the house and saw a parade streaming out the back door.

Uh-oh. That hadn't been part of the plan.

But since his goose was cooked no matter what he did now, he wasn't about to ruin a clean breakaway. Ryan raced toward the goal that faced backwards, three feet out from the back boards, cut behind it, and roofed a shot into the top of the net.

"Gooooooooaaaaaallllll! The Bruins win the Stanley Cup!" he yelled, thrusting his arms into the air. "Ryan Andersson with the game-winner in overtime!"

And then, since he figured he might as well go out in a blaze of glory, he completed the Stanley Cup-winning celebration, throwing his stick and gloves into the air and looking for his teammate, Aiden, to hug.

Only then did he see the attractive brunette wearing an elf's cap of green with red stripes. He wouldn't have pulled this stunt if he'd suspected even one of the Amigos' girlfriends would come out. But that wasn't their way. They did their own thing inside, whatever that was.

But this was a million times worse. Not one of the other guys' girlfriends. A total stranger.

And not just any stranger. A beautiful stranger.

"Oops," he said.

It seemed to Julia as if the entire world was apologizing to her. The man-boy in the boxers. His parents. The other parents, presumably his aunts and uncles. Even the other players.

"He likes to make us laugh," said the one they called Connor. "He isn't sicko crazy. Just funny crazy."

Julia just nodded, unable to take her eyes off the Adonis in the boxers, even after his mortified mother came rushing out with a yellow blanket to drape over him. Julia had never seen a stranger before in his boxers, and she was quite sure in almost every other case, she would have been revolted. She'd only seen two old boyfriends in just their boxers and that had been long after their relationship had started, fully clothed. That was how things worked. A boy seemed good-looking dressed in slacks or jeans with a nice button-down or pull-over shirt.

Eventually things worked their way down to the boxers, and then beyond. She'd never imagined starting right out at the boxers.

But holy shinola, there was an exception to every rule. And when he took his helmet off, steam rising off his plastered hair, apologized, and flashed the boyish, embarrassed grin of a kid caught with his hand in the cookie jar, Julia thought she might melt.

She'd never believed in love at first sight, and perhaps this man-boy might prove a little too crazy for her—the Billy Joel song "You May Be Right" came to mind—but if there was such a thing, this was it. She could barely collect herself enough to talk.

"What would you like me to sing?" she finally managed, briefly tearing her eyes away from the Adonis to turn around and ask the adults.

"I think after exposing you to this—" Mr. Andersson said, then blinked rapidly, "—and I swear to God that pun was totally unintentional. Or Freudian or something. But after this … this situation, I think *you* should pick the song. You've earned it!"

Everyone in the crowd agreed, so Julia made her choice. Her favorite was Mariah's version of "Joy to the World," but that desperately begged for a backing choir. *A cappella*, the choice was easy. And so with the stars above twinkling, a smattering of snowflakes floating in the cold air, and her eyes inevitably drawn to the hunk now huddled in a yellow blanket, she began.

"Oh, Holy Night, the stars are brightly shining!"

Ryan stared in wonder as The Vision, as he'd come to think of her, sang with the voice of an angel.

It was a voice he wanted to hear for the rest of his life.

He checked himself. What was that? What was he just thinking? He barely knew this girl. But what a voice! It was like listening to Mariah or Whitney or Beyoncé. He was no expert, but this girl had pipes! She should be on the radio. Topping the charts. Selling out the Garden. Thinking of crossing over to the movies like Lady Gaga. She was amazing!

He didn't want to be creepy, but huddled beneath the scratchy yellow woolen blanket, he slid slowly across the ice to get closer to the girl. He wanted to hear every note with total clarity. He wanted to see her smiling in all her astounding beauty. There was only one word for what he was feeling.

Thunderstruck.

When she neared the end and opted for the ultra-high note and hit it dead on, Ryan realized he was holding his breath, and only exhaled when she finished the last few notes.

No one cheered harder. No one cheered longer.

"That was awesome!" he said, skating to the edge of the foot-high boards, fifteen feet away from the girl. Trying to be as discreet as possible, he said softly, barely above a whisper, "I know I've made a bad first impression, but I'm really not a creep. I like to have fun, but I'm really not crazy. Even if it seems that way. Could I get your phone number? I'd like to make it up to you. Let me take you out. Wherever you want to go. You name it."

She blushed, glanced at everyone around her, and opened her mouth to speak, but said nothing.

"How about tomorrow?" he asked. "We can do a fancy place or just pizza. We can go to the movies or just talk. Talk at some place like a Starbucks or Dunks. Whatever you want."

A bemused smile came over her lips. "Tomorrow is Christmas. I'll be spending it with my family."

Ryan wanted to whack himself across the head. As if her first impression of him weren't bad enough, he had to make himself look like a moron. Geez, what day is tomorrow? It's Christmas—he had forgot.

And he was having to ask her out in front of everyone else with no privacy at all. But what was he supposed to do? Let her walk away, shaking her head at the lunatic who played hockey in his boxers, never to be seen again?

Hell, no!

"Then how about the day after tomorrow?" he asked. "I'm sorry if I'm embarrassing you in front of everyone, but"—he wiggled his arms beneath the blanket—"I don't know what else to do."

Panicked thoughts that this vision might get away ricocheted inside his brain. But she hadn't said no. At least not yet.

What else could he say? What else could he do?

"Stay for Christmas Eve dinner tonight!" he blurted out.

Julia felt her face grow hot. She liked this boy, at least as much as you could like one you'd just met, albeit with him wearing nothing but his boxers. And it really wasn't just that he was built like a Greek god. She'd enjoyed his goal celebration almost as much as he had.

Goooooooaaaaaallllll! The Bruins win the Stanley Cup! Ryan Andersson with the game-winner in overtime.

The pure joy. The boyish enthusiasm.

He seemed like *a lot* of fun. And she felt like she could use some of that right now. Every day seemed to be push, push, push. Twelve hours at the bakery, six days a week, except when she had to cut out early for gigs that lately had become nonexistent.

Julia loved performing. She loved to sing. That was her fun, even when it was hard work. But since there'd been no performing lately, there'd been no fun. At least until the carol-singing promotion.

She wasn't going to give up on those dreams. Dammit, she was going to keep trying. But right now, she needed a huge dose of *fun*.

And who better to provide that than the boy in the boxers?

But she certainly couldn't intrude on his family's Christmas Eve dinner. That was simply out of the question. It would be rude and awkward.

"I'm sorry, I couldn't do that." Julia gestured to his family behind her. "This is your family. I'm not family. I couldn't intrude."

"Three of them are my cousin's girlfriends," he said. "I wouldn't presume to be lucky enough to call you my girlfriend." He smiled broadly. "Yet." His eyes twinkled. "But we could call you my possible future girlfriend and you wouldn't be intruding any more than they are. Or just join us because you have the voice of an angel, and we'd all love to hear more."

When Julia paused, the boy's mother jumped in.

"You've seen my son in his boxers," the woman said. "It doesn't get much more family than that."

Everyone laughed, including Julia. She was thinking that she still couldn't accept, it just didn't seem proper, when her phone rang.

Julia jumped with a start at the ring tone. The famous birdlike aria from Mozart's *The Magic Flute*. Her mother was calling.

And it looked like she'd sent five texts

Julia looked at her watch. Twenty-one minutes. One minute late and her mother had already sent five missed texts and now the phone call.

"Excuse me," Julia said, holding one finger aloft and walking away from the crowd for some privacy.

"Mom, I'm okay," Julia said in greeting to ease her mother's mind.

"I was scared out of my mind!"

"It just took a little longer," Julia said, figuring that trying to explain the exact "why" it took longer

wouldn't be a good idea. "But I'm with the Anderssons right now, so I have to go."

"I knew this crazy promotion was a bad idea!" her mother said.

The words struck just enough of a nerve that Julia rebelled. The promotion hadn't been a bad idea, it had been a *great* idea. It had boosted sales, given her the welcome opportunity to sing, and even introduced her to the boy in the boxers. It had been anything but a crazy promotion. Crazy? Well, if her mother wanted to know crazy, there was this boy she needed to meet.

"Mom, I'm going to have dinner with the Anderssons. They've invited me and I've accepted."

"What?"

"Mom, it's a boy," Julia whispered. "A young man about my age. I'll see you tomorrow. Love you. Merry Christmas."

It felt to Ryan that dinner was over before it started. Freshly showered and neatly dressed in dark slacks, a light blue shirt, and a light blue sweater, he hung on Julia's every word.

When asked, she admitted that she thought *sill*, the pickled herring dish with onions, often served on the crispy bread known as *knäckebröd*, was disgusting, but it couldn't hold a candle in that department to *lutfisk*, cod treated with lye. Only the sturdiest of die-hard Swedes went for *sill*, and only mentally unstable ones for *lutfisk*.

The opinion, which she insisted was off the record since her parents sold both traditional delicacies, was met with much laughter, and they all congratulated themselves for not ordering any *lutfisk*.

According to her, it wasn't really Christmas without Jansson's *frestelse*, a creamy potato and anchovy casserole that the group had shown the good taste to order and consume in quite reasonable amounts.

And no desert was complete without *vitabra*.

Ryan was smitten.

He listened to Julia's explanation for the phone call out by the rink, and her mother's insistence on a twenty-minute alarm system.

"She's the most caring mother possible, and I love her to death," Julia said, "but sometimes she does drive me crazy."

"Wow," Ryan said. "We have so much in common!"

"Hey!" his mother said, waving a fork, but laughing.

Then Julia made the mistake of asking about the construction of the outside rink. Ryan groaned as his father launched into the need for the plastic to go down first or it would rip, then the foot-high boards on top in sixteen-foot-long planks, laid butt-to-butt and joined by four-foot-long patching pieces that overlapped the long planks by two feet on both sides. And of course, before all that, the ground had to be leveled.

It was a mind-numbing discussion that could go on for what felt like days, with his father barely needing to come up for air. Fortunately, his mother interrupted.

"He's an engineer," she said with a smile.

Mr. Andersson grinned sheepishly and shrugged.

"That was interesting," Julia said pleasantly.

"Don't encourage him," Ryan said in a stage whisper. Everyone laughed, including his father.

But then suddenly everyone was clearing the table, which meant his dinner with Julia was ending. The night was ending.

"Stay for our Yankee swap!" Ryan said.

"Oh, no. I couldn't. I really should be going." Julia said.

"No, stay!"

"How can I be in a Yankee swap if I didn't bring a present?"

"We'll make one up," Ryan said, sensing he had a chance. "Mom and Dad, would that be okay?"

"Sure!" they said in unison, and his mom added, "We'd love you to stay."

A bolt of inspiration struck Ryan. "Your present can be that whoever gets it, can request two more songs for you to sing. Their choice."

Julia smiled. "That's not much of a gift."

"We'll be the judge of that!"

And after one more protest that she didn't know every song written and some don't lend themselves to *a cappella* performances, she agreed.

The large front room included a fireplace, a large-screen TV, and enough easy chairs and sofas to seat twice as many as were here. And of course, a large, beautifully decorated Christmas tree.

Julia sat on a leather sofa next to this intriguing, boyish young man, Ryan. The more time she spent with him, the more Julia liked him. And not just because he was gorgeous. Whenever he teased his parents, it was always in a loving way, never cruel. He made those around him laugh and enjoy themselves.

Including her.

And when it came time for him to either trade for an already opened gift or open a new one, he went right to the envelope that contained her promise of two songs. And looked around the room and said, "Don't anybody even think about it."

When the opening and swapping was done, she asked cautiously, "So what songs would you like?" She supposed he could give her something totally embarrassing to sing, like the Donna Summer song, "Love to Love You, Baby," with all its orgasmic moans and cries, but she didn't believe that was him at all. And if it was, she'd walk out, insulted beyond belief, and never come back.

Instead, he turned himself in the sofa so he could look directly at her and said, "It's an old song. Maybe you don't know it. But you have the voice of an angel, and I can see you recording it some day and it being a thing of such total beauty that anyone who hears it, loves it."

The words took Julia's breath away. It was as if Ryan had looked into her soul and seen that those words were exactly what she needed to hear right now. She almost began to cry.

"Please sing 'Bridge Over Troubled Water,'" Ryan said.

It *was* a beautiful song, one of her favorites from generations past. She poured her heart into it, and when she was done, everyone in the room jumped up from their sofas and easy chairs and gave her a standing ovation. Especially Ryan. Of course.

She brushed the tears from her cheeks, and choking said, "Thank you everyone, but I'm not sure what I can do now for an encore." She smiled at Ryan. "What's the finale?"

He handed her a folded sheet of paper. "I've written the names of three songs here. Pick the one you'd most like to sing."

Julia opened the sheet and scanned the names of the songs. She smiled broadly. It was the easiest choice ever. There were two vanilla choices, nice songs she'd be happy to sing anytime. And then the one that was perfect for this moment.

She looked into Ryan's eyes, channeled her best inner Gladys Knight, and began to sing, "You're the Best Thing That Ever Happened to Me."

Ryan beamed with a radiance that Julia thought just might rival the Sun's. It was an impish, yet innocent, loving smile she wanted to see a lot more of.

And she would.

An award-winning author and an Amazon bestseller under a different pen name, Olivette Devaux writes LGBT contemporary and paranormal romance. Her novel Like a Torrent, *book two of the Disorderly Elements Series, has won a Honorable Mention in the 2017 Rainbow Awards. She enjoys swimming the rivers in Pittsburgh, PA and can be reached at www.olivettedevaux.com.*

THE MUSIC OF LOOSE SPRING

by Olivette Devaux

Berkley Springs sat halfway in West Virginia and halfway in Maryland, but Roan had come up from Virginia, which was only a few miles to the south. Little intertwining tentacles of the three states' borders tried to grab as much of the Hot Springs Creek's valley as they could. The long-dead colonials, who had established these borders, must have had a notion that someday, the valley and its hot spring would bring them untold advantages.

The Main Street, where Roan stood, was all gussied up just like the Commons to his right. Main Street was Route 522, whose civilized four lanes shrank to only two while passing within city limits. Cars crawled along the cheerful, quirky tourist traps, local folks going places. Delivery trucks with their produce and goods, pickup trucks with their occasional Confederate flag statement, and tourists with their money.

If the colonists who had tried so hard to claim this little valley rose from their historically protected graves, they'd shake the dirt off their bones in shock at how insignificant and poor their descendants have become. Good thing the valley had the springs that drew the moneyed sorts from elsewhere. Roan's family had visited Berkley Springs in his teens, and they had been the tourists back then.

He was one of the locals now. New, still a fresh face in town, but he bought his basics in Dollar General with the rest of them. Roan Christy worked four blocks up and one block over as a nurse practitioner. His pay at the clinic would be lower than elsewhere for the next five years, but his position came with a modest apartment, and would satisfy his debt to the state. Some scholarships were like that—go to school for free in exchange for serving in a rural area for a time.

"Come on, let's get some lunch," Rachel said. She elbowed him, then jogged ahead toward The Common Cup. "I can smell their chicken soup all the way down here, and their sandwiches ain't half bad!"

"Quit bossing me," Roan said, barely putting one foot before the other.

"I'm older, I get to boss you all I want," Rachel said. "And they'll have biscuits!" She tossed her head and laughed, and as she did so, her auburn hair sparkled like burnished gold in the thin, dappled shade. The leaves, chartreuse and thin, let the sun shine right through as though they were made of stained glass. Vernal breeze caressed his smooth-shaven skin, whispering of fragrant crabapple trees in full bloom right across the Commons, by the hot springs.

Roan smiled, stopped, and looked up again. So pretty. Life was so beautiful, sometimes it just took his breath away.

"Hurry!"

Roan gave her a look of irritation. "You're just nineteen minutes older than I am, but that doesn't give you the right to boss me nineteen times a week." He pushed off and walked, forcing his stride into that youthful, springy step he should still have at his twenty-nine years of age.

His knees hurt.

His feet hurt.

His heart hurt, too, knowing that Rachel was taking him to a new lunch place the long way only to make him move. She shouldn't have to worry about him and his stupid lupus, twins or not. She should've been out on the high seas, having adventures of her own. Maybe even a husband and a family.

Yet every time a guy got close enough to Rachel to find how attached she was to Roan, he skeedadled.

Roan sped up. Their lunch break would last only so long, and so would he.

Lunch traffic was slow on a Tuesday. Nothing to worry about, Tristan reminded himself. Of course, this was only his second year running Fairfax Antiques by himself, what with his dad laid to rest and his mom off to her sister in Nashville.

The old watch his dad had left him hung around his neck, feeling heavy with portent. Like he was

supposed to do something or was forgetting something important.

But what?

He filed the taxes on time, he got the water heater replaced, the car's inspection wasn't due till November.

So much to do and so little time. He knew the ropes; he had the routines down. The other antique store owners had more experience in business than the thirty-one years he had in life, and if there was an area where age was an asset, accumulated knowledge of old things was one of them.

Tristan pulled the old wooden chair to the card table behind the counter and opened his laptop. All those lovely things his dad, granddad, and ancestors going back generations had accumulated lived not only on the cluttered, eclectic shelves of his store, but also on the pages of eBay and Amazon. A quick glance at door and window showed only a lovely spring day outside, and a tourist feeding the parking meter. He'd go check on Loose Spring later, after he was officially closed. With his dad gone, the duty of keeping the spring's stone enclosure fell upon him. At least it was just twigs and leaves, and not the sort of plastic trash he often fished out of the two main springs, which were enclosed within a concrete square wall. Their water flowed into the Hot Spring Creek and was pleasant even with snow on the ground.

For now—or at least until a customer showed up in living flesh—he'd do the housekeeping necessary to running an online store.

The old brass doorbell clinked as the wood and glass door swung in. Not sure how much time had passed, Tristan looked up.

Visitors. A young couple, he a bit reticent, she full of enthusiasm.

He stood up. "Hi, welcome to Fairfax Antiques." He smiled. Probably tourists. He knew everyone in town, and he sure didn't know these two.

"Hi!" The woman bounced over to the counter and stuck her hand out. "I'm Rachel Christy and I haven't been inside *here* yet." She gave him a once-over, not making a secret of checking him out. "What's your specialty?"

Barking up the wrong tree, honey. Tristan's thought had no malice in it. Just a wishful yearning for a bit of company of the masculine kind, one that was hard to find a town like Berkley Springs. A town that had almost as many little churches as it had antique stores. "Oh, old things. All kinds of little bits. This store's been in my family for generations." He smiled. "Where're you folks from?"

"From here," the man behind Rachel said. "Don't let my sister run you over. I'm Roan Christy and we both started working at the clinic not too long ago."

Oh. *Oh.* Not a couple, then. Siblings.

Tristan gave them both an assessing look. Her eyebrows were finer, but both Roan's and Rachel's were set on a similar angle, and their eyes were set the same distance apart.

And the cheekbones. He could cut glass on those cheekbones, not just on hers but on his, too. Her chin was small and pointy, giving her face a cute heart shape, whereas his extended into a lean jawline.

Peppered with just enough midday scruff, too.

"Twins?" he hazarded a guess. "And let me see, Rachel's older?"

"Yeah," Roan said, and glanced at his sister with a fond smile. "And she never lets me forget it."

"Our eye color's different," she said. "Come to the window where there's more light!"

Tristan lifted the partition that closed off the space behind the counter and followed them. New folks in town, and twins! They were obviously fraternal, he reminded himself as he fumbled for what little information he recalled from school.

And they were quite different. "Is your hair natural?" he blurted out. "Sorry, I know women don't always advertise dying their hair, but …"

"No, it's not that red," Rachel said, unconcerned. "It makes my eyes greener, is all. It makes them pop!"

Tristan nodded with appreciation, then he turned to Roan. His hair was brown with just a touch of warmth to it, shorn short on the sides, with a longer flop-over on top. Like city folk.

But his eyes. Not as green, no, but their hazel was speckled with amber drops of sunshine. They were deep, like pools of ever-changing water. There was just something … *multi-layered* about them, like the art glass paperweight with all its swirling colors and light and—

A light, amused cough startled Tristan and brought him back to the here and now. He didn't land in the here and now with grace. No, that would be too easy.

Instead he straightened so fast he teetered back. His foot hit a display and he was sure he'd fall and wreck hundreds of dollars worth of merchandise, but Roan grabbed his arms and pulled him forward, hard.

Into him.

The clashed together like kids in the playground, and Rachel's laughter was cut short by the sound of glass shattering on the floor.

Once they stabilized and detached, Tristan rubbed the back of his neck with an awkward grin on his face. "Well. You do have the most interesting eyes. Let's see what I broke."

The pressed-glass pitcher had been kind of rare, but when both Rachel and Roan insisted on paying for it, Tristan shook his head. "No way. That would be no way to welcome you into town. But, tell you what." He cocked his head at Tristan. "Since you and I kind of broke it together, you can buy me lunch later this week."

Roan's eyes widened, then he nodded. "Deal."

They shook on it.

As Roan opened the door for his sister, she turned to look at Tristan over her shoulder, and winked.

Their one-bedroom apartment over the Guns'n'Ammo Emporium was starting to look like home. The building was old but well taken care of, and the low ceilings and broad wooden boards hinted that it has seen a lot more than the fussy Victorians in the nearby Winchester. Tristan settled into a reading chair he brought home from a flea market and pulled out a medical journal. The wingback's leather creaked under him, but the horsehair stuffing was still good and the brass tacks around the arm rests were all present and accounted for.

Just as he immersed himself into the intricacies of modern Lyme disease treatment, Rachel piped up from the sofa next to him. "What are you gonna wear tomorrow?"

"Clothes." His reply was automatic. Hm … so the team at John Hopkins managed to eradicate the *Borrelia burgdorferi* bacteria in rodent using a three-prong approach of—

"Roan. Roan!" Rachel was standing over him now, arms crossed and lips pressed together.

He pulled himself away from the text. "What? I'm reading. This is for work."

Her expression didn't soften. If anything, she was digging her heels in. "Your date after work tomorrow, Roan. With Tristan. Are you changing out of your scrubs? What are you wearing?"

Oh. That old saw again. He plopped the journal on the scarred coffee table upside down so's not to lose his place and glared up at her. "It's not a date. It's just a meal."

"From the way he was looking at you, it just might be a date. He seems nice."

"And I seem sick." Roan stood up and stretched. He had to do that on a regular basis or else his joints would stiffen, and his muscles would grow sore. Lupus was unpredictable and its management was funny that way. He tried to stay ahead of trouble through drugs and preventive maintenance, a system that worked only most of the time. "I've already told you I'm not interested in a relationship. And you know why."

"Tristan seems nice. I stopped by yesterday after picking up coffee. He's funny—and did you notice he wears two watches?"

"Never mind his two watches." Roan wasn't going to be pushed around by Rachel again. "Look. If I'm so fine, why don't you go and live your life and go sail the high seas? That's what you've always wanted to do. But instead you're here to help me with my periodic episodes, and, well …" He frowned. "I like Tristan. I can't possibly ask him to take care of me."

Rachel burst out laughing. "Just listen to yourself! You're making it sound as though living with you is a horrible fate and only your twin sister will ever put up with an occasional bout of inflammation and fever. If it's so horrible, why do you let me stay?" She smiled her sweet, daggers-on-the-ready smile. "I'm your sister, after all."

And she had a point. "I'm so sorry." Roan said it the way he always did when she ended up taking care of him and driving him to see his specialist. "I know it's a lot. I wish … I wish there was another way."

"There *is* another way. Date the guy and see if he's nice, if you get along. Don't worry, I'll stick around. I kind of like the receptionist job at the clinic. Do you even realize the amounts of gossip I hear every day?"

He was grateful Rachel had stayed with him ever since his diagnosis two years ago. Being with her reminded him of their years as kids in high school, as college students who came home from their respective fields of study to reconnect over the summer.

He'd been healthy back then.

Now he was shackling her, stifling her. She was safe. No matter how irritating and high-maintenance Roan got, he knew Rachel would never leave him.

But a boyfriend might.

If it didn't work out.

If Roan's condition became too volatile.

If he became disabled.

Dark thoughts ran through him like raging river, cold and treacherous. He shivered and immediately compared the quality of the tremor that had run through is frame to an onset of a flare-up.

Would he be able to walk tomorrow, or would his joints swell and ache, making him double over in pain?

"You're not living, Roan," Rachel said as she sidled up to him and pulled him into a hug. "You've got to do the things that make your days worth sticking around. Just shake it up and let the dice fall."

Maybe she was right. Maybe he had a lot less to lose than he thought.

The Crow's Nest was a white-cloth restaurant attached to a nearby hot spring spa. Roan pored over its online reviews, drawn in by its dark wood, white walls, and warm lighting accents. When he had called to make a reservation, the staff had reassured him he'd be able to "eat clean." So far, the place didn't disappoint.

"I should ask you to help me break an old glass pitcher more often," Tristan said. His spoon hovered over his desert, a lovely *creme-brulee* with a crust of caramelized sugar on top. "You sure you don't want a taste?"

"No tastes for me but thank you." Not unless the desert was low in sugar and dairy-free. The consequences of sliding off his low-inflammation diet didn't bear to think about—and he wasn't going to spoil a lovely evening with explanations. Instead, he pushed his bowl of berries toward Tristan. "Try it with some raspberries. They're delicious!"

As they ate and sparred over whose meal was better and whether Apple's ecosystem was really worth its price, Roan's gaze kept landing on the old-fashioned pocket watch that hung around Tristan's neck like a large necklace. Its tarnished silver case was chased with a design Tristan couldn't quite make out. He tried to focus on the conversation, but the silly watch kept staring at him.

A lull in the conversation gave him an opening. "Speaking off, I see you have that Apple Watch. You seem pretty happy with it."

Tristan nodded. "I am. It has more bells and whistles than a railroad crossing!"

They laughed.

"So what's the story behind the watch around your neck?" Roan had almost said *the cheap watch around your neck* but had stopped himself just in time.

"It's been in the family for generations," Tristan replied, weighing his words with slow care as though he had to compose each sentence word by word. "It's …" and here it was again, that effort to even speak. "It's special," he finally hurled out.

"Does it even work?" Roan's curiosity was now assuaged. Its beauty was the one of old, beat up things that were beautiful, but it wasn't *pretty*. He hadn't seen Tristan even open it, even though he had glanced at the sleek, dark screen of his fancy Apple watch more than once.

"It's a Loose Spring watch, so not always." Tristan gave him a disarming smile, the kind that had his dimples pop. "You mentioned that time your folks gave you a guitar. Do you still play?"

Nice change of subject. The watch intrigued Roan, but he had time. For now, he rolled with Tristan's new direction.

Next time was Tristan's turn. The blossoming trees were at their peak, and the Commons gleamed with the polish of recent rain and fresh grass growth. The maples and chestnuts began to leaf in, but the cherries and plums across the creek were still holding their own.

He led the way across a stone foot bridge. The Hot Spring Creek was bound by a straight channel of concrete, its bottom a level surface of sand punctuated by smooth rocks. Several springs bubbled up from the ground, surrounded by carefully maintained walls, the mineral spring water gushing down narrow channels to join the creek where children played almost year-round. Even when their par-

ents stood around in winter coats, the hardiest kids slipped into the tepid spring water and stayed there.

He had been one of those urchins, the ones who ended up in the creek and didn't want to exchange its warm embrace for the bite of December air.

Maybe that's why the watch came to him and not to his cousin.

"Are you getting in?" Roan's voice stopped him, and Tristan realized he'd been in a world of his own.

"Sure. Yes, yes I am," he hurried to explain. "And I suggest you do the same. "It's quite pleasant."

Roan hesitated, but he did roll up the pants of his navy blue scrubs, kicked off his shoes, and peeled off his socks. "You promise it won't be cold?"

"I promise." A wave of trepidation broke against Tristan's self-confidence with a crash even as he said it. There was something about Roan, something careful. He reminded him of a lovely glass gazing ball with a tiny crack on the bottom.

Trouble on the horizon.

His watch grew heavier around his neck, warmer against his chest.

That had never happened before, and Tristan didn't know what to make of it. He only knew what to do if the ancient chronometer's little music box began to play.

The air weighed heavy and oppressive in the air and Roan hoped the storm would break already. Weeks have passed, and over those weeks he had met with Tristan for dinners, for lunches, for excursions. Rachel was always invited, yet she joined them only when they went hiking.

"So I know you are absolutely *not* dating Tristan, but you should know he has a birthday coming up," she said from behind her book. The way she was holding it, she might as well be using it as a shield.

"Oh? When?" Of course, Roan wouldn't miss out on getting to do something special for Tristan, not after all the time Tristan had taken to show him around and help him settle into the area.

"June twelfth," she said.

Roan didn't need to see her face to know she was smirking.

Were they dating? Tristan had pulled out his old bass guitar to play along while Roan worked on regaining his finger skills. He'd stopped playing after a bad flare-up, but … but maybe the act of playing was a good for him.

Were they really dating? Like, dating-dating? Even after Roan told Tristan about his illness? Tristan's reaction came in the form of new recipes, and that made him different. Accepting of Roan's reality. Not trying to explain it away, and Roan realized he could, for the first time since his diagnosis, relax in the company of a person other than Rachel.

Were they dating? Tristan waded through the Loose Spring's water. This one was cool enough to form a bit of ice by the edges over the winter. Because of its cooler temperature, and because it sat hidden behind the old Roman Baths, it didn't see many visitors. Tristan liked it that way.

He shuffled over to where the crystal-clear water stirred pallid grains of sand as it came up from underground. Lit by a sunbeam, the crystalline textures of almost translucent sand and sparkling water hypnotized him. The silence helped, too, as though the trees and the bath house shut out all civilization and let Tristan truly relax.

His shoulders dropped, his spine straightened, and air came in and out of his lungs easier, and the watch around his neck lightened as though in response.

Tristan's commensurate lightening of spirit made him wish he could bring Roan here, just fifty feet away from their usual hot spring hang-out. Except this spring didn't have a population of little tropical fish which probably escaped from somebody's aquarium a long time ago. It was too cold, too cold for guppies and too cold for Roan.

Roan and his Persian flaw, his joints that swelled and ached at random, and which Roan took for granted and *not as bad as it could be*, even though his fingers could barely wrap around the fret board of his guitar last week. Yet his Persian flaw was also part of his charm. It showcased his resilience, his courage. His compassion, too, because only a nurse-practitioner with a condition of his own was likely to have enough compassion for his patients to win the hearts of even the oldest and most hardened gossips in town.

As Tristan stood in the creek with his feet cool, his neck hot and a grumble in his empty stomach,

he came to realize that Roan was as close to perfect as he could wish for in a partner.

The question, however, stood. Were they dating? Was Roan's refusal to be a burden a real concern or just an excuse of a man who was letting Tristan down easy? Because Tristan wasn't a quitter, and when his heart sped up at the sight of Roan's smile, Tristan thought he'd take flight like a poorly tied helium balloon.

A roar of a motorcycle on Main Street broke the screen of silence he fancied the spring could provide. He glanced at his Apple watch and jumped up the stone wall with alarm. If he didn't go back right now, he'd be late, and Roan was bringing him a birthday lunch in a proper picnic basket. His stomach growled again at the thought of savory sandwiches and pickles and pie.

The air within the antique store was cool and pleasant, for which Roan was grateful. Another muggy week brought another moist air mass which took its sweet time before it rode up the mountain, where it would cool off and drop its load of rain on them all.

His eyes adjusted. "Tristan? You here?"

A call from two rooms away, and moments later Tristan slithered around a new shelf loaded with antique household implements. Roan hadn't thought a hand-drill or a meat grinder with a hand crank and a clamp that would bolt it onto the kitchen table would go over well, but he'd been wrong. Preppers loved old hand tools.

"Hi, Roan!"

Roan wanted to say something sweet, almost cloying, now that he had resolved to be brave and allow himself the luxury of a relationship. "Happy birthday," he said instead, and set the picnic basket on the counter.

Tristan set his armload in a wooden crate, then took a few steps toward him.

Expectant. Also, looking like he was hesitating. "Thanks."

Brave. Roan had to stick his neck out and go after what he wanted, he reminded himself.

But starting small was a good idea.

He spread his arms out. "I brought you a birthday hug!" He tried to be all casual and cool while suspecting that his expression looked like a cat startled by a vacuum cleaner.

"Ooh, a special treat." Tristan's smile lit up his world as he entered his personal space.

They touched, arms around each other, and suddenly this wasn't just a regulation bro-hug anymore. No, it was the real thing, chest to chest and thigh to thigh.

The air crackled with dangerous potential. The potential for heartbreak. Roan was just about to let go when Tristan buried his face into the crook of his neck. "I love birthday hugs," he mumbled. "So much."

Something warm and ephemeral blossomed in Roan's chest. A relief for not being shot down. *Are we dating?*

Just before he blurted out something rash and made a fool of himself, the old beat-up watch that always hung around Tristan's neck began to play a simple melody.

Tristan let go and stepped away. He looked down. "Wow," he said, touching the old watch with reverence. "It's time! Quick! Let me get my pickle jar!"

He leaned over the counter and pulled out a clean jar with a lid on it. "I hope the lunch will keep. Come on! We gotta hurry!"

The watch kept chiming on, and as Roan jogged after Tristan and cursed his sore left knee, he realized that the melody wasn't repeating at all. A wind-up music box would play a short tune over and over, but this?

A chip?

No.

Tristan would never retrofit an old chronometer with something electronic.

They crossed the bridge and turned right. The old Roman Bathhouse was to the right and the forested hillside was on the left. It had never occurred to Roan to see if there was anything back here.

A narrow, grassy path opened into a clearing surrounded by a ring of trees. He could see the yellow stucco of the ancient building flash between the trunks. A spring sat in the middle of the clearing and as they got closer, the music of Tristan's watch grew louder and louder.

Tristan kicked off his sandals, set the pickle jar on the spring's old stone enclosure with gentle care, and climbed in. The water ran only up to his calves, much like in the other springs. Roan untied his shoes, removed his socks, and carefully made his way in.

"Holy moly! This one's not warm at all!"

"No, I know," Tristan murmured as he stooped over a place where water burbled up through the blush-colored sand. He filled his jar, capped it, and took a step to reach over and set it on the wall.

As soon as he did so, the melody emanating from his watched stopped.

"This spring doesn't get as much appreciation as it should." Tristan straightened up and waved his hand, encompassing the stone walls and the water within their curved embrace. "Welcome to the Loose Spring!"

The connection. There was a connection between the spring and ….

"You don't have a watch with a loose spring," Roan whispered, shocked into a state of amazed stillness. "You have a Loose Spring Watch!"

Tristan's uncertain expression turned serious. "That I do. That's because I'm the Loose Spring watchman." He stroked the old chronometer, and as he did so, Roan tried to wrap his mind around a concept that no longer obeyed the laws of Newtonian physics.

"I thought it was just a steam-punk affectation," Roan said with an uneasy chuckle. "You know … before you told me it was a family heirloom."

"My family …" Tristan drifted off, then stopped as though an idea occurred to him. "I want you to drink some of the spring's water!"

Roan rose his eyebrows. "Dude. You do realize the Rocky Mountain fever has spread all the way east, don't you? And what about the natural bacterial load? We're under a hill," he said and pointed helpfully, as though that fact wasn't obvious.

Tristan bent his knees, stroked the water surface as though in a greeting, and cupped his hands. He took a long, slow, comfortable drink, and stood back up again. "See?" he said, turning back to Roan. "There's nothing to it. My family drinks this water all the time and they've never gotten sick!"

Roan took a step forward, then another. He came close to where the upwelling water stirred the sand. He touched the water surface, then looked up at Tristan. "I don't know about this."

The sandy bottom shifted underfoot as though he was at the beach and a wave washed the sand from under him.

Roan stumbled, then landed in the water.

Deep water, as though the crystal clarity had been misleading.

The gasp that was meant to be a scream got water in his mouth. A hand gripped his arm, and soon Tristan was helping him stand up away from the part that had looked so innocent and stable only moments ago.

"You okay?"

Roan swallowed his mouthful, then nodded. "Yeah. Wow." He glanced back at clouds of silt that got stirred up in the water. "It's deeper than it looks."

"No, it's not," Tristan whispered. "Something loosened underfoot. It's a geothermal spring, after all, and the earth can shift this way and that." He looked him up and down. "You're soaked! You've got to be freezing!" Except he didn't try to shoo Roan out of the water. He had asked him to drink, after all.

"I'm fine!" Roan said, to starve off worry. Then he realized, for the first time in two years, he wasn't worried about what might go wrong; it was as if a weight had been lifted off his chest. He reached up to shuck the water out of his hair, and the motion felt natural, easy. His eyes widened. He had not felt pain. "I'm … wow! Check this out!" His voice held wonder. Disbelief, even.

He stuck his hands out and wiggled his fingers, then circled his wrists. "I bet I can play those riffs now. And look!" He squatted, not caring about the water with his shorts already soaked. He stood up again. "My knees seem fine."

Tristan gazed at him with a look of satisfied wonder.

"Is it the spring, Tristan? Is the Loose Spring some kind of a, I dunno, a magical healing spring?"

Tristan shook his head. "I don't know. All I know is, the watch recognized you as family. When you gave me that hug, I mean."

"And not before?"

"No."

Roan grinned. Feeling courage was easy when his joints didn't ache. Being brave was a piece of cake when you believed—truly believed—that something outside of this plane of existence decided to give you a nudge.

"Roan?" Tristan's voice held both questions and answers in one big bundle of happiness.

Their eyes met.

"That means we're dating," they said it unison.

As Roan pulled Tristan close for his birthday kiss, he reflected that the cold water of the Loose Spring didn't bother him at all.

Copyright © 2019 by Olivette Devaux.

Kathryn Nolan is an adventurous hippie chick and loves to write steamy romance. Her books are filled with slow-burn sexual tension, memorable characters, tons of heart—and are often set in wild and beautiful locations. Kathryn is a wanderer at heart, and loves to spend her free time hiking, camping, and traveling in her camper van ("Van Morrison") with her cute husband and Walter, their rescue pup. Kathryn is a Philly girl who just moved back home after spending more than 8 years living in Northern California—and six months traveling across the country in her camper van.

QUEEN CLEOPATRA AND THE BASEBALL GOD

by Kathryn Nolan

CHAPTER ONE
Wyatt

The woman standing behind home plate wore a wedding dress and held a sign that read *Will You Marry Me Wyatt Nash?*

It was my first marriage proposal of the night—lower than average for me. It wasn't unusual to see a handful of women and men leaping the fence and racing toward me in the outfield with a question they *had* to ask.

Will you marry me?

Security always caught them before they got too close—not that I was really afraid of a few love-struck fans. I was Wyatt Fuckin' Nash, after all. If they sent additional proposals through the mail, or online, I tried hard to answer each one honestly, which drove my publicist up the wall.

But it was a big deal, asking for someone's hand in marriage. Even if that person *was* asking an absolute stranger on a baseball field.

The Philadelphia Revolution was playing against the Georgia Nationals. I'd smacked out a powerful home run in the first inning, earning us a triple play. A hit like that used to send me flying into the stratosphere.

But tonight? I didn't feel like a young, cocky phenom.

I felt desperately, utterly, *painfully* homesick.

And tired as hell.

As the Nationals struck out our batter, I walked toward center field, glove in hand. The wedding-dress-woman was waving ecstatically. I took a fair amount of ribbing from my team-mates Cash and Sawyer as she called my name in a near-scream.

"Jealous," I said. "Both of you are just jealous." In the stands, I caught a flurry of white signs go up that spelled out my name in giant letters. I chuckled softly, shook my head at the absurdity of it all.

"Nothing but the greatest for *the greatest*," Sawyer smirked.

I smacked my glove, shook out my shoulders. "Maybe she's legitimately meeting her groom here," I offered. "You think of that?"

"Or maybe she's legitimately running on the field right now to meet you."

I turned around to take a crack at Sawyer—who was no longer laughing.

And that woman was barreling toward me like a linebacker.

"Oh *shit*," I said, but it came out in a laugh. Because I was fairly certain she wasn't wielding a knife—but she did have a wedding ring for me in her hand. Cash and Sawyer were a blur of motion to my right. The security guards were hauling ass across the field. But in a blink of an eye, the wedding-dress-women was skidding to a halt in front of me as the audience screamed their heads off. Her arms latched around my waist and she *squeezed*.

"Ma'am," I said, still laughing. Trying to wave to the audience and untangle us at the same time. "Ma'am they're going to arrest you if you don't let go."

"I knew it," she breathed. "I knew we were soul mates."

I hid a grimace—I hated this part. "Ma'am."

"My name is Karen."

Guards were pulling her off now, but she didn't seem to mind—she was beaming at me.

"Karen," I said gently, dropping my glove to the ground, "I know you believe us to be soul mates but we're not. I'm sorry to tell you that."

Her eyes widened—and she tried to wrench her elbow from the guard, attempting to get to me. I was the best defensive baseball player in the Major League and a wicked short-stop. I did grueling workouts with a smile, sang obnoxious songs on the plane, tried to keep my teammates' spirits up when we lost games. I was Wyatt Nash. *The Greatest.*

But this stranger in tears made my chest feel like it was being punched with a sledgehammer.

Cash clapped me on the shoulder—of all of my teammates, he had an intense empathy I always appreciated. "You did a good job. She'll get over you."

"They all do," I said, with a booming—fake—laugh. The audience was wolf-whistling, but I didn't want to make fun of her, so I yelled at the coaches to start the damn game back up and spit in the grass. I felt tired, and badly for Karen—who was being led away in handcuffs.

What would it feel like, to be so sure you were meant to be with someone you actually *broke the law* to propose to a complete stranger? Having never been in love before—only experiencing a long-running continuation of hot, heavy, *lust*—I had nothing to compare that too.

Although there was *one* woman I could compare that too, and she was back home in Starfish Bay, probably concocting the world's best Pina Colada.

And I blamed *all of this* on the reason why I was so distracted in that moment; why I reacted three seconds later than usual to a 200-pound-man hurtling toward me as he rounded the bases, arms pumping, legs kicking up red dust; why instead of getting out of the way I stared, dumb-founded, as he collided with me.

Sharp cleats jammed into my right knee at high speed; there was a sickening twist, a pop, and the distinct feeling I was being stabbed with a knife that was also on fire.

Someone—I think it was me—let out the strangled yell of a wounded animal. I was only aware of my face in the dirt, that fiery knife sensation, the other player frantically asking me if I was alright. Cash and Sawyer, faces pinched and worried. The audience suddenly hushed.

I was Wyatt Nash, *the greatest*, screaming as a medical team tried to lift me. Catching a glimpse of my knee and experiencing that bone-deep realization that it wasn't *right*.

And before I passed out my only thought was: *At least I'll get to go home.*

CHAPTER TWO

Cleo

I turned up Starfish Bay's local reggae radio station and dimmed the lights, so the bar lit up in hot pinks and jungle greens. Red, yellow and teal lamps dangled from the ceiling. I flipped a switch and the indoor palm trees burst with strands of white lights.

The back bar wall was opened to the ocean and sand covered the floor. I wore sandals and jean shorts, about to make my first Pina Colada of the night. It was Memorial Day weekend, the busiest tourist weekend of the year.

And The Siren was officially open for business.

Granted, The Siren was open year round in Starfish Bay—the only Tiki Bar in our tiny, coastal town and a favorite of both locals and tourists. Gwendolyn, who'd been The Siren's bouncer since the days when my uncle had owned it, screened each patron thoroughly, ensuring the privacy of Starfish Bay's incredibly famous local "the baseball player," Wyatt Nash. The prodigal son of our beach town, beloved by all who lived here. Wyatt's family—two parents and a married sister—still lived and raised their children here. And every year during the winter, for the few months that Wyatt wasn't on the road, he lived in a small house, right on the beach.

It was a testament to the awe-inspiring love this town had for Wyatt that he was able to come and go as he pleased with *minimal* interruptions from the paparazzi (courtesy of Gwendolyn, who ran a friendly bike gang just menacing enough to scare off any reporters). Thus, Wyatt was able to sit in The Siren and drink beer whenever he wanted. Which, ever since he'd come home with a horrifying knee injury in the middle of his baseball season, he'd been doing every single night.

I waved to a few friends and slid frosty bottles of beer down the bar to three regulars. Then I danced my way towards Wyatt, who was staring into his drink.

"What kind of secrets is your beer whispering to you, Nash?" I asked. I poured white rum, cream of coconut and pineapple juice into a blender. He looked up as I pressed *on*, drowning out his words. I winked at him, nodded at his drink, and a slow grin spread across his face. His baseball hat was pulled down low, but it still couldn't hide the fact that Wyatt Nash looked like a big, muscular, blond-haired, blue-eyed baseball god who clearly knew the effect he had on women.

He was an egomaniac heartbreaker with a goddamn twinkle in his eye and a dimple in his cheek. And every year, when he was back in Starfish Bay, I played a little game with myself. The game was called: *Don't Be Attracted to Wyatt.* It was a simple game with a point system: I tried my hardest not to notice anything sexy, attractive or appealing about the ruggedly handsome athlete I'd known for ten years. Because I *knew* he was hot, and *Wyatt* knew he was hot, and knowing that Wyatt knew that *I* knew he was hot was fucking infuriating.

The only way I ever won the game was to count the number of times I flustered him.

"I'm sorry, what?" I repeated, turning the blender on just as he opened his mouth to speak. I smirked, popped my hip. Wyatt smirked, and watched my mouth.

The blender stopped. I took out a knife and a cutting board and began hacking into a pineapple.

"I was going to say—" Wyatt drawled.

I hit the on button again. The answering *whirrrr* buzzed like a chainsaw. Wyatt's eyes crinkled at the sides and I tossed my pink hair like I had all the time in the world. But then—before I could bat an eye—Wyatt's big hand was covering mine as he leaned across the bar. He pushed my finger down with his own—the *whir* sound stopped.

And his face was barely six inches away from mine.

"I was going to say how beautiful you look tonight, Cleopatra."

I forced an eye-roll and ignored my thready pulse.

"You don't have to tell me, Nash," I replied.

Another grin—this one somehow *sexier.* A grin that turned into a hoarse laugh as he sank back onto his barstool. Some friends of his wandered by, clapped him on the back, and I went back to making him a drink. I half-listened to their conversation: lots of sympathy about his torn ACL, an injury that had the potential of permanently affecting his baseball career. As usual, Wyatt was light-hearted with those who asked, declaring himself *ready to be back to being the greatest in no time.*

As they wandered over towards the back, I looked up from the pineapple slices that fanned out on my cutting board like a tropical flower.

"No time, huh?" I asked, avoiding his eyes. I saw him shrug his broad shoulders, sip his beer.

"What's a busted up knee?" he said. "The doctors say I'll be good as new, or even better, well before the predictions. They're supposed to call me on Sunday with the final results."

"Can *the* Wyatt Nash actually get any greater?" I widened my eyes.

His lips curved. "I don't know, Cleo. You tell me."

He was flirting, but there was a glimmer in his expression I couldn't quite decipher.

With a flourish, I presented him his drink. "*Ta-da.* A Pina Colada for the greatest baseball player who's ever lived."

"You shouldn't have," he said, hand to his chest.

I held his gaze and leaned all the way across the bar, knowing that the white tank top I wore exposed the tops of my breasts and the lace of my red bra.

Wyatt's jaw clenched, nostrils flaring, the closer I got. His fingers reached forward and caressed a strand of my hair. "Did you dye it *pinker?*" he asked.

"It's called Magenta Dream. And you're not allowed to touch the bartenders, Nash."

Wyatt *tsked,* shaking his head. "Except I'm pretty sure you want to be touched."

It was a smooth line, delivered in his deep, rasping drawl. But as I ran my tongue along my lower lip, Wyatt dipped his mouth toward the straw in his new drink and missed entirely, poking himself in the eye.

"Ow, *shit,*" he said. As he grabbed for a napkin he knocked the drink over, spilling sticky liquor everywhere. "Oh my god, I'm so sorry, I'll clean it—"

"Stop, let me see your eye," I said, waving away his protests. I came around the bar and gripped his face. Did not notice his impressive jawline or the light stubble that grew there. "I'm not a doctor but you look perfectly fine."

Actually Wyatt Nash did not look fine.

He looked *embarrassed.*

Fluster Wyatt: point 1.

But I'd reacted so quickly I didn't realize I'd stepped between his giant baseball-player thighs; didn't realize my hips were squeezed against a solid wall of flexing muscle.

Or that he'd smell like soap and sunshine.

"Cleo, I'm sorry about your bar. I'll clean it, okay?" he asked without an ounce of his usual swagger. And for a glorious second I felt like I was falling into those dark-blue eyes, which were starting to crinkle at the sides from smiling too much.

Don't Be Attracted to Wyatt: -10

My phone vibrated in my pocket, startling me from my stupid reverie. I attempted a graceful exit from between Wyatt's powerful legs and grabbed the towel on my shoulder to mop up his drink. Read my text messages as I mopped.

"Mother*fucker*," I bit out. Read the messages again.

"You okay?" Wyatt asked.

"Both of my bartenders just called out sick for the holiday weekend," I sighed. This wasn't good. It was only Friday night and I was already feeling slammed. I drummed my nails on the counter, sorting through past bartenders I could call up in a pinch.

"Brilliant idea," Wyatt said, "what if *I* was your bartender this weekend? I've got nothing going on until I hear from the doctor."

"Can you make drinks?"

"Sure," he shrugged.

"*Well?*" I arched a brow.

"Cleo, I can do *everything* well." The swagger was back—along with a smile that should have been illegal in every single fucking state.

"Yeah, yeah, why don't you shove it—"

But I was interrupted by a bright, glaring *flash*.

Wyatt and I turned to find a beet-red tourist holding a cell phone.

And taking Wyatt's picture.

CHAPTER THREE

Wyatt

There was only one rule that Cleo enforced at The Siren: no taking photos of *me*. Like everyone in Starfish Bay, the locals made it possible for me to come home and just be *me*. Plus, the friendly folks of the Bay didn't really want a steady stream of fans

and paparazzi showing up and turning our quaint beach town into some place garish or seedy. And if I needed another reason in the midst of recent shittiness to love this town even more, it was watching every head in that bar swivel menacingly towards the red-faced tourist like it'd been choreographed.

And standing in the middle of it like a magenta-haired Valkyrie was the only woman I *continually* made a fool of myself in front of.

Cleopatra Hendrix.

She'd moved to Starfish Bay ten years ago to take ownership of The Siren after her uncle, the bar's original owner, had passed away suddenly. So she was not a *true* local, but in the eyes of Bay folks she was as good as born here. I hadn't spent a summer in Starfish Bay since getting signed when I was 20 years old, but every winter I sat in this quiet bar, drinking some tropical wintry beverage she'd make me, and try to come off as effortlessly cool as she did. Which was fucking infuriating, since on the road it was easy as pie for me to meet women, pick up women, fuck women. But faced with this confident bad-ass, I ended up tongue-tied more often than not. She was the kind of woman who accepted ownership of a bar at twenty-two with a steely level-headedness; who surfed terrifyingly large waves without batting an eye. Cleo could take a shot of whiskey like a champ and then mix you a Tiki drink you'd *swear* had washed up from the magical shores of Hawaii.

I spent more time dreaming about what it would feel like to kiss this woman more than anything else—more than I'd once dreamed about winning the World Series. Because I'd done that—twice—and in the end, I felt fairly confident that Cleo Hendrix would show me a better time.

Who was I kidding—I had a *monster*-sized crush on her. Could submit it to the Guinness Book of World Records, that's how big it was. I'd just stabbed myself in the eye with an umbrella straw. And now I was watching her size up Red-Faced-Tourist like he was a bug she couldn't *wait* stomp on.

"Did you take a picture of him?" Cleo asked, hands on her hips. Cleo had wild pink hair, pale skin, green eyes. And I was trying—fucking unsuccessfully—not to stare at her ass in those cut-off jeans. I'd managed not to look down her shirt when she'd teased me a moment ago, although I'd gotten a glimpse of full flesh pressed against lace.

"Yeah? So? That's Wyatt Nash," the tourist said. He gave Cleo a sneering, repulsive up-and-down look that made my skin crawl.

I stood up.

Red-Faced Tourist caught the movement, probably because I was at least 6 inches taller than he was.

"Did you see the sign we had on the wall?" Cleo asked, voice deadly soft. To be fair, there was a sign, right next to a string of coconuts, that read *No Taking Pictures of Wyatt Nash*. Cleo had drawn it herself years ago.

His eyes flicked up, brow furrowed. And then he took my picture again.

Cleo snatched his phone from his hand with dizzying speed. "*Asshole*," she muttered.

"Hey, you want to put your number in there, sweetheart?" He was leaning in close, swaying a little. And I knew if anyone could handle this piece of human garbage it was Cleo. But a protectiveness rose fiercely, tightening my chest, and before I knew better, I'd stepped right up to him.

I ignored the ache in my knee. No, not an ache—a violent little *stab*, that reminded me just how human I was.

"Hey there," I said, enjoying the way he had to crane his neck to catch my eye. "She's going to delete those photos and you're going to leave this bar. And if Gwen has anything to do with it, her gang will ensure you leave this town."

He gulped.

"Here's your phone back, dickweed," Cleo said, tossing it at him.

So much of my interactions with Cleo came with a bar between us. Had I ever spoken to her elsewhere? Standing right next to me, with no bar as a barrier and her shoulder brushing mine, I took a deep breath: citrus, sunscreen, rum. *Heaven*. I knocked back a strong urge to lean down and sniff her hair like a weirdo.

"You put your number in it?" the tourist asked her.

"*This*," she said, indicating her curves, "is not something you could handle, dickweed. I'm damn sure of it. So you can go now."

It happened right before my eyes. I could swing a bat and hit a ball hurtling 90 miles per hour at

my face. But put me an inch away from Cleo's sunshine-smell and I was operating like a man with a blind-fold on. Red-Face leaned in as if to grab her waist—with one hell of a leer—

Cleo nailed him right in the balls and he dropped to the floor.

"Way to *go*, Queen Cleopatra," I said, starting a slow clap.

She gave me a mock curtsy, and I didn't mistake the flirtatious gleam in those sea-witch eyes. But Red-Face was standing up (barely) and giving Cleo a look I'd officially qualify as *illegally creepy*.

"Come with me," I said. I hooked my arm around his neck, careful not to lean too much on my knee, and half-dragged him through clumps of locals who were loving this evening's entertainment. The Night Wyatt and Cleo Beat Up A Guy would be a tale heard in Starfish Bay for years to come. Once through the door I tossed him hard; a bit harder than I meant to.

"I didn't think the great Wyatt Nash would be such a fucking dick," he spat out. Fans did this all the time. If they weren't cheering for you, they had some random bone to pick and over these many years I'd developed the thickest skin imaginable. Because it was impossible for me to make every single stranger that came to see a baseball game *happy*.

"I'm not a dick, man," I said, stuffing my hands in my pockets. "And I think you know that. But this is my home. And I wouldn't fuck with it again unless you want Cleo to *actually* try and hurt you. Oh, and thanks for calling me *the greatest*. It's the truth."

He sputtered something again, but I was already making my way back into the tropical atmosphere of The Siren. Cleo was back behind the bar, cleaning glasses and laughing with a few patrons. The vibrant lights of the bar danced across the smooth curve of her shoulders, glittered in her pink hair, and were reflected in her eyes as she looked up and saw me.

I felt forever drawn into her orbit.

But beyond that—the bar was swelling with patrons and beneath her jaunty attitude I knew not having another bartender was affecting her. I leaned forward and scooped up a towel, tossed it over my shoulder and strode behind the bar, which was small and packed with bottles. Cleo was fluttering around it like a butterfly. She hauled a massive case of beer up onto the bar, flipped two glasses over, tossed maraschino cherries into a frothy drink and handed me a knife and a pineapple. I held them up, bemused.

"You were right," I said. "That guy could never have handled you, Cleo."

"Not a lot of men can, Nash," she said airily. "And I'm not sure what you're doing back here, but since you are, chop that, will ya?"

"Yes ma'am," I drawled and thought I caught her cheeks flush. "You're definitely in a pinch without your staff, huh?"

She shrugged.

"Allow me to help this weekend. Please?"

Cleo glanced over at me. "America's favorite baseball hero is gonna pour beer and empty trash cans?"

"I'm pretty sure we'd make a great team."

Her eyebrows shot up. "You'll take my orders?"

I'll take it all, I wanted to admit. But instead I said, "I've always enjoyed being bossed around by you."

She snorted. Sized me up with a jaunty tilt of her hips. "You'll do in a pinch, I guess."

"These hands?" I said, holding them up for examination. "Have only set a home-run record two times over. Pretty sure you'll be thanking me profusely by the time the night's over."

"That happen to you a lot?" she asked. "Getting profusely thanked by every woman you come in contact with?"

"You know it," I winked. "But I'm a benevolent god. I use my talented fingers for good, not evil. Say the word and I'll—"

And then I accidentally tipped over an entire rack of wine glasses, sending them shattering to the ground, shards of glass flying. It was a record-scratch moment, the sound hushing every conversation so that an entire bar had cause to stare at me.

"It's fine everyone," I said, elbowing over the blender and spilling freezing-cold pineapple juice down my shirt. It *dripped-dripped* down the fabric, down the front of my pants, landing in the pile of broken stems.

This was worse than the fucking straw. I felt like a hormonal high-schooler, desperately searching for a hole to crawl into and die already. But instead I looked up at a smirking Cleo and said, "You're welcome."

CHAPTER FOUR
Cleo

By 2:00 am, Wyatt had managed to stop breaking glasses left and right and had only spilled one more beer down his shirt, which was starting to look like a pirate's map of juice stains.

Fluster Wyatt: 5

But he'd also turned his baseball cap around and grinned devilishly at me as he hauled boxes of booze and poured shots *almost* like he knew how to bartend. And stepping in like that to help me behind the bar—besides the fact I'd enjoyed seeing him haul off that tourist—meant that I was battling a bad case of Wyatt Nash Nearness Nerves. Being squeezed together with a Baseball God behind a narrow-ass bar meant he was constantly brushing my arm, brushing my back, breathing on my skin, leaning over my shoulder.

Don't Be Attracted to Wyatt: - 28

"You don't have to stay," I told him, wiping down the bar as he stacked chairs on tables. The back wall was still open and the stars were bright pinpricks of light in the black sky. I was always wide awake the hour after we closed and I knew if I didn't distract my hands I'd be climbing Wyatt.

"Aw, I'm happy to, Cleo," he said. He was limping slightly, and I cursed when I realized I'd essentially had an injured athlete on his feet for hours. I hopped up onto the bar, feet dangling, and patted the spot next to me. Then I poured us both a shot of smooth coconut rum.

"Have a drink with me and rest that leg," I said. "It's a Siren tradition. We can watch the waves. And, most importantly, you can *sit.*"

His brow furrowed. "I keep forgetting I've got a busted knee."

I patted the spot again. He was so big he barely had to lift himself to sit on it. I was shoulder-to-shoulder with a baseball hunk, sipping rum, with no one else around.

"Thanks for jumping in to help," I said, clinking our shot glasses together. His blue eyes twinkled with mirth.

"I'm basically the greatest bartender who's ever lived," he shrugged. "You don't have to put it into words. I can tell by your expression you agree with me."

I bit my lip, but a smile appeared anyway. "Something like that."

We watched the waves for a long, peaceful minute. Every night, even when it was cold, I sat and enjoyed a view that I never wanted to take for granted. Starfish Bay was the most beautiful home I'd ever known. Down-to-earth but filled with quirks.

"Did you always know you were going to inherit this place?" Wyatt asked.

I looked at his handsome profile, realized that in all our years of casual bar-top flirting we'd never had a real conversation before. "I started spending ever summer here when I was ten," I said.

"I was in baseball camps," he grimaced. "Always. That's why I never saw you when we were kids."

"I wish we had," I said. "Anyway, that's when I fell in love with the Bay. I'm from Baltimore, but my parents always knew I was a beach baby. And my uncle and I had a real strong connection. He loved his home, loved the spirit of this place. It's earthiness. Big cities, even bigger beach towns, rubbed him the wrong way. He wanted to see me grow up in a town with a sense of purpose in its soul. When I was 18, he told me that I was in his will as sole inheritor. I loved The Siren but didn't give much thought to it. I was thinking about college and all over the place, mentally. But he died right as I was finishing my degree." I took a sip of rum and thought of him. There was a picture of my uncle hanging over the bar that the locals tended to touch with their index finger when they passed.

"Did you know your uncle used to sneak my sister and I fudge ice-cream cones when I was in middle school?" Wyatt asked.

I smiled at that, grateful for every new memory I received. It'd been almost ten years, so my grief had settled into a dull ache at the back of my heart. And memories now brought me a lot of comfort instead of tears.

"Twenty-two years old. Cleo Hendrix, no fear," Wyatt shook his head. "Behind that bar like you always knew you'd be there."

I laughed a little, nudged his shoulder. "I wasn't afraid. It felt like … my destiny. Maybe that destiny is small potatoes compared to being a nationally ranked baseball player, but I could spend the rest of my days living this life and be happy. Ocean, neighbors, surfing, sand, rum."

Wyatt's jaw clenched; brow furrowed again. "That's not a small destiny. That's a perfect Cleo-shaped destiny."

I pointed at Wyatt's knee. "And how is your destiny?"

"Fucking awesome," he said, then took the rest of the shot. "Minor setback. I'm not even a little bit worried."

I smelled *bullshit* from a mile away.

"So once you're healed you'll … go back?" It wouldn't do me any good to think about the first few weeks of Wyatt's absence every year, when he left Starfish Bay and headed to spring training. I only ever saw him at The Siren, but his presence was like a winter tide, an ebb and flow I craved. The first few weeks of March I'd look up to his usual corner and wince at the empty space.

Wyatt rubbed his hands together. "Can't wait." He cast a sly look at me. "I, uh, miss home though. A lot."

"Starfish Bay's prodigal son gets homesick?"

"All the time," he said softly.

Don't Be Attracted to Wyatt: -40

He covertly lifted his white-tee shirt and sniffed. "Sweet Jesus Christ I smell like a drunk pineapple threw up on me."

"Is that some kind of line that you use to pick up women, Nash?" I leaned back on the bar while he stood up, catching his eyes dropping to my legs for all of a second.

"I don't need lines, Cleopatra." He pointed at his face. "One look at *this* is all it takes."

"According to the gossip rags, it's not your face that's popular."

"How often are you reading about me?"

"Constantly," I said, drily. "In my apartment is a stack of magazines with just your face on them."

Which wasn't entirely untrue—it was only a *couple* magazines, not a full stack.

"What did these gossip rags say about my most popular attribute?" His voice had taken on a silky danger I hated to find alluring.

"Cock as big as a baseball bat," I blurted out— hopefully with *some* measure of cool.

Wyatt threw his head back and laughed a big, throaty sound that was contagious. And the worst possible thing for my self-control was happening.

Wyatt Nash was stripping out of his shirt.

"Whatcha up to, Magic Mike?" I said, startled.

There was a reveal of muscular, rippling, golden skin; pecs you could bounce a quarter off of, Paul Bunyon shoulders, and his grinning face as he tossed the shirt behind me. "That's better."

"What's better?"

"Cleo, I smelled horrible." But his eyes had a flirtatious gleam and, yet again, I knew that Wyatt knew that this move got him laid.

Not today, Nash.

"Plus, isn't this a better view?" He flexed his pecs with a cheeky grin and I rolled my eyes with more drama than was necessary.

"Are these your little moves? Like when you're on the road and want to fuck a stranger?"

"Big moves," he clarified. "Huge, baseball-sized bat moves."

Not today not today not today.

"Well they don't work on me," I hedged. "You must not be my type of guy."

"Such a goddamn liar, Cleopatra," he said. And there was no mistaking the scrape in his voice.

"Bare chests don't really do it for me. *Or* baseball bats."

The waves outside were an angry roar, mirroring the sound of my pulse in my ear. Because Wyatt— shirtless Wyatt—took two confident steps until he was standing between my legs. First his right hand, then his left, landed next to my own. We were nose-to-nose.

"What does do it for you?" he asked.

"Basketball players," I half-moaned.

He actually chuckled—although it was dark and laced with intent. "Do you want to see my moves or not?"

I shrugged carelessly. And Wyatt was leaning his handsome, sexy-as-fuck face into the crook of my shoulder, the most sensitive, erogenous patch of skin on my entire body. I was instantly aware of *man*: muscular thighs pressed against my own, his phero- mones, his nose, *just* touching my skin. "What's this move?" I managed shakily. "Sniff a girl like a weirdo?"

"No," he said. His lips were ghosting up and down the column of my throat from the crook of my neck to the edge of my jaw.

My fingers gripped the bar.

"I call this move *show a girl I know just what her body needs.*"

I swallowed hard. "Doubt it." But he was still do- ing it, the barest brush of lips, and my eyes were fluttering with pleasure. "I'm still not the kind of woman you could handle, Nash."

His mouth was at my ear. "Don't I fucking know it, Cleo."

Wyatt was far from flustered. He was six foot four inches of confidence and as his face moved toward mine, I knew this sexy motherfucker was going to try and kiss me.

Abort! Abort!

My point system had been exploded and left for dead the moment Wyatt had ripped his shirt off. But I could still win, could still grip the tendrils of my willpower.

I placed my palm in the middle of his chest. *Whoa.* Skin-on-skin with Wyatt was a series of heart- stopping fireworks. He felt it too. I saw his expres- sion change from casually flirtatious to a powerful understanding.

"I call this move," I taunted, dragging my palm down his hard stomach, "*show a guy I know just what his body needs.*"

"Smart girl," he said, but his breathing was ragged.

So was mine.

Like a pompous jerk, he speared his fingers into my hair and held my face still.

"Is this what you do next?" I asked. Gasped, really.

"Cleo," he said, but it was more of a reverent *plea*, stripped of ego.

I couldn't handle it—couldn't handle this wick- edly open Wyatt. So with a purr I slid off the bar, dragging my body down his with an indulgent de- liberation. There was a low sound in the back of his throat I knew I'd be thinking about later when I touched myself.

I turned around in his arms—bent *all* the way over to grab my keys and my phone from the bar. "You're right, Nash," I said, over my shoulder. "We do make a great team."

"I know, baby."

I reached forward and gripped the top of his shorts. Pulled him toward me. Tilted up on my tip-toes until my mouth was right at his ear.

"Show up at work at 4:00 pm tomorrow." I sighed. "And don't be late."

CHAPTER FIVE

Wyatt

I was trying (and failing) to run along the ocean, trying my hardest not to think about the stabbing pain in my knee. Or the fact that before this injury I was the kind of athlete that could run ten miles on this beach easily because my body was a finely-tuned machine that ran on protein and home runs. Plus, ever since my baseball talent had been discovered at a young age, I'd been running this beach—hard—since middle school. It was usually as easy as breathing, like slipping on a pair of worn pants that fit you comfortably.

Today I felt like death. Grimey, panting, wheezing death. It'd taken me weeks of physical training and intensive work with the team's doctor to even work up to this casual, loping half-jog, half-walk. And really, I only jogged when people were in sight. It wouldn't do for the entire town of Starfish Bay to collectively worry about their Favorite Baseball Player.

But as soon as I was out of sight, I walked. Worried a little myself. Or a lot, really. Because my homesickness and persistent disillusionment with baseball aside—if I couldn't heal from this injury, if I couldn't *be* a baseball player ….

Then who the hell was I?

I had two more days before The Call, when my agent, coach and team doctor would put their heads together, examine all of my range-of-motion tests and deliver my future to me in none-emotional medical jargon. But really, the question was: can he play or not? *Playing* meant a triumphant return to my fans, and at least five to ten more years of professional baseball.

Not playing meant leaving in the middle of my prime to do ….

My mind was nothing but blank space.

To do … what?

I jogged *extremely slowly* through the marina, waving at friends and neighbors who were already untying their boats for fishing, for crabbing, for drinking and partying. Sails flapped in the breeze—that *snap* sound of fabric and wind never failed to make me feel home. The water was a tranquil blue at the Bay, compared to the roaring waves I'd just jogged past. At the end of the dock I took a left, moving down Main Street. Starfish Bay burst forth every Memorial Day like a rainbow-colored umbrella, popping open on the beach. Sidewalks became cafes, the boardwalk became crowded, the air hung with the smell of sunscreen and hot dogs.

I swung by my sister's house under the pretense of needing a glass of water when I really needed a break.

"Knock knock," I called into her little blue beach cottage. "It's only me, Wyatt Nash, greatest baseball player of all time. Can I bother you for a glass of water?"

My little sister, Frankie, flashed me the middle finger from her kitchen where it looked like she was main-lining coffee. "Of course you can have water but I'm unleashing the dragons on you for five minutes so I can shower in goddamn peace."

"You shouldn't say *goddamn* in front of children." I smirked.

"I'll goddamn do what I goddamn want," Frankie replied. But she grinned as she walked past me, punching my shoulder. "Also you're all gross and sweaty. How's your knee?"

"A-okay," I lied.

And from the look on my sister's face, she knew it.

"Where are the dragons?"

"Outside," she said, waving her hand airily. But her eyes narrowed when she caught my slight limp.

I grabbed a glass of ice water and stepped into Frankie's giant backyard, where my twin nieces were hurtling through the grass like Olympic-level sprinters. Charlotte and Zoe were five-years old with the stamina of, well, *me* in my prime. And before I could warn them about my knee, they crashed into me with a jubilant squeal.

I winced. "*Oof.*" But I landed on my back, remembering to cradle my knee, and avoiding additional career-ending injury.

"*UncleWyattPlayCatchWithMeNow*" was the gist of what they were screaming at the top of their lungs.

"Get a glove, rookies," I said, still panting heavily. "You've got four minutes before I have to continue my run."

I tried to remember the last time I'd craved four blessed minutes of rest. I was always happy running, batting drills, warming up, stretching. Those movements were ingrained in me so deeply, my brain was still having a difficult time comprehending I was injured.

Charlotte sprinted back, throwing a glove that smacked into my stomach and winded me all over again.

"*Jesus,*" I muttered, eyeing my nieces with a wary appreciation. This is what happened when you were a professional athlete, you spent eight to nine months on the road every year and you missed *everything*. My little hellion nieces were growing up fast, and where was I? On a flight over the Midwest somewhere, playing for massive crowds that idolized me but never knew me.

"Three minutes," I said, tapping my running watch. "You got your gloves?"

They nodded in unison.

"Bend your knees, remember," I coached. I pretended to wind up, old-school-pitching style. They laughed, spurred me on, and loped the ball underhand.

Zoe caught it easily and then hurled it back so fast I almost dropped it.

"I can't believe 'the greatest' deigned to come by."

I turned, finding my sister wet-haired and teasing. "Oh, you know," I shrugged, tossing the ball again. This time Charlotte caught it. "Gotta stay humble."

My sister made a disbelieving *hmmmm* sound. "And this wouldn't have anything to do with that knee, would it?"

"Nope," I lied again.

Frankie took the glove and my now-empty water glass. "We still on for babysitting on Sunday?"

"Wouldn't miss it." I walked over and patted each niece on the head, much to their chagrin. "I'll have these dragons running sprint drills in the backyard before moving up to two-a-days."

"More like *they'll* be sprinting around you," Frankie said with a knowing look.

I began jogging in place and tried not to wince. "Don't tell the paparazzi I was here," I said in a mock stage whisper. Frankie mimed zipping her lips, tossing the key.

"Hey, Wyatt?"

"Yeah?"

My sister gave me a wistful smile. "It's nice to have you home."

I gave her a quick hug and a kiss on the cheek. "You're only saying that because you need a babysitter."

She laughed as I was leaving. "Guilty as charged, big brother."

Frankie's street led to an old hiking trail I usually enjoyed running on, but my entire body felt like I'd been disassembled and put back incorrectly. And I would have stopped, would have slinked home for a good sulk and a hot shower, but up ahead I saw a flash of bright magenta, long legs in shorts, a black sports bra.

Cleopatra.

I'm still not the kind of woman you can handle, Nash. Her palm on my bare stomach. Her lush mouth at my ear. The filthy fantasy I'd indulged in last night, as I fucked my own fist, of hoisting her up on that bar and spreading her wide; burying my face in the paradise between those luscious legs so I could lick until I'd had my fill.

Of course, I was so deep in my Cleo-fantasy that I didn't see the massive, snarling bed of roots. Which I hit head-on, sending me sprawling forward.

And landing right at her feet.

CHAPTER SIX

Cleo

I'll admit that my *very first thought* was a selfish *damn.*

Wyatt looks good at my feet.

But then I realized he hadn't sprung there from the force of the *very* dirty sex dream I'd had about him last night.

No. This was *real* Wyatt stumbling over a bed of roots and falling on his face.

"Oh my god," I said, dropping to the ground. His white shirt was see-through and wet with sweat, now covered with dirt. When he rolled over, he was panting and looked, well, *flustered.*

But I didn't like Wyatt being flustered *and* injured.

"Don't mind me," he panted. "Just wanted to get a closer look at this … unique root formation."

"Is that so?" I arched a brow. "And what are your findings?"

He was still flat on his back and I was on my knees, leaning over his broad chest. I wasn't trying to be flirtatious, but I was, again, nose-to-nose with Wyatt and trying not to kiss him.

"Beautiful," he said, brown eyes searching mine. "The most stunning root formation I've ever seen."

"Why *thank you*," I said, tossing my hair. His grin was a slow-burn I felt all the way to my toes. I stood up, extended a hand to yank him to his feet.

"Sure about that?" he asked, eyes narrowed. He was half-sitting up, knees bent.

"Yeah, take my hand." He did, clasping mine. They were big hands; baseball hands, and there was a tensile strength in every finger. "Did you hurt your knee?"

I tried to yank him up, like I'd yanked up countless friends and boyfriends past, without realizing I was seeing Wyatt out in the wild, not stuck behind a Tiki bar. All six-foot-four of solid muscle naturally resisted my tug, regardless of how badly I wanted to yank him up. I routinely hefted a surfboard over my head that weighed more than I did, so I was no weakling. But still. This was an American Baseball God and I felt, for the first time ever, out of my league.

"Don't sweat it." Wyatt climbed carefully to his feet, brushing off branches. He passed a hand over his hair, biceps bulging, and I momentarily forgot to breathe. "And no, my knee's okay. Luckily I hit the roots with my left foot."

"Oh, cool."

We were suddenly shy—for all of ten seconds—before I clapped him on the shoulder. "Will the great Wyatt Nash join me on a run? You might have to slow down to allow this mere mortal time to keep pace."

He laughed, but it was bashful. "Uh … yeah." He looked behind him, like we were being spied on. "Actually, can we go a little slow?"

"Slow?"

"My knee's bothering me, but the doc says I gotta run, keep it loose. Company would actually make me feel less like I want to die of shame, so …"

He was jaunty and light-hearted, but there was a sadness behind his humor that had me aching for a different reason entirely.

"Your *slow* is my normal speed."

"I don't think anything you do is normal, Cleo." He winked. "And you're not slow. I've seen you run."

I started from a stand-still to a dead sprint, laughing a little as he caught up with me immediately. It was nice of him to be bashful but even injured Wyatt was a force to be reckoned with. I set a nice, even pace as we arced around a corner on the trail.

"Like this?" I asked.

"Yeah, perfect," he said.

"So why are you watching me run?"

"It's impossible to ignore Cleo Hendrix running down Main Street with hot pink hair," he said.

I tried to ignore the schoolgirl-crush-feeling that gave me. So I said: "Pervert."

He huffed out a laugh—and stopped. Bent over at the waist, hand on a trunk.

"Wyatt?" I was instantly at his side, unsure where to put my hands but compelled by an urge to comfort.

"It's fine," he said. "Listen, remember when I asked if we could go slow thirty seconds ago?"

"Yeah?"

"I actually meant: can we walk? And if you so much as breathe a word of this to anyone I will …"

"What?" I teased.

He stood up, gave me a wink that had my toes curling. Could Wyatt still flirt while having some kind of … well, whatever he was having?

"Kiss you," he panted.

"Well, that's not really a threat now, is it?" I said breezily.

His eyes flashed with heat, but then he reached out and squeezed my shoulder with that massive hand of his. "I'm only supposed to lightly jog once or twice a week. And only a mile, maybe two. Walking's good for it but I'm used to …" he shrugged, "you know."

"Being a world-class athlete?"

"Yep," he said grimly. "I'm not saying my recovery isn't going well. It's just—"

"Going," I finished.

He nodded, brushed a hand through his hair again. "I wouldn't have kissed you, so you know."

"I'll try not to die of disappointment," I said dryly.

Liar. You're already dead.

We settled into a comfortable walk through the slightly wooded trail, ocean to our right, the bay behind us. "I run this trail almost every day," I said. "How come I never see you on it?"

"Because I'm never home," he replied.

"I'm sorry you're getting so homesick," I said, remembering his confession last night. "Does that happen to the other players?"

"It's kind of the tragic underbelly of being a professional athlete," Wyatt said. "Some of us can handle it well, which makes us stay. And that competitive drive is part of it. Easy to forget your loved ones if you're aiming to be a world champion. But others …"

"Like you?"

"I'm one of the greatest baseball players of all time, Cleo," he said, but there was no ego to his tone. "I'm definitely aiming to be a world champion."

"*Are* you though?" I prodded. "Because whenever you're home you seem truly happy. Like yourself. The real Wyatt."

He chuckled a little. "And who's the real Wyatt?"

I placed a hand on his chest, right against his heart. The contact startled us both but my hand had moved of its own volition. "Who you are in here, of course."

Wyatt wrapped his fingers around my hand for all of a second, but his dark eyes filled with … *something*. I couldn't read it.

"Tell me about the waves this morning, Queen Cleopatra."

He dropped my hand. And I sensed the diversion but allowed it. Maybe it was his slight limp, and the pain I could see etched around his mouth, but I wasn't trying to harangue Wyatt Nash about his life choices right now.

"Perfect swells," I said, trailing my fingers along the coastal scrub brush. Sea gulls were calling in the distance. "Only wiped out once, but it wasn't so bad."

"So you closed the bar, surfed all morning and then came for a run?" He looked impressed.

"I do that most days, weather permitting."

"Looks like I'm not the only world-class athlete in this town," he said.

I felt his eyes travel the length of my body and I didn't hide my natural preen. I *was* strong and proud of it. "It's one of the things I think we have in common actually," I said. "Physicality."

"Moving our bodies." Wyatt nodded—and I wasn't sure if he realized that he was pushing my walking pace, pushing us faster. His loose running shorts kept exposing thighs so muscular I wanted to bite them, drop to my knees and sink my teeth into his leg.

"Speaking of bodies," I said, "I saw a very interesting Google alert on you today."

"Oh yeah? More baseball-bat-sized-cock rumors?"

I snorted. "Apparently you are loving-and-leaving a slew of women all up and down the Eastern seaboard during your rehabilitation."

"*What?*" he laughed. "I have to call my agent. That shit can't be flying around the news. My parents could read it."

"The women would be angry?" I asked—so *glaringly obvious.*

Wyatt's eyebrows shot up. "You think it's true? Cleo, you've seen me basically every day I've been home."

"I don't see you after the bar closes." We turned a corner, and both stopped to take in the view of the morning waves.

"I'm not seeing anyone right now," he said. Then he turned to me with an expression so intense I took a step back.

"Oh," I said. "Interesting. I thought you were kind of a casual guy. Don't you sleep with a lot of women while you're on the road?"

"I don't know what *a lot* is," Wyatt said. "But yeah. I fuck around. When you travel nine months out of the year it's hard to have anything stable that lasts. And that'll be my reality for the conceivable future."

Right, I reminded my rapidly-beating-heart. *Because he's a famous baseball player.*

"How about you?" he asked.

The breeze was tugging apart my ponytail. I tugged off the holder, flipped my head down to finger out the strands. When I stood back up, hair blowing in the wind, Wyatt was staring at me like a starving man.

"What about me?" I asked.

"Who do you fuck, Cleopatra?"

Wyatt was bouncing on his feet a little, like he wanted to run again. So I picked up a very, very slow jog, and he joined me.

"I'm a casual girl," I said. "I sleep around. I have a few steady hook-ups in town. Plus the *occasional* tourist."

He made a sound of derision.

"Some of them are quite cute," I mused. "Hot even."

Wyatt tugged on a strand of my hair as we ran. "Baby, you haven't *seen* hot."

"You mean, like tripping over a pile of roots and falling on your face?"

"Well, that was because *you* are hot," he grinned, "so really, it's your fault."

I laughed. I couldn't help it. "You're fucking ridiculous."

We were nearing a slight hill, which I used to race my friends up all the time when I was younger. There was a smattering of trees at the top and a gorgeous view of the coast.

"Race you to the top?" I asked, taking off in a dead sprint towards the furthest tree.

"*Cheater*," Wyatt called, but he was on my heels in an instant. We were both laughing, arms pumping, and I could feel the heat of his body near mine.

And at the absolute last second—his palm slapped the tree first.

"I forgot to tell you what the winner gets," I panted, beaming up at his stupidly handsome face. But I'd barely caught my breath before Wyatt Nash had his palm on my chest.

And he was pushing me hard against the tree.

CHAPTER SEVEN
Wyatt

I had Cleo up against a tree. We were both sweating, panting. I was slightly wired from our breathless race to the top, adrenaline a sweet edge in my bloodstream. I dropped the hand that had pushed her to my side, let my other land above her head. She stared up at me with wide, sea-witch eyes, full lips parted. Her nipples were hard against her sports bra; flesh pressed to the fabric, almost spilling out. "What does the winner get?" I asked, voice dangerously low.

"I guess I didn't … really think about it," she admitted. Her chest was heaving with breath. "What does the winner want?"

I hovered my mouth over her ear. "You know what it is that I want. It's the same thing I've wanted since the first moment I laid eyes on you behind that bar."

"Tasty … rum drinks?"

I chuckled darkly. I let my finger slide up the middle of her stomach, between her breasts, up the elegant line of her throat. She tilted her head up like a good girl. "If you're so casual, why didn't you let me do some *casually filthy* things to you last night?"

"What kind of things, Nash?"

Cleo was taunting me now. I ghosted my lips over hers, but like she did last night, I never kissed her. Just teased her with the thought of my mouth.

"You first," I said. "What did you want to do to me last night?"

"Teach you how to properly mix a drink," she purred.

I growled like an animal, pressing our foreheads together. "*Cleo.*"

"I would have shown you how to use that baseball-bat-sized cock the right way," she whispered.

Another dark sound escaped my lips. "Oh baby, I'll show you how I use it." I swiped a thumb across her lower lip. "One word and I'd fuck you on that bar until the only word you understand is *please*."

Cleo's fingers were tightening and twisting in my shirt, dragging me hard against her. We were practically climbing this tree together.

"Why not?" I asked, *almost* kissing her. She arched up, tried to capture my mouth. "Even casual sex with me would be mind-blowing and you know it."

"Because." She panted, exhaling out a big breath. "Because."

"*Why?*" My teeth closed around her earlobe.

"Because you're not going to stay," she gasped.

That stopped me cold. Cleo? Concerned if I *stayed?*

"I'd stay the night with you," I said, brow furrowed. "Anything you wanted, beautiful. As many times as you needed it."

"That's not what I mean," she said, eyes closing.

Stay, you idiot. Stay in Starfish Bay.

"I thought you only slept around?" This conversation had taken a serious turn I wasn't expecting. "Who cares if I stay?"

Was she serious? A woman like *Cleo?* This brazen, bad-ass, pink-haired goddess would want me for what … a boyfriend?

The concept startled a smile from me—a big, dopey grin I thought she'd return.

But instead she reached down and gripped my cock with lowered lashes.

"Holy—" I smacked the bark over her head, sensation flooding me almost violently.

"Forget I said anything, Nash," she said, kissing my cheek. "And I'll still see you at 4:00 pm for your shift, right?"

"*What?*" I panted, already utterly lost. Cleo was stroking me through my shorts with talented fingers. What was *happening* right now?

And then she let me go. Gave me a wink and a pat on the shoulder. "See ya there, champ."

She sprinted off down the hill, pink hair flying.

I looked down at my hard cock, back up at her. Down-up-down-up. From afar I probably looked like some kind of insane bobble-head doll.

But once again, Cleo Hendrix had reduced me to nothing more than a jangling mess of lust and desire.

And confusion.

CHAPTER EIGHT
Wyatt

It was 3:59 pm and I was strolling up to The Siren—freshly showered and with a head bouncing with thoughts from the Dick Grip Heard Round the World. After Cleo had sprinted away, I'd thought I was heading home for a hot shower and to jerk off to dirty thoughts of Cleo on her knees.

Except that hadn't happened. I'd sat on the tiny patio of the cottage I owned on the beach, watching the waves and wondering what I was going to do.

You're not going to stay.

Strange that Cleo's honesty mirrored the thoughts I'd been fretting over for a few years now. That coming home to Starfish Bay every year felt more and more right—and leaving for spring training felt *deeply* wrong. That playing catch with my nieces in my sister's backyard brought me more satisfaction than the hundred and sixty-five games I played non-stop, year over year.

Could I stay … here?

And every time I let myself glide into that fantasy, Cleo was there—laughing with me, teasing me, tossing her hair and challenging me. Instead of a shower and a self-induced orgasm all I did was stare

moodily into the waves until pure excitement sang me towards the cheerful tropical lights of The Siren.

Cleo was behind the bar, wearing just a black bikini top and cut-off jean shorts because she wanted to *actually kill me*.

"Cleopatra," I said, running a hand through my hair as she glanced up from cutting a pineapple in half.

"The great Wyatt Nash," she said lightly, but I could see the flush in her cheeks.

I leaned my elbows on the bar and pinned her with a direct gaze. "Do you want to talk about what happened at the tree this morning?" I asked softly.

Cleo looked surprised.

"What?" I said. "You think I'm some kind of asshole that wouldn't bring it up?"

"Professional baseball players with big egos and big dicks aren't always super honest." She popped a slice of pineapple in her mouth.

"Fair," I said. "But I'm a little more three-dimensional than that, don't you think?"

Cleo assessed me. "I got a little swept up in the moment, is all. You wanted to kiss me. I wanted to touch that famous cock."

"Anything else?"

I made my way behind the bar, which was crowded immediately by my size. Took the knife from her hands and began dutifully cutting limes like I'd seen her do the other night.

"Maybe," she said. "Maybe there was something else there." She glanced at the wall-clock, which was a coconut with sunglasses. "But I do need us to prep for tonight's mad rush. Could we talk later?"

I tugged on her ponytail and she grinned at me.

"Yeah," I said. "We can do whatever you want, baby."

"I'm not your *baby*," she said, but she was still grinning. "And tonight I'm showing you how to make a Zombie, which is the most famous Tiki cocktail there is." She laid out the ingredients: a few types of rum, orange liqueur, lemons, limes, passion fruit puree, grenadine, bitters and began a magical mixing process that seemed like alcoholic alchemy.

"You remember all this every night?" I said, watching her work.

"I've got cheat sheets here if I forget," she said, pulling out a box of index cards. They were handwritten recipes that looked older than she was. "My uncle's notes."

"He had great taste," I admitted, chopping lemons now. "Who would have thought a tiny Delaware coastal town would take to a Tiki Bar so fervently?"

Cleo laughed. "Or that I'd end up running it."

A few wisps of hair had fallen from her ponytail. I reached forward, tucking them behind her ear. "I'm happy you're happy here."

"Exceedingly so," she said, a little breathless. "Okay, taste this rum."

She held out a shot glass with just a splash and I tipped it back. "Tastes like … summer."

Cleo was layering everything with care, painting me a picture of this tropical drink as the ocean roared outside and the sea breeze tickled my nose. It was warm, humid, sticky and something about this moment felt important in a way I couldn't put my finger on.

"I meant to ask you," she said, sliding past me to grab more rum, "how did you end up tearing your ACL anyway?"

I was momentarily distracted by Cleo's ass sliding across my groin.

"A marriage proposal," I said, dazed.

She stopped, turned her head. I was still behind her, the position powerfully intimate.

"What?" she asked.

I moved away, sliding to the far end of the bar and pretending to pick up a stack of napkins for no goddamn reason. Then I turned and sent a basket of limes flying.

"Wyatt Nash for the *win*," I said dryly. When was I ever going to *cool* around this girl? She went to clean my mess but I waved her off. "Make your drink," I said hastily. "I got them."

Of course this put me eye-level with her bare legs, which she seemed to notice.

And enjoy. She turned, leaned back against the bar on her elbows. Crossed her right leg in front of her left.

"Were you sent to this earth to destroy me, Cleopatra?" I asked.

She gave a coquettish shrug. "Tell me about the marriage proposal."

"I get like three a game," I said. I stood up with my arms overflowing with limes. "My agent and I try to handle the letters and the emails and the social media messages that come in, asking the same thing. Or sometimes it's, you know, men or women offering to do any number of explicitly sexual things."

"All of America wants to fuck you, basically," Cleo said.

"Yeah," I laughed softly, "which gave me a pretty big head when I was a rookie. But it's been more than ten years and the whole thing makes me sad."

"Sad?" Cleo was shaking up the cocktail, hair flying with the movement.

"That's why I was distracted," I admitted. "This woman, Karen, ran onto the field in a wedding dress and declared me her soul mate. I try to be honest every time with them, you know? Let them down easy. But she was so *distraught* as they led her away. I've never proposed marriage to someone but I'm sure it would take all of your courage, right?"

"You answer the proposals?" Cleo asked, brow lifted.

"Yeah, Am I a monster?"

I took out Cleo's uncle's handwritten recipe and started to dutifully follow it. If I could break the current standing record for home runs, I was pretty sure I could mix this drink.

"Wyatt."

I looked up at the earnestness in her voice. "Yeah?"

"That's …" she swallowed. "That's really nice of you. And unexpected."

"*The greatest*," I mouthed, pointing at my chest.

She laughed, shaking her head.

The lemon sheared open, juice running everywhere. The bar was starting to look like some kind of fruit-stand massacre. I took a slice, grinning at her until she returned it. Watched this confident, happy woman beam in the late-afternoon sunlight.

"Why do you like casual?" I asked. "Do you have a romantic end-goal in mind?"

Cleo bit her lip. "Fucking around is fun."

"That's extremely true."

"And I guess …" she thought for a moment, "I guess I always thought when it was time for me to find the *one*, we'd have a spark. A real spark. Something utterly electrifying. I like the guys I fuck. They're a fun way to spend a night. But it's not always …"

"What?" I prodded, attempting to wrangle a surge of dark jealousy that was trying to tackle me by the throat.

"Satisfying." Her eyes were clear, no teasing. "I don't always come."

She said those words as I was bringing a lemon slice to my mouth. The sudden spike of acid sent me into a coughing fit. Cleo was there, slapping me on the back, but I waved her away. I needed time to choke like a fool while processing two equally intriguing, yet upsetting concepts:

Cleo … coming. I pictured flushed skin, and fingers in sheets, head back, body shaking with release. I would have bet my baseball career that Cleo climaxed so beautifully the man she'd allowed the privilege of pleasuring her would have no other choice but to make her orgasm all over again.

That was the intriguing concept.

The upsetting one was the thought of this woman being unsatisfied. Ever. In anything.

"So what …. I mean, uh, why?" I croaked out.

"They don't fuck me the way that I like," she explained.

Yeah. She was definitely trying to destroy me. "What do you do in that situation?"

"Toss them out on the street, where they belong," she winked. "And bust into my world class collection of vibrators and dildos."

Cleo, masturbating. Cleo, legs spread, fucking herself with a dildo. Cleo cupping her own breast as she buzzed a sex toy against her—

"Is that one done?" Cleo's gaze let me know she knew *just* what I'd been thinking about.

"Yeah," I managed. "This one is done. Prepare to enjoy the best thing you've ever tasted, baby."

"You sure about that?" Her eyes were narrowed with suspicion.

"Your mouth is gonna be so happy."

Her lips twitched.

"Full taste-bud orgasm." I wiped my hands together. "I'm not sure if you are aware of what these hands can do."

Cleo placed a straw into the frothy red mixture. Slid it up and down with a lascivious gaze. She was such a goddamn tease and it made me want to bend her over this bar. When she licked her way onto the straw to take a drink, I had to run baseball statistics rapid-fire to keep from reaching forward and yanking her towards me.

Her gorgeous face contorted in a grimace. "Oh my god."

"Stop joking," I said breezily.

"No. Here, taste it."

I took it with an arrogant smirk. Placed my lips where Cleo's had been. And swallowed something that tasted like passion-fruit brine.

I spat it into the sink. "I made that? Is there something wrong with me?"

Cleo was laughing, wiping her eyes. "Nope. You're a rookie again, Nash. But it's okay. I successfully fucked up every single drink for the first two years. Practice makes perfect. You know that." She glanced up at that clock again. "We've got twenty minutes until a slew of customers are coming in. Try again."

I shrugged, although I quickly mopped up the bar and set about with the ingredients for a second time. "I'm just a lowly baseball player, Cleo. Apparently my skills end at fucking and home runs."

I was trying to wring a laugh from her, but there must have been something in my voice. Some hidden fear or yearning I was desperate to cover up. Because her eyes were kind as she said: "You're a lot more than that, Wyatt."

CHAPTER NINE

Cleo

"You really think so?" Wyatt asked, pinning me with a crooked grin so charming I knew why this guy got three marriage proposals a day.

When Wyatt had me up against a literal tree this morning, I'd made a grave error in my logic. Because I *was* a casual girl. I lived for summer-flings and one-night-stands that went nowhere. Wyatt and I were alike in that way—hook-ups were my speed. But pressed against Wyatt's body my heart had whispered something vital and true:

If I was lucky enough to get Wyatt Nash into my bed, I'd want him to stay.

For good.

Admitting that my years-long, embarrassing crush on him was *more* than a passing phase was a tough pill to swallow.

Seeing the look of open vulnerability on his face right now though?

Tougher.

"Of course," I said, watching the muscles in his forearms flex as he cut into a lime. "You're a son. A brother. An uncle. A beloved member of a town that loves you so much they beat up paparazzi for you."

"They are somethin' else," he said dreamily. "But I guess, with this," he glanced down at his knee, "there's actually a real chance I won't play professional ball again."

My heart stuttered. "You're serious?"

"I am. I haven't told many people that except my parents and sister. I'm on the slightly older side for a baseball player, with knees that have been put through hell. A torn ACL is bad enough for a lot of people. But an athlete that needs to go from a stand to a sprint, every day, for nine months out of the year …" Wyatt shrugged his broad shoulders and avoided my gaze. "Might not be in the cards for me."

I let him chop in silence for a minute before asking: "How does that make you feel?"

To my knowledge, Wyatt Nash lived and breathed baseball; he was a man that embraced his life and dreams fully. Anyone who knew him could see that.

"Honestly? Not as sad as I expected to be."

He diced in silence for a minute and I let him, sensing his need for focus. Or maybe distraction. I flipped on the music and classic reggae poured through the speakers. On came the lights, the lanterns, the Tiki torches.

"Actually, that's not honest," he said. And I expected him to change his mind. But instead he looked me right in the eye and said: "I'm really not sure I want to play baseball anymore."

And then he went back to quietly dicing.

"I miss you," I offered, because that kind of honesty deserved honesty right back. "When you leave every winter for spring training. I miss you. That's why I keep track of you in the gossip magazines."

A lazy grin slid up his face. "I knew you were spying on me, Cleopatra."

I started to stack cocktail napkins, needing a task that hid my blush. Customers would be here any minute and I was enjoying Wyatt way too much. "It's not spying. I have a responsibility to my bar patrons. They want me to report back on your shenanigans."

Wyatt was moving closer—and closer still. Suddenly a wall of heat and muscle was behind me.

"Sorry," he whispered, "just had to grab this." He reached forward, bringing his mouth into the crook of my neck, and closed his hands around a bowl of cherries.

"Excuses excuses," I mumbled.

"Do you have a favorite rumor about me? Besides, you know, my record-setting dick size?"

That record-setting dick was pressed comfortably against my ass. "Um …" I said, swallowing hard. Wyatt's rough palms left their place on the bar, dragging themselves to my hands. I was unbearably aroused by the sight of my small hands engulfed by his; the rippling strength in his tan forearms, his thick wrists, fingers that could tear these shorts in half with ease. Somewhere, deep in the recesses of my mind, was a chant of *fluster Wyatt fluster Wyatt* but that train had long left the station. Because giving in to *this* felt like that first decadent lick of ice cream on the fourth of July. *Delicious heat and fireworks.*

"Oh, I know the one," I said breathlessly. Wyatt was inhaling me at the crook of my shoulder, lacing our fingers together. Cock urging against the swell of my ass. "The one about Shayla what's-her-face. The actress."

"Barely remember her," he murmured.

"She told … she told the magazine you'd um … that you made her pass out."

He placed an open-mouthed kiss on my neck. "And why would I do that, Cleopatra?" His voice was silky, dangerous. Wyatt gave a deliberate roll of his hips, causing me to shoot up onto my tiptoes to receive it.

Then he did it again.

And sweet *fuck*, I knew why the actress passed out now. Wyatt's clothed, covered cock was bringing me more pleasure than my last string of fully naked hook-ups.

"You gave her too many orgasms." I said this in a breathless rush—but there was an edge of jealousy there. And Wyatt, ever the champion, pounced on that vulnerability like a wolf pouncing on its prey.

"Cleo," he said. But it came out like a plea, an aching prayer. His lips traced an erotic path up the entire length of my throat while his slow, teasing dry-fuck had me gripping his fingers.

"Ye—yeah?"

"Do you think that's true, baby?"

"I think the great Wyatt Nash could fuck a woman so good she passed out." There it was—my last coherent sentence before I became nothing but raw, demanding need. And it was all honesty.

"Such a good girl," he whispered and every hair on my body stood *straight* up. His mouth caressed my ear and I was *all* the way up on my toes, leaning forward, pressing *back*, begging for it. "Because they call me *the best* for a lot of reasons, and I won't lie and pretend to be humble."

Heat rippled in my belly, a delicious *coil* of pleasure. I lifted my leg up, pressed my knee high up on the bar, and was rewarded with a growl that ripped from Wyatt's chest.

"And look at you. Begging for it like the gorgeous queen that you are, Cleopatra. Because it's only the best for you, isn't it? Best ball player. Best hitter. Best *fuck* you'll ever have."

My head dropped to the bar—I couldn't help it. Cradled between our entwined arms, I let years of sexual frustration work its way through me. I was half-sobbing and we hadn't even *kissed*. Wyatt ground against my ass and nosed up the back of my neck, mouth in my hair.

"Those men you take home," he whispered, "why don't they ever satisfy you?"

His hand dipped to cup my breast. We both produced a moan that was years in the making.

"It's the way they fuck," I gasped. My nipple pebbled against his palm and he stroked it. Lightning sliced through my vision. I was endlessly searching for the sex partner who would fuck me the way I needed—a dirty, filthy, dominating possession that left me with bite marks and bruises. I was a casual girl and I was a *dirty fucking girl* and I'd torn through the men in this town, and half the men one town over, attempting to find that right fit.

And of course it was Wyatt Fucking Nash all this time.

Of course. A week ago I would have hated to give this egomaniac the satisfaction but I was learning he was more than that. Deeper than that. And so I turned my head on the bar and purred when his hand smoothed up my throat to my cheek. I sucked

his entire thumb between my lips and watched his eyes go storm-black.

"How do you need to be fucked," he demanded. It wasn't a question.

"Rough," I hissed.

Not a second passed before Wyatt's palm was on the back of my head; his fingers, twisting in my hair. And then my hair pulled, yanked, head coming all the way back until I was entirely bowed. That single motion sent me rocketing towards the edge. A big baseball god with a big cock and the kindest eyes I'd ever seen was handling me like his fuck-toy.

"Like this, you mean?" he asked, turning my face so I could meet his eyes. He was seeking permission and approval and I gave him both by biting hard on this thumb.

"Yes," I said, clearly. "Those women you take home on the road, do they ever satisfy you?"

"No," he said, mouth ghosting over my own.

"And why not?"

Wyatt brushed his lips against mine. "Because they're not you."

CHAPTER TEN

Cleo

Because they're not you.

Both of us stilled completely—gazes trapped and filled with a mutual longing. A real *understanding* of the depth of this shared attraction. Oh god, I liked Wyatt. *Liked-liked.* And no amount of flustering or games or teasing could steal that thought once it'd blossomed in my brain.

"Cleo," he started to say—but there was a raucous cheer from outside the bar that had us springing apart. The first band of locals and tourists were coming in and Gwen was roaring up on her motorcycle. It was 5:00 pm on the Saturday of Memorial Day weekend and the town of Starfish Bay wanted a mai-tai in their hand and their toes in the sand.

"Meet our new bartender," I said shakily, fixing my pony-tail and straightening my bikini top.

Wyatt gave a mock bow, but his jaw was clenched tight and there was no hiding the shape of his erection in those boardshorts. But the locals were cheering, and I gave Wyatt a tap with my hip.

"Your Zombie-making skills aren't quite up to par, but you can tap a keg, can't you?"

"Yes ma'am," he said, eyes dark.

I swallowed again, chest heaving. "You should know," I said, "that you're more than just a baseball god."

"You think I'm a *god?*"

"Absolutely not," I said, sliding past him to grab a bottle of rum. But Wyatt had me around my waist, tickling up my ribs. I squealed with laughter.

"Cleopatra Hendrix thinks I'm a *god.*"

We were right in front of people, in front of our *neighbors*, but Wyatt wasn't afraid or secretive.

Maybe Wyatt and I had been burning the same candle for each other.

Maybe Wyatt and I could be more than what we were.

Much, much more.

I was still giggling. "A small god. Like the weakest one. The runt of the litter, if you will."

"I'll take it." He handed me the rum with a lascivious look. He leaned back down to my ear. "Tonight I'll be showing you otherwise, pretty girl."

Wyatt kissed my cheek with a *smack* and went to grab the keg.

When I turned back around, grinning like an idiot, half the fucking town was suddenly there. And every expression said *I told you so.*

"You can order drinks, but you can't give me that look," I said, exasperated.

But Gwen called from the door: "If you two get together tonight, a *lot* of us will be winning bets."

CHAPTER ELEVEN

Wyatt

By 10:00 pm, the town was thoroughly drunk, and Cleo and I were having the time of our lives, laughing and enjoying the sultry breeze, the good music. I managed not to knock anything over (much) and even made a Pina Colada that didn't suck. This was Starfish Bay—my great love besides baseball—and with Cleo by my side, I didn't feel like I had to say a damn thing about my knee. My future. Whether or not I'd play again.

Whether or not I *wanted* to play again.

"But before baseball though," Cleo was saying, "what are your favorite memories of Wyatt? Remember I wasn't here really until I was ten, so I missed out on some of the best Wyatt Nash moments."

"Wyatt had a paper route when he was about eight," Todd said. "Although he was terrible at it."

"Lies," I laughed. "I was the best paperboy this town has ever seen."

"What made him so bad?" Cleo asked.

"He would stop and chat each person's ear off. Took him hours just to make it down the street."

Cleo grinned. "That's very cute."

"I like people." But I had loved that job. Had it up until baseball took over my life in high school. Frankie would join me sometimes, and then we'd *really* take our time. "Also, I got paid in cookies."

"What else?" Cleo prodded.

Leslie tapped her chin, thinking. "There was the time Matthew's dog Sammie got pulled out on the riptide and couldn't swim. Wyatt rescued him. I remember that day being really scary. Your mom and I were so proud of you, but also terrified that you'd get trapped in the current."

I sipped the tequila, the burn welcome. "The current that day had been stronger and more terrifying than I'd let on. "Sammie needed a little help, is all."

Cleo bit her lip. "Was Sammie okay?"

"Oh yeah. Good as new when I got him out."

Leslie added, "Also he was Homecoming King *and* Prom King every year. Although he never *ever* had a date."

"The great Wyatt Nash, international playboy, didn't have a date for *prom?*" Cleo asked.

I took the shot all the way back, fighting a smile at her. "I, uh, didn't like turning girls down. It felt shitty. So I went stag every year and tried to dance with everyone."

Cleo stared at me for a long time, her expression undecipherable. As the locals got distracted in some gossip about potholes on the highway, I hooked my finger in the loop of her shorts. Gave her a tug until her feet landed on top of mine.

"What's the look for?"

"More than baseball," she said. "You're more than just baseball to this town."

"I love baseball," I admitted. Because I *did*, dammit, which is why my feelings felt so fucking complicated.

"I know," she said. "Sometimes changes aren't abundantly clear. They're more subtle. You'll figure it out."

I wanted to yank her against my chest and claim her with my mouth. But instead I said, "Drink your drink."

She narrowed her eyes at me, lips twitching. She took the shot all the way back.

"Good girl," I praised. A bit of tequila had slipped from the glass as she'd knocked it back, dripping down the front of her throat. I leaned in. Inhaled the tantalizing blend of Cleo's skin and the tequila. Placed my tongue at the base of her throat and licked it all the way, stopping along the way to press one, two, three open-mouthed kisses.

Cleo shuddered, sucking in a breath.

"Delicious," I said. She looked stunned, dazed. A clap of sudden thunder rattled the windows at The Siren. A thunderstorm barreled towards us. They flared up like this along the coast, resulting in torrential downpours and lighting racing across the sky.

"We should uh … close down early if there's going to be a storm," she whispered.

"You think so?"

"Uh-huh."

I liked this turned-on Cleo, it sent power arcing through my veins. If Cleo wanted a dominating fuck I'd give that to her in spades—it was my specialty, in fact. And I'd happily put this pink-haired princess on her knees if that's what she—

Cleo dropped to her knees.

I almost passed out.

"What are you doing?" I hissed.

"Just getting more glasses," she purred, limpid eyes filled with sex. As she searched with one hand, she trailed her palm up my shin, my knee, my thigh, dipping beneath the fabric.

What power? What dominance? The little *minx* knew who was really in control and she was calling me on it.

"I know what you're doing," I hissed down at her. Her fingers inched up my inner thigh and my cock jumped.

Cleo bit her lip, fluttering her lashes. Then she stood back up and assessed me with a cool gaze. "I guess you'll do for tonight. If I have to close down early and all. You haven't seen any basketball play-

ers, have you?" She was trying not to laugh, but I'd reached the point in the night where I was done with jokes.

I grabbed her wandering hand, stilling her. Yanked her to me with force. "Close this bar down now," I growled against her ear.

Cleo gulped; pupils dilated. She gave an overly dramatic shudder at the heavy storm clouds covering the stars, gasping when lightning struck in the distance. I flipped off the music, leaning against the bar with crossed arms.

"Final call," she said, to a chorus of boos. "Oh, whatever, you've been here since five," she laughed. "Storm's comin'. We all should get home to bed."

When she turned back, I pinned her with a look so intense she gulped again, wetting her lips with her tongue.

My bed, I mouthed to her.

Because I was making this woman mine tonight.

CHAPTER TWELVE

Cleo

Wyatt was waving people off and locking the front door, while I stood barefoot in the sand facing a furious ocean. Soft music still played, but lightning danced across the sky and the water was frothy as it crashed against the shore. A low rumble of thunder mirrored the ocean sounds, which is why I didn't hear Wyatt as he stepped up behind me

A drop of rain hit the top of my head. On instinct, I tipped my head back, caught the next one on my tongue.

"On the road, this is how I picture you," Wyatt said, moving next to me. He was facing the water, and I was once again entranced with how *big* he was, how forceful, how strong and mighty.

"How?" I asked, voice already trembling.

"Living your life with pure need," he said. "Need for adventure. Need to surf, to run, to be around the people you love. No bullshit, no pandering to society's ideas. Being who you are. Drinking the rain on a stormy night, bare feet in the sand."

I flushed, grateful for the darkness. "That's one hell of a compliment, Nash."

"You're a hell of a woman, Cleo," he said quietly.

Rain drops fluttered down, sliding across my na-ked arms, down my back. A sheet of it hit the ocean, warm and humid, and Wyatt tipped his head back and let it cover his face for a second.

"Starfish Bay rain," he sighed. "Summer rain. There's nothing like it in the whole world. When I'm on the road, I miss this place so fucking much it hurts. Worse than this damn knee. It hurts here."

Wyatt placed a hand over his chest, and I felt my heart jump at the motion. I was suddenly deeply afraid of my feelings for this man—this brash, tal-ented ball player that took the time to answer mar-riage proposals from strangers and danced with every girl who asked in high school. Who rescued dogs and loved his town with a fierce passion. Sud-denly, I wished I'd never seen this Wyatt—because this Wyatt was the kind of man a girl like me fell in love with.

But Wyatt was also the kind of man to leave— nine months on the road, year after year, women throwing themselves at him wherever he went.

"I, uh, should get the glasses," I said. The waves pounded, the thunder pounded, my heart so loud in my ears I felt dizzy. "I'll be right back; you can stay here." I turned to move, sliding away in the sand, anything to put real distance between me and this gorgeous man.

But Wyatt was *the greatest* for a reason.

Because no sooner was I turning than Wyatt had me by the arm and up against the bar wall.

Thunder *cracked* and reverberated across the beach. Lightning bleached the sky. A warm mist of rain drenched us immediately.

Wyatt's palms had me boxed in, his hips pushed firmly between my legs. "It's hard for me to admit this Cleo," he said, "because this injury has caused me tremendous pain and tremendous doubts. It's not fun, worrying about your future, wondering if you're important to anyone without a bat in your fucking hands."

Wyatt's palms left the wall to cup my face, fingers spearing into my hair. He was so goddamn *perfect* I couldn't breathe.

"But I think this injury was the best thing that's ever happened to me."

"Wh—why?" I stuttered out. My breath was com-ing in short, fast pants.

"Because it brought me to you."

There was another crack of lightning, another roll of thunder.

And then Wyatt claimed my mouth.

There was no other word to describe our first full kiss—it wasn't gentle, or exploratory. There was no delicate tasting, although there was an illicit sweet-ness to being possessed like this. Wyatt's mouth was hot and demanding, lips moving over mine like we'd always *been* kissing.

I moaned deeply against his lips, nails scratching up his back as I desperately tried to climb him. Wy-att complied, lifting me easily and spreading my legs against the wall, pinning me with his cock and the weight of his deliciously heavy body. Wyatt's tongue swept against mine and my fingers moved up his back to grip the strands of his hair, giving them a hard yank. I was rewarded with a thick, deliberate roll of his hips. His erection rubbed my clit through my shorts.

I bit his lip, harder than I intended. And Wyatt growled, kissing me harder, one rough palm landing on my breast over my bikini top. His thumb stroked beneath the thin fabric, finding my nipple, and I cried out against his mouth. I was rolling my own hips now, desperate for contact, desperate to *come*.

"Cleo, baby, I'm always ready for a hot fuck against a wall," Wyatt said, biting my throat. I shuddered and sighed. "But not for our first time."

Wyatt stepped back and I admired his rain-drenched body, his white shirt clinging to edges of muscle I didn't know existed. "Our first time is go-ing to be in my bed. Got it?"

I nodded—struck speechless. And I let the great Wyatt Nash drag me home.

CHAPTER THIRTEEN

Cleo

At his cottage, Wyatt banged the front door open so hard it left a mark. And I knew he wanted me in his bed, but I was desperate to regain some sense of control. So I dragged Wyatt into what I assumed was his living room, which had wall-to-wall win-dows facing the ocean. Lightning kept flashing, il-luminating Wyatt's hungry, animal look as I shoved him backwards onto his couch.

"*Come here,*" he growled, reaching for me. But I danced out of his grip, untying my bikini top and tossing it at him like his own private strip tease. Wyatt matched me by stripping off his wet white shirt.

"Look at how beautiful you are," he rasped, staring at my bare breasts.

I tore off my jean shorts, leaving just a flimsy scrap of panties. With a rough swallow, Wyatt shed his remaining layers. And I watched as the biggest cock I've ever seen jutted straight up, veined, smooth, already beaded with moisture. Wyatt gave it a lazy stroke, leaning back on the couch like a king, eyes bright with mischief.

My knees weakened.

He smirked. "Told you the rumors were true."

"I never doubted them," I said. Rain fell like pebbles against the roof of his house. A flash of lightning lit the sky. "Do you remember what I told you earlier? About what I like?"

Wyatt's eyes went black. "I do."

"Can you do that for me?"

Wyatt leaned forward, elbows on his knees. The predatory look he gave me sent a shiver up my spine. "You want it rough, pretty girl?"

I nodded, too out of breath to speak.

Wyatt rubbed his jaw, like he wasn't sure I could handle it. "You trust me with your body?"

"Yes," I said, clear as a bell. "You can have it all."

"Well that's good," Wyatt drawled. "Because I plan on taking it all." He ran a hand through his hair, settled back on the couch with his massive thighs spread and his cock at full attention. "Come here."

I took a step closer, then another, then another, bringing my breasts directly in front of his face.

"You're the most beautiful woman I've ever seen, Cleo," he said, running his palms up and over my breasts. I cried out, gripping his wrists to keep steady. "I've been waiting for this night for a long time. Rough or not, you're in control, you understand? It's always been *you.*"

His palms left my breasts, slid up my throat and gripped my face. His kiss felt like a promise, a teasing, hopeful brush of lips and tongue. "Give me everything, Wyatt," I whispered. "There's no one I want more than you."

That mouth descended to my nipples and I almost blacked out.

"*Oh my god,*" I cried, clutching his head to my breasts, holding him there. Wyatt licked and sucked my nipples with a deliberate precision that sent my head spinning. One arm wrapped around my waist, the other caressing whichever breast wasn't in his mouth. He made hungry, aching sounds as he pulled and licked and sent my body floating up and into space.

Wyatt leaned all the way back again against the cushions. "Now come up here and fuck my face."

I didn't have to be told twice. I shoved Wyatt back again and climbed up to his shoulders, knees on the top of the couch and my pussy pressed to his lips. Both hands landed on my ass cheeks, spreading me, pulling me closer so he could breathe me in. I gripped his hair and rolled my hips against his face and his tortured groan had my toes curling.

"Cleo, baby, *baby,*" he growled. His mouth opened, tongue sweeping over the wet fabric of my panties. "I could eat this sweet pussy all night."

I was hovered over him, held tight by his strong arms. I ground my hips again and he gave my ass a ringing *slap.* I inhaled sharply, eyes rolling back.

"Look at me," he said firmly. I did—and almost fainted at the sight of Wyatt Nash's face between my legs. "Was that okay?"

I nodded, struck dumb again. So he spanked me again. And again. Each time the sharp pain hit, I rolled my clit against his mouth. *Slap,* lick, *slap,* lick, and I was wantonly fucking Wyatt's face like a wild woman, hips rolling, hands in his hair, his palms raining down on my sensitive skin. I'd always been a little spank-addict and Wyatt had perfect fucking form—fingers landing right beneath my ass cheeks, sending vibrations through my sex and delicious bites of pain up my spine.

"Yes, Wyatt," I chanted.

He was tonguing through my panties, the material soaked, the rough fabric making me delirious. "Scream my name again," he rasped. His eyes lit up with mischief as his tongue swept past the material to dip inside my pussy, tongue-fucking me with a talent I'd never experienced before.

And out came his name. "*Wyatt Wyatt Wyatt fuck.*" Mindless now, half-babble, half-prayer.

"I used to jerk off to fantasies of you every fucking night," he said. I was aware of being shifted, lifted, then thrown backward onto the couch. My knees were spread roughly as his mouth landed back on my pussy. "I fucked you for hours while you screamed my name until you lost your voice."

There was a *rip* and my panties disappeared, torn in half and tossed to the side. Wyatt wrapped my legs around his head and let loose the full speed of his tongue on my sensitive flesh. One big arm slid across my stomach to palm my breasts, tweaking my nipples as he danced tantalizing circles against my clit. The hot, aching, coiling sensation that had been building in my belly broke apart, exploded, sent the most powerful orgasm of my life ripping through my body as I screamed Wyatt's name. His eyes never left mine, urging me on, urging my climax—and just as I thought I might come again, the great Wyatt Nash flipped me over onto my stomach and yanked me to my hands and knees.

And his big palm landed on my ass with a *slap*.

I groaned against the pillow, clutching the fabric, half-sobbing with pleasure.

Wyatt reached down, fisted my hair, and tugged me all the way back. His kiss was awfully sweet for the dirty things we'd done, things I could taste on his tongue.

"We're just getting started, baby," he crooned, mouth in my hair, lips on my neck. I was a heaving, panting mess of raw nerves. "Now be a good girl and come for me again."

CHAPTER FOURTEEN

Wyatt

Give me everything. I'd had one simple directive from the pink-haired beauty I was falling hard for and I intended to obey with all that I had. And what I had was a bone-deep compulsion to make Cleo come again and again and again. She wanted rough? I'd bring her to her knees and make her beg for my cock; fuck her senseless against every flat surface in my house with my name on her lips and bruises on her neck.

Except as I stared at a very naked Cleo, on her hands-and-knees in front of me, I knew *I* was the one who'd be begging by the end of the night.

Begging for her to want me the same way I wanted … no, *needed* her.

I slapped her ass and she let out a high-pitch moan.

"Do you like that, Cleopatra?" I taunted. I let a series of strategic slaps land on her gorgeous ass cheeks, the backs of her thighs. Pink hand prints blossomed against her pale skin, feeding my desire for possession.

"*More,*" she pleaded.

I laughed darkly. This woman was going to be the death of me.

I slapped her harder and she yelped. Her pussy was wet, glistening and I let my fingers dip between her folds, seeking her heat. I slid one, then two fingers into her cunt, growling when her internal muscles squeezed. Cleo was shuddering. I slapped her ass with my other hand, and she started chanting my name again. "So wet, so ready to go off again for me." I slid my fingers all the way out, all the way back in, mimicking what I planned to do to her later with my cock. Her arms stretched in front of her, back curved, beautiful hair spread everywhere. She was my every fantasy come beautifully true.

"Touch yourself," I commanded. "I want to see your fingers on your clit while I finger-fuck your cunt."

When her fingers found her clit, I spanked her. Stroked her g-spot harder. I watched her arm work, mouth open in pleasure, eyes squeezed tight.

"More?" I asked. Cleo nodded. I gave her three, four, five hard slaps and she started bucking against me. Cleo liked pain and pleasure and I was happy to oblige. Every slap seemed to get her closer, every stroke of my fingers in time with her own ministrations. And within moments, Cleo was flying apart, screaming my name against the pillow as she shuddered through another orgasm.

I slipped my fingers out gently, sucking them between my lips. As Cleo lay flat against the couch, I moved my mouth over her thighs, the swell of her ass, kneading her softly. I massaged my thumbs into her lower back and slid up, massaging muscles knotted from sex. When I reached her hair, I moved it aside and kissed the back of her neck, her ears, her jaw.

"The other article was right," she murmured.

"Which one?" I stroked her hair, feeling each strand between my fingers. Silky, smooth, smelling like Cleo.

"You made that woman pass out. I'm passed out right now."

Cleo rolled over and I pulled her all the way up until she was straddling my lap. When my cock slid through her wet folds she shuddered again, panting against my neck. "And I haven't even fucked you properly yet."

Her pupils dilated. She gave a delicious, slow grind against my cock. I gripped her hips, stopping her. Shook my head. "We fuck when I say, pretty girl."

Cleo bit her lip, coquettish. "Yes, sir."

She was teasing but I fucking *liked* it. "On your knees."

Cleo dropped in a flash—just as loud thunder cracked over our heads. Cleo was sliding both hands up and down the length of my cock with a look of pure lust on her face.

"Cleo," I choked out.

Her eyebrow arched. She dipped her head, sliding my entire cock through wet lips and a hot, hungry mouth.

"*Cleo*." My nostrils flared, breath coming in hot pants. I wrapped my fingers in her hair and twisted and she let out a needy moan. Deeper, deeper …. Cleo was deep-throating me and my world was going to end like this, with a perfect woman on her knees, servicing me like it was her only joy in life.

"What the *fuck*," I growled, almost *angry* at the onslaught of erotic sensation. Cleo was beating me at my own game *again*.

I couldn't have that happen. I hauled her up by her elbows, gripped the back of her legs, and lifted her up around my waist as I stood. We were kissing passionately as I walked her back toward my bedroom, kicking shit out of the way, knocking over a lamp I didn't gave a fuck about. My hip collided with a pair of water glasses on a table that fell, shattered and when I shoved open my bedroom door it hit the wall with a *bang*.

I threw Cleo onto the bed with more force than I intended but it only seemed to turn her on more.

"I want you to fuck me bare," she said.

I attempted to steady my roaring heart. "I get tested every month. I'm clean."

"Me too. And on the pill," she said. "I want to feel you. No barriers."

But I barely let her get the rest of that sentence out before I was prowling toward her naked body on my bed. I landed on top of her, punching my cock down between her thighs, grinding hard against her clit.

And then pain stabbed through my knee. I winced, pressed our foreheads together, blowing out a breath that didn't help with the pain.

"Wyatt, what is it?" she asked. "It's your leg, isn't it?"

"It's nothing," I lied. "I want you like this."

But Cleo was shaking her head and shoving me onto my back with more strength than I was prepared for. She lowered herself like a queen onto my cock, rubbing the head through her folds in an erotic, teasing display of flesh.

"Does this feel better?" she asked.

"*Fuck*, don't stop." I gripped her hips, rolling them, grinding up against her. Cleo leaned down, pink hair hanging like a curtain around our faces.

"Just to be clear," she said, brushing her lips against mine, "I'm also sorry about your injury. Anything that causes you pain causes me pain. But I *am overjoyed* that you're home, here with me." Cleo kissed me, lowering herself down my cock inch-by-agonizing-inch. She was hot, tight, slick with arousal—and suddenly I was inside Cleo, *fucking* Cleo and I'd never felt more complete in my entire life. My jaw dropped, eyelids fluttered, as I took in the sight before me. I drifted my hands up her lean stomach to cup her breasts as she threw her head back, riding me with a sinuous twist of her hips. My thumbs caressed her nipples before settling back on her hips; lifting her, moving her, thrusting my hips up in a rhythm that went from slow to punishing in a matter of seconds.

"Wyatt," she said on a low moan, "your cock … I've never … never been so *full*."

I gave another roll of my hips that had her eyes rolling back. "That's right, pretty girl." I stroked my finger across her clit, and she screamed. "Ride this cock like it's yours. Because it *is*."

She whimpered, a deep flush working its way up her chest. My body was so primed to come I had to chant baseball statistics in the back of my head to stop the driving need to climax. Because she was too beautiful, too sexy, and I'd wanted her for too long.

Cleo dropped to my chest, hands by my head, and ground against me. My fingers twisted in her hair, holding her in place, giving her a rough kiss that had us both gasping into each other's mouths. My other hand caressed her ass, gave her a spank for good measure.

"I'm so close." She panted, licking her tongue between my lips. She tasted like good rum and sunshine. My teeth grazed her jaw, fingers tightening in her hair as I licked up the column of her throat. I let my fingers dip between the seam of her ass cheeks, knuckles grazing the tight ring of muscle.

"Yes," she chanted, "yes, *Wyatt, yes.*"

I teased that muscle, kissed her throat, worked my hips as hard as I could as Cleo came with a wild, gorgeous scream. I sat up, wrapping her legs around my waist, and with three brutal thrusts emptied inside of her, our lips fused together as the most intense orgasm of my entire life ripped through me. My vision went black as sensation roared from the top of my head to the tips of my toes

My forehead landed on her sternum as I tried to catch my ragged breath. Cleo stroked my hair and murmured words against my skin. I licked a drop of sweat from her collarbone.

You're not going to stay. Cleo's honest admission from earlier reverberated through my skull. Because all I wanted to do was wrap myself around this goddess, cook her breakfast in the morning, and do what we'd just done over and over again. But I had a call with my agent tomorrow that could mean any number of things: I was out of baseball for good or, and right now this felt worse, I could come back in a matter of weeks.

Cleo's green eyes searched mine. I kissed the tip of her nose and she giggled. I pulled us both backwards onto the bed, dragging a cool, crisp sheet over our sweaty bodies.

"You're going to stay, right?" I asked.

Cleo bit her lip but beamed a grin at me. "Of course."

I kissed her palm, hooking her leg over my hip. "Was that … to your liking?"

"You mean was it rough enough?" she asked. She shrugged. "I don't know. I guess it was fine."

"Liar," I declared, tickling her ribs until she was laughing loudly.

"Okay okay," she said, wiping her eyes. "I guess it was … you know … the best sex I've ever had or whatever."

She was going for sarcasm but she and I both knew that what had happened between us was more than a release of years of flirtation and sexual tension. She'd told me her feelings for me were anything *but* casual.

"What happens now, Wyatt?" Cleo asked, mirroring my thoughts. "Your knee. I mean, you'll probably go back, right?"

I stroked my hand up her thigh, the curve of her hip. Behind her, the beach I'd loved my entire life shimmered in the moonlight. "I haven't been a very happy baseball player in a long, long time. And I know …. I mean, thanks to you, I can see how I'm more than just that. But just leaving like this in the middle of an incredible career would be …" I blew out a noisy breath, "I mean … a lot of people would tell me I was making the worst decision any professional athlete had ever made. The money, the fans, the fame."

Cleo was silent, watching me in the darkness. "What would … what *could* you do instead?" she asked.

"Work at The Siren," I shrugged.

She grinned but shook her head. "Nah, that's my gig. What would make *you* happy?"

"I don't know," I said honestly. "Is that okay?"

"Yes," she said, kissing me. "That's very, very okay."

And then Cleo laid her head on my chest and fell deeply asleep. And I held her like that, stroking her hair and memorizing the sound of her breathing.

Wondering how I'd ever gotten so lucky.

CHAPTER FIFTEEN

Cleo

I woke up from the most incredible dream—one where I'd finally slept with the man I'd had an intense, tortuous crush on for years and it had been the most passionate and erotic sex of my entire life.

I rolled over in a giant bed, still warm from Wyatt's body heat, and realized it had been real, real, real. I sat up blearily, hair a rat's nest of snarls, body bruised and aching and so so so *satisfied*.

I touched my swollen lips. Smiled to myself. I was terrified to be falling in love with a man who might leave—but also so hopeful. I couldn't help it. After years of being the *casual girl* my body and heart recognized Wyatt as the antithesis of that.

Permanent.

That's what Wyatt felt like to me.

I could smell bacon, hear its sizzle, and the alluring scent of coffee. I reached down and grabbed Wyatt's shirt, throwing it over my naked body. Wyatt's beach cottage was even cuter in the daylight. It had a vintage beach-look to it and a sunny yellow kitchen where the great Wyatt Nash stood shirtless in nothing but sweatpants. Hair mussed, stubble on his jaw, eyes a little bleary. He was flipping bacon, the motion causing his arms to ripple, and when he looked up and saw me, he dropped the spatula, knocked over the skillet, and spilled a bottle of orange juice all across the floor.

Fluster Wyatt: +10

"Good morning," I said, voice froggy from screaming through two orgasms that sent me flying into the stratosphere. Wyatt's cock ... Wyatt's *cock* ....

Wyatt stood up from mopping up juice and I could see every inch of it outlined through his sweatpants. He rubbed the back of his neck sheepishly and sat down at the kitchen table. "You're too beautiful for your own good, Cleopatra."

Don't be attracted to—oh fuck it. I was well past games anymore. Happy and smiling in the early-morning light, I basically skipped over to the American Baseball God, who dragged me onto his lap with a sweet, passionate, slightly-sloppy kiss.

"Did last night really happen?" I asked.

Wyatt grabbed my palm, placing it right over his chest. I could feel the steady beat of his heart. "It did. Way to rock my world, pretty girl."

"Right back atcha," I winked, but the kiss he gave me in response was serious, searching. When he pulled back, I saw him swallow.

"Hey, I, uh, am supposed to have a call with my agent and my coach later today. About my knee."

I remembered what he'd said last night ... an open and honest *I don't know.* Strange that that sentiment had put me more at ease, having this man express a *real* feeling of doubt when all he usually did was brag.

I brushed a strand of hair from his temple. "How do you feel?"

"Well, my knee feels like dying," he said. I went to move off his lap, but he held me firm. "Please don't ever move, okay?"

I smiled. "Okay. So beyond excruciating pain ..."

Wyatt stroked a big palm up my spine. "How would you feel if I—"

"*UncleWyattComeOutside,*" came a chorus of childlike shrieks. Wyatt's eyes widened and he hit his forehead with his palm. "Oh *fuck,* I forgot I'm babysitting my nieces this morning."

"Oh, I can go ..." I said, sliding off his lap for real. But Wyatt gave me an abashed look. "Are you serious? Come hang out with us. We're going to the Boardwalk to eat too much funnel cake and run on the beach."

"Okay," I said, almost shy. "That sounds ... fun."

"It *sounds* like a date." Wyatt winked.

"First dates don't usually involve children," I pointed out.

But Wyatt merely kissed my temple. "I don't believe this is our first date, Cleopatra. After last night? We're on like date 250, feelings-wise."

My heart slammed a strange metronome against my ribcage, and I let out a shaky breath. I ran around his house grabbing my clothes and yanked on my jean shorts and twisted my hair up into a sloppy ponytail as Wyatt was pulling open his door. Two blond-haired toddlers jumped up and he caught them at the same time, tickling them as they laughed.

"I totally remembered I was doing this today," Wyatt said to his sister, Frankie. She smirked, handing him a bag filled with toys.

"Yeah, yeah," she said. "Oh, and *hello* Cleo. You just won me a lot of money, babe."

Wyatt dropped the twins, who ran past me screaming into the house. "Town bet, huh?"

Frankie nodded.

"Those bastards," I said, and Wyatt laughed. He also pulled me for a side hug that surprised me, brushing his lips across my hair.

"So you two ..." Frankie said, eyebrow arched.

"Pretty cool, huh?" Wyatt said. He and his sister shared a meaningful look.

"I think it's perfect."

I didn't expect any of this—not for me to stay over at Wyatt's, not for him to imply we were more than one night; not to be paraded in front of his family like some kind of *girlfriend*.

"Just so you know, I'm not paying you for babysitting," Frankie said.

"You know most people would pay a lot of money for the great Wyatt Nash to watch their children."

Frankie gave Wyatt a hug and kissed me on the cheek. "Go have fun, you two. And don't let my daughters eat too much cake."

As she strode off, I watched Wyatt gaze at her with brotherly affection. "You have an amazing family, Nash."

"A family that I never see," he said.

I squeezed his side. "That's so sad."

But he shook his head. "It's only sad if you're not able to change it," he said. "And I think I might be able to change it."

CHAPTER SIXTEEN

Cleo

Our 250th date was one for the record-books. After Wyatt cooked us breakfast, he escorted all of us to the Boardwalk where we spent a classic Starfish Bay day: funnel cake, soft pretzels, hot dogs. Silly Boardwalk games and a long time in our bathing suits, jumping through the waves. If I'd wanted to keep my feelings purely *lustful* with Wyatt, I should have scooted out of his house before I had a front-row seat to him being the World's Cutest Uncle. It was a regular heart-and-ovaries explosion to watch a 6'4" baseball god carrying twin girls as they licked ice cream cones and made him laugh.

With his easy grin—and endless winks in my direction—I was a heart-sick mess by the time the sun was setting behind us. Wyatt and I sat on the boardwalk, toes in the sand, as the girls built a sand castle in front of us. I'd taped up a sign at The Siren that said "On a date with Wyatt Nash. Closed for tonight," and, as I'd expected, half the town walked past us with sly, knowing looks.

Wyatt lifted my hair from my shoulder, stroking my neck. "Truth time, pretty girl. How long have you had a crush on me?"

"About a day or so," I shrugged. Wyatt leaned close, nipped my shoulder. I laughed.

"Beautiful liar," he growled.

"Um … it must have been your third year or so, playing. I was twenty-two and had recently taken over The Siren and you were probably twenty-four, twenty-five? I was trying really hard not to give you any extra attention because of your celebrity status, but that night you were making everyone laugh and you looked," I cleared my throat, "like the handsomest man I'd ever seen. You probably don't remember this, but you stayed late that night and helped me clean up. Even though I'd just seen you on the front page of *Sports Illustrated*."

"The first night we met, then?" he clarified.

"Yeah … yeah, I guess it was," I admitted. "Every year, when you'd come home, my crush would get worse."

Wyatt laced our fingers together, pressing his lips to my palm. "That was the night I developed my crush on you, Cleopatra."

My entire body shivered. How was this moment *happening?* How were Wyatt and I enjoying an adorable night with his nieces and licking ice cream cones at the beach?

"What does your future look like?" he asked.

I looked in his dark blue eyes and saw a lot of things. But mostly, against all odds, I saw our life together.

"I want to expand The Siren," I said, "add a second location over in Dewey Beach. I want to surf every morning and see our neighbors every night as we drink rum cocktails. I want to get married and have a bunch of kids, own a big house on the beach. A simple life, but a profound one."

Wyatt gave me a smile as bright as the sun. "Where am I in this future?"

"Next to me," I said.

There was a buzzing sound—Wyatt's phone. His agent and coach were calling to talk about his knee, his career, The Big Decision.

But Wyatt looked completely calm. He cupped my cheek and kissed me.

"I need to take this call," he said, "and then let's talk about that future."

EPILOGUE
Wyatt Nash

One year later

I'd been right all along. Asking someone to marry you *was* terrifying. Evidenced by the fact that the formerly-great Wyatt Nash was scared shitless.

It had been easy to get all of Starfish Bay in on it—while I wanted the actual moment I asked Cleo to marry me to be private, I needed all the help I could get to set it up. The timing had been everything: we'd recently put in an offer on an old pink-and-yellow Victorian right on the beach, and I'd found out yesterday that our offer had been accepted. Luckily our real estate agent took bribes in the form of baseball autographs. Cleo still had no idea.

Gwen, Frankie, the twins, my parents and Cleo's parents, as well as a handful of other well-meaning residents, had worked with me all day to string up a series of lights on the wall of our new house that read *Will you marry me Cleopatra Hendrix?* I had a remote in my pocket I could *click* when it was time. All of Cleo's rotating bartenders showed up and told her to take the night off (per our plan) so she was on her way. If she said yes … *when* she said yes … the entire town was going to come by for a huge surprise engagement/housewarming party. Although I gave us at least an hour in between to have wild sex, of course.

The day I took that call from my agent and coach had been one of the hardest and best days of my life. Because it would have been easy if my knee was busted for good—but it wasn't. They were calling to welcome me back to the team.

And were flabbergasted when I turned them down, terminating one of the most lucrative contracts in the history of professional baseball. But I had enough money—what I needed was more love. And *no one* had been supportive; no one had been excited, and the professional sports establishment dragged my name through the mud quite a bit. Fans called me nasty names, and even my teammates had some unkind words for me. I wasn't sure what I'd had expected, but I was so happy, so joyful with Cleo by my side, I assumed everyone around me would *know* this was the right choice.

Which made it harder—leaving in the face of stalwart criticism forced me to truly consider my decision. And as Cleo and I laughed our way through a dinner that night—and then had wild, heart-pounding, headboard-shaking sex—I knew in my heart that difficult decisions didn't necessary mean they were wrong. And the moment I officially moved home to Starfish Bay, I stood in my parents' house, with my family members hugging me for dear life as they cried happy tears over my decision, and I just *knew*.

Plus, it helped that I was hired to coach the high school baseball team as soon as I came home—like I'd imagined, coaching baseball filled my life-long love for the sport without crushing my spirit. Every day I got to stand on that green and listen to the perfect, poetic sound of a ball hitting a bat.

And every night I came home to a pink-haired goddess named Cleopatra. Although most nights I finished with her at The Siren, where we made drinks and danced and more often than not, we hard-core made out on every available flat surface. The future she'd envisioned for herself a year ago—expanding The Siren, getting married, having a family—was something I very, very much wanted to be a part of.

Forever.

But I couldn't help but flash to that last woman who had proposed to me—Karen—who I hoped was happy now. It *did* take a lot of bravery to do what I was about to do—bare yourself, express your undying love, hope and pray the other person felt the same way. I'd spent the past year goofy-in-love with Cleo, and I hadn't ceased being clumsy and tongue-tied in the face of her extreme beauty. And if Karen hadn't distracted me by running onto the field in a wedding dress, I never would have been hurt—never would have come home and opened myself up to a love like Cleo's.

"Nash?"

"Queen Cleopatra," I said, coughing a little to hide my shaking voice. "You made it."

Cleo was wearing a long sundress, hair wild around her face, and big, beaming grin. "Did we get news on the house?"

"Yeah," I said, pulling her in for a long hug. "It's ours." We swayed for a moment.

"Wyatt," she said, voice choked. "This is … this is *our house?*"

"Forever, if we want it."

Cleo stood back, taking in the funky colors, the many designs, the slightly dilapidated but clearly very loved wrap-around porch. "Is this why everyone came to take my shifts at The Siren? So, you could show me the house?"

I felt in my pocket for the ring. Frankie had helped me pick it out.

I took a deep breath—it was now or never. If I could hit a home run during Game 7 of a neck-and-neck World Series game, I could find a way to propose to my soul mate.

My right knee hit the sand.

"Wyatt," Cleo said, hands flying to her mouth. "Wyatt Nash, what are you doing?"

"Cleopatra Hendrix," I said, holding a rose-gold ring up in the moonlight, "it turns out we were meant to be together from the very moment we meant. You challenge me, you make me laugh, you helped me see a life where I was more than a professional athlete. I want to live in this house with you and make a ton of babies and have all the sex forever and ever."

Cleo fell to the sand, wrapping her arms around my neck and kissing me.

I laughed. "You're supposed to wait for me to ask the question, pretty girl."

"What if I propose to you too?" she asked.

I pushed the pink hair from her face. "Okay. Show me what ya got, Hendrix."

Cleo bit her lip. "I'm not sure why I denied my attraction to you for so long. Probably because I was scared to experience the full force of my feelings for you, Wyatt. I think …" She closed her eyes and tears spilled over, "I *know* it's because my heart recognized you as the one. My person."

We grinned at each other for a minute as I swiped the tear away. I fumbled and pressed the tiny button and I watched Cleo's face light up as she saw what I'd made for her. I turned—saw the entire side of our house blazing with the words *Will you marry me Cleopatra Hendrix?*

"Will you marry me, Cleo?" I asked, kissing her hands.

Cleo tackled me to the sand—besting me as usual. Laughing into the sky. "Yes," she whispered, kissing me. "Yes, yes, yes."

Our columnist, Julie Pitzel, has been a receptionist, radio DJ, bill collector, telemarketer, administrative assistant, community college instructor, and an expediter (a.k.a. professional nag). She's been involved in the Houston writing community for many years including two years as president of a local Romance Writers of America chapter. She writes paranormal fiction from a geodesic dome south of Houston, where she lives with her husband and a pair of cats. Most recently, her story "The Dance" was published in The Death of All Things *anthology.*

YOU READ *THAT*?: SAVED BY ROMANCE

by Julie Pitzel

Books, especially romances, save lives.

I don't mean physically. A book isn't going to give you the Heimlich if you're choking or carry you from a burning building. And though books can, and do, deliver instructions for saving lives, I'm not talking about saving someone from thallium poisoning or providing instructions for how and when to tie a tourniquet.

Books save us emotionally.

I'm the sixth of seven children. Being a younger sibling in a large family meant that I had no privacy. I shared a bedroom with two of my sisters. The bottom bunk and a couple of drawers were mine, but I couldn't reasonably expect to be left alone if I went to my room. And the lock on the bathroom door was only there for show; anybody could and would let themselves in. If my mother was getting ready to leave the house, I could only pray that I'd be able to exit the room before she broke out the Aqua-Net.

I soon discovered that although I couldn't get away from the chaos and havoc of a house full of people, I could hide in the *Island of the Blue Dolphin* or Dracula's castle or Asimov's *Foundation*. It didn't matter what was going on around me, I had fictional worlds to explore. That ability to escape helped me endure my teen years and some ugly family drama. Years later when my first marriage was ending, romances and their promised happily-ever-after (HEA) helped me through a difficult, emotional time.

I always knew fiction, and especially romance, was my personal escape. Until a few years ago, I didn't realize that for some it's so much more than just a mental vacation. At the 2015 Romance Writers of America National Conference, Julia Quinn gave the keynote address. One of her points was that romance writers provide a valuable commodity—important for much more than simply its entertainment value. As proof, she read a letter from a fan explaining how Quinn's books had been a lifeline during a tough and troubling period. After that, I've heard similar stories from other romance authors—heartfelt thanks from readers grateful for a break from reality.

This year at RWA National, the keynote was given by Jennifer Armentrout who admitted she owed thanks to many of the writers in the audience for saving her life as she'd dealt with depression and suicidal tendencies. Armentrout was quick to point out that books did not cure her depression. However, reading about someone else's life, immersing herself in a fictional world that she knew would end with an HEA, provided a calm port in the storm. It was enough of a buffer that she could take the steps necessary to seek help.

Armentrout noted that it was more than having an HEA that made those stories lifelines. It was identifying with the protagonist. Recognizing herself in the characters helped her live vicariously through those fictional lives. There are too many people who need that support, who need the hopeful message, but can't find characters like themselves in stories about romance and happily ever after.

I've touched on the importance of diversity in publishing before, and *Heart's Kiss* makes an effort to publish stories with a range of voices and characters. But that's only one small slice of a massive industry that is still out of step with the real world.

It would be wonderful if the major publishing houses recognized the need and published a greater variety of own-voices stories. I won't hold my breath. Fortunately, we do have other outlets because we need more stories about people of different races and religions, people of different genders and sexuality, and people with disabilities. An LGBTQ Navajo who's on the spectrum should be able to find stories about others with similar challenges who've found happiness and hope.

But in order for others to find those stories, in order for someone hurting in their real life to find someone like them in a fictional lifeline, those stories need to be written and published. This is an open invitation to the would-be-writers out there to be those needed storytellers.

This is your tacit* permission to write the stories you want to read. Write the novels, short stories, poems, and/or essays that examine your struggles. Write your tales of hope and sadness, of success and frustration. Write your fantasies and wishes; share your experiences and your truth.

I understand many of you will think, "I can't. I don't know how to write." And that's a legitimate concern. Writing isn't easy, but the mechanics and the craft can be learned. There are a bazillion blogs and articles on the interwebs that provide the basics. Even *Writer's Digest* has a wealth of information freely available. Besides the free online sources, there are books and magazines covering all phases of the process from the basics of plotting, to understanding deep point of view, to selling your book. And many communities have writing groups where you can attend meetings with likeminded individuals to learn craft, or trade manuscript critiques. For such a lonely profession, there's an active support network.

Some of you will have the excuse, "No one wants to read about someone like me." Maybe not, there are no guarantees. But you want to read about someone like you. That's at least one, and where there's one there are more. Don't hold yourself back because there may not be a market. The romance industry—and all of its subgenres—is the product of readers creating the stories they couldn't find on the shelves.

Earlier I said writing wasn't easy. That's not the full truth. Some aspects are easier than others. Most writers are readers first and we've absorbed techniques simply from seeing how our favorite authors do it. The real difficulty comes from putting ourselves in our stories. For readers to truly connect with our work, we must reveal inner thoughts and feelings. Doesn't matter if it's comedy, drama, or even non-fiction, readers connect through emotion.

---

* Tacit because you don't actually need my, or anyone's, permission.

We must dig out our fears and wants and put them on display.

Writing has been referred to as bleeding on the page because it's very difficult to make a reader laugh or cry or get angry if we don't feel the same. As difficult and exhausting as it can be to expose pain, shame, and other emotions on the page, I find that it's also cathartic. During my teen years, reading helped me escape, but writing angst-ridden poetry (My name is Julie ~ like the fragrance patchouli …) helped me deal with the issues happening in my life. Focusing my thoughts into rhyming couplets was a useful outlet.

Writing and reading aren't panaceas. They won't cure all of our ills, but they are tools we can use when the world becomes too much—or not enough. And if you have experiences or fantasies or dreams that you can put in words, that story—your story—may become someone else's lifeline.

Copyright © 2019 by Julie Pitzel.

C.S. DeAvilla writes award-winning science fiction, fantasy, and romance under another pen name. She has been a romance fan since she sneaked a peek at her mother's massive historical romance bookcase and fell in love with all the characters. She reads every romance genre—as long as two people are falling in love, she'll give it a read. Her favorite authors are Jennifer Crusie, J.R. Ward, Darynda Jones, Suzanne Brockmann, Sarah MacLean, and Christina Lauren. But she always has room for one more.

RECOMMENDED BOOKS

by C.S. DeAvilla

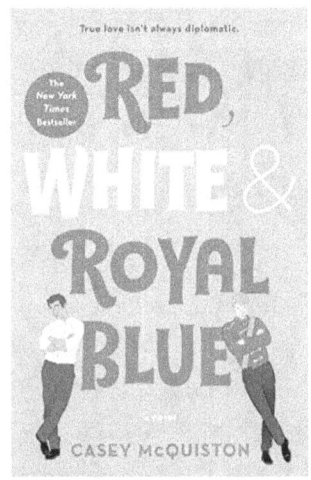

Title: ***Red, White, and Royal Blue***
Author: Casey McQuiston
Publisher: St. Martin's Griffin (Macmillan)
ASIN: B07J4LPZRN
Release Date: May 14th, 2019

Casey McQuiston comes out with all the writing fireworks for the debut of the season. Red, White, and Royal blue takes readers to a fictional set up where the president is a woman and she has older children who are just out of college and causing all kinds of foreign affairs—pun intended. The romance between Alex (first son) and Henry (prince in line for the throne of England) was adorable and refreshing. It all starts with a mutual rivalry then a forced meeting to assure the public that Alex and Henry are friends, not mortal enemies—but after getting to know one another better they realize that the line between love and hate is actually pretty slim. This book is a reminder of how far our society has come regarding LGBT rights and the remaining work to be done for those in the media spotlight. At points I really thought that Alex and Henry wouldn't be able to make it work—heck, I didn't think of the legal implications of treason until the storyline brought up the issue. McQuiston does a fantastic job of layering very real and tangible conflicts for the two main characters and the barriers they faced after falling in love. This is a new author that is worth putting on your permanent auto-buy list. She's on mine now!

Title: *Twice in a Blue Moon*
Author: Christina Lauren
Publisher: Gallery (Simon & Schuster)
ASIN: B07O5H13YQ
Release Date: October 22nd, 2019

It's Tate Jones' first trip to England. Her first time flirting with a fellow tourist. First love. Then first devastating heartbreak. In Christina Lauren's newest book readers are treated to what feels like two books in one. The first part details Tate and Sam's young love—falling hard for each other while both are on vacation with their grandparents. Tate with her rule-making grandmother and Sam with his adventure-seeking grandfather. The four quickly become a traveling team and late nights are reserved for Sam and Tate to sneak out of their respective

hotel rooms to meet on the grass outside of the hotel and stargaze. They share their deepest dreams and fears. Sam believes his grandfather is dying and Tate reveals she's the long-lost daughter of a famous actor. The trip ends abruptly when Sam disappears, Tate is betrayed, and her identity leaked to the press. It's clear that she trusted the wrong person. Fast-forward to present day and Tate is now an actress herself—a dream she shared with her young love—and takes on a role with her Hollywood star father in a much-anticipated drama. This role could elevate Tate to the next level, but her game is thrown when Sam appears back into her life and she has to spend several weeks of filming with him watching on the sidelines. Will he be able to redeem himself? I really enjoyed this book and I have to admit that main-characters-as-actors is a hard trope for me. I tend to veer away from books with that description because it's hard to imagine myself being able to relate to that lifestyle (which is funny because I would read about an astronaut anyday … so why not some other profession I would never ever have? We all have interesting blind spots to challenge ourselves on). However, I gave it a chance because I love Christina Lauren so much and I don't regret it. Now I know I've been missing out.

Title: *Top Secret*
Author: Sarina Bowen and Elle Kennedy
Publisher: Tuxbury Publishing
ASIN: B07RD7ZPPM
Release Date: May 7th, 2019

When two of my favorite authors team up I know I'm going to be guaranteed something fun. Considering the last time Sarina Bowen and Elle Kennedy wrote m/m romance they won the RITA award for best contemporary, it would be a sure bet this book would be a smash hit too. No pressure. Keaton needs to get used to the idea of having a man in his bed if he's going to give his girlfriend the threesome she keeps saying she wants for her birthday, so he signs up for Kink, an app that will help him find the perfect third to their plan and also allow him to explore the idea. The surprise is that he's more into having a man's hands all over his body (and sexy parts) than he's ever allowed himself to realize. He's more energized for this new sex adventure than he has been with his girlfriend … maybe ever? Luke Bailey, Keaton's roommate, frat brother, and rival turns out to be the guy on the other end of those texts—which is a shock to both of them. And if readers think this is your average guy-has-threesome-and-decides-he-likes-guys-more m/m romance, they would be wrong. I loved watching these two fall in love in an unexpected way and also grow as characters.

Title: ***How to Date A Douchebag: The Lying Hours***
Author: Sara Ney
Publisher: Self-Published
ASIN: B07RM6FJ6Z
Release Date: May 7th, 2019

Abraham Davis is an honest, hard-working wrestler who spends most of his free time cleaning up after or preventing his teammates' messes. So when his teammate needs a girlfriend he gets him all set up. But Abe's teammate doesn't have the confidence to message girls because he doesn't have great writing skills (or people skills, but readers will figure that out right away). So Abe takes over that task as well, setting up the dates without getting too involved and turning over the rest to his teammate. Except one night a conversation with a match interests him a little too much and he finds himself wanting to know more and meet her. When his roommate keeps messing up dates, Abe hurries to smooth things over, wondering why Skylar and his teammate are not clicking, until he sets up a double date and meets Skylar in person and now he'll never be able to let his teammate date her. She deserves the best and normally he'd say that would be him, but will she forgive him for lying to her? I'm a sucker for Ney's books, any series. She writes jocks well. Just the right touch of strength and unexpected vulnerability. There are no cardboard cut characters either—readers might think that jock romances in New Adult get repetitive, but not Sara Ney. She's carved herself a spot in the genre and it's clamped in with reinforced steel and cemented.

Title: ***I Dare You***
Author: Ilsa Madden-Mills
Publisher: Self-Published
ASIN: B07CPFLKD9
Release Date: April 26th, 2018

Sometimes a book keeps coming up in my radar and I begin to wonder if it's the universe telling me it's time to check out a new-to-me author. Sometimes those encounters lead to flops and other times to greatness. *I Dare You* was definitely greatness. Ilsa Madden-Mills has earned those high review counts and more. Orphan Delaney Shaw is at her lowest after her long-time football player boyfriend cheats on her with her nemesis Marsha "Muffin." But mysterious texts from a flirty admirer help her get over that relationship fast. She can't help but fantasize they're from hunky talented football player Maverick Monroe. They shared a brief kiss freshmen year, though he did seem a bit of a flirt and full of himself. Also, Delaney has sworn off football players for the foreseeable future. Best to land a nerd into science fiction who's a little more like her. The texts keep coming and she slowly falls for whoever is on the other end, meanwhile Maverick keeps showing up in her life and being there for her when she needs someone most. When he reveals himself as the mystery texter it's a dream come true, but that's not his only secret—which if he doesn't come clean to Delaney, they could lose any chance at happily ever after before they even have a chance to get this hot romance off the ground. I loved the layered conflicts the couple faces together and individually. It gave the story dimension and the characters a raw, real feel. *I Dare You* won't be my last taste from this author!

Andrea was drawn to Chicago to the famed Charlie Trotters Restaurant. There, Andrea was exposed to one-of-a-kind wine cellar in which she received one of the best wine educations in the world, tasting & serving some to the most rare and most special wines ever produced. She worked with some of the world's top ingredients, Chef's, Farmers, food lover's and wine aficionados, but homesick, Andrea returned to Santa Fe, NM, where she was Partner & Head Chef at Rasa Juice Bar & Ayurveda. Andrea received many rave reviews and won the Local Hero Award two years in a row for her organic, plant-based café. Her attention to detail to her beautifully plated and delicious food is enhanced with the love and care she infuses into every bite! She is currently the Owner and Chef of The Temptress Private Chef & Catering operated out of her home town of Santa Fe, NM.

THE TEMPTRESS PRESENTS: LENTIL SOUP WITH TOMATO, POTATOES & FRESH HERBS

by Andrea Abedi

Fall is upon us and it is time to get back to the warm, cooked yummy dishes we all love and missed. The leaves are falling, the weather is changing and temperatures are dropping ever-so-slightly. I love to cook a nice pot of lentils with fresh herbs, grab my book and curl up. I love this recipe so much and I hope that you get to enjoy this lovely bowl of homemade lentils!

INGREDIENTS

2 cups of green or red lentils

1 small onion, diced

2 cloves of garlic, minced

1 tablespoon of ghee

1 bunch of tri-colored carrots, stems off, chopped into small rounds

2 sweet potatoes or 2 russets, peeled and diced (medium size)

1 bunch of fresh spinach, stems off

1 large can of crushed tomatoes

2 sprigs of fresh thyme

½ bunch of fresh parsley

3 cups of fresh chicken stock or vegetable stock

DIRECTIONS

1. Measure all ingredients.

2. Chop all ingredients.

3. Heat the pan with 1 tbsp of ghee.

4. Add onions and turn down heat to a medium flame

5. Stir the onions until translucent, then add the minced garlic.

6. Sautee for 2 minutes, then add the chopped carrots.

7. Add the lentils and stir into heated mixture.

8. Add can of crushed tomatoes, stir.

9. Pour the chicken or veggie stock and bring up to light simmer.

10. Add the fresh herbs and let the soup lightly boil.

11. Let it go for about 30 minutes, check lentils.

12. Add chopped potatoes and salt and pepper.

13. Let simmer for another 30 minutes and check for doneness.

* Garnish with vegan yogurt if you would like a little extra tang

Enjoy!

xo

Copyright © 2019 by Andrea Abedi.

CLOSING EDITORIAL

by Lezli Robyn

Hurricane Dorian whirled into my life and swept me off my feet for my birthday. Not the best of presents, or the most romantic—I prefer my dates to be a little less destructive. But Myrtle Beach survived and during the storm I was able to curl up with my computer and read some new fiction for this issue of the magazine. I was so swept away by the romances our authors created that I forgot all the turmoil around me. That is how you know you have read a captivating love story.

Next issue we bring you yet another Kayla Perrin novella, interviews with Darynda Jones and Anna J. Stewart, and some holiday-themed stories that would warm the coldest winter heart. We're also excited to announce that we are sponsoring a romance fiction conference—on a cruise ship! With bestselling authors Beverly Jenkins, Anna J. Stewart, Melinda Curtis and Kayla Perrin on board as our panelists—as well as Harlequin editor, Kathryn Lye—our "Love Boat" cruise is a "must do" event for all romance fiction fans and aspiring writers. Who doesn't want to meet their favorite authors while cruising the Caribbean? Go to www.HKConference.com for more information, and remember: there are only fifty slots available on this exclusive cruise. Sign up early to avoid missing out!

Until next time…read, live, love. Life is short—embrace it like a sexy hero in your favorite romance novel!